CHASE THE DEVIL

THE JAKE SAWYER SERIES (BOOK 5)

ANDREW LOWE

GET A FREE JAKE SAWYER NOVELLA

Sign up for the no-spam newsletter and get a FREE copy of the Sawyer prequel novella **THE LONG DARK**.

Check the details at the end of this book.

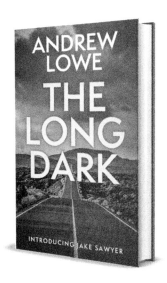

Email: andrew@andrewlowewriter.com
Web: andrewlowewriter.com
Twitter: @andylowe99

First published in 2020 by Redpoint Books
This edition April 2024
Cover photographs © Shutterstock
Cover by Book Cover Shop

ISBN: 978-1-9997290-9-7

For Tom and Josh

What consoles me a little is that I'm beginning to consider madness as an illness like any other, and accept everything as it is.

— *VINCENT VAN GOGH, LETTER TO HIS BROTHER THEO, 21ST APRIL 1889*

PROLOGUE

Grinding, as the bolt is pulled away.

The door rolls aside, and the gloom of the barn is banished by a flare of late evening sun.

The man startles out of his stupor, shields his eyes. By the time he has shifted upright, sitting with his back against the wall, his captor has stepped inside and rolled the door closed.

The man tugs at the chain, rattling the base link against a metal plate fixed into a rim of thick stone at the bottom of the wall. His wrists are squashed together by a tight metal cuff, and his legs are secured to the chain by a clasp around each ankle.

The captor lingers by a storage unit just inside the door. He is still, shoulders rising and falling. Is he watching the man? Facing the unit? Impossible to tell at this distance.

He moves towards the storage unit and crouches, preparing something. As he stands and approaches, taking slow, lumbering steps, he passes beneath a filthy skylight, and the man catches an outline of his head: unnaturally large, with two protruding points sticking upright, near to where his ears should be.

Horns?

The man squints into the darkness, trying to catch more detail. But his captor turns and faces a workbench in the corner. He sets down a heavy bag, and the contents jangle. Metal, glass.

The man licks his lips with a dry tongue. 'Please. Who are you? What am I doing here? This must be... mistaken identity.'

The jailer takes an item out of the bag and sets it down on the workbench. He pauses and reaches down for a second item. The man flinches at the sound of metal on metal. Rasping. Sharpening. He tugs at his chain again, sucks in a breath, tastes the stale air: faecal and rancid. 'I've been here for a long time and... I don't know what I've done. Please. Tell me. Why? Who—'

'Close your eyes.' The jailer's voice is deep and low. He doesn't turn; he nods to the bench. Again, the horn-like tips on either side of his head are caught in a weak shaft of light. 'You don't look at me. You don't see anything.'

The man takes another breath; it catches in his throat. He closes his eyes. 'Okay. I've done it. Now what?'

'Keep them shut.'

The captor walks to the man and stoops beside him, breathing hard. The man can smell him now: pungent, unwashed. A hint of ammonia.

The captor moves behind the man and covers his eyes with a blindfold, securing the knot.

The man turns towards the jailer, panic in his voice now. '*Please*. Whatever you think I've done, I'm sorry. I don't know unless you tell me. Please tell me. Let me explain, defend myself.' He hears the captor walk back to the bench. 'Jesus Christ. What are you doing to me? Why? What's going to happen to me?'

'You're going to die. But not yet.'

PART ONE

DARK & LONG

MARCH 2008

Three knocks on the office door.

Detective Chief Inspector Ivan Keating slid the scene photos back into the blue file folder and called out. 'Yes?'

But the door was already open, and a tall, slender man in his mid-twenties, dressed in full uniform, had stepped into the room. He took off his cap and shook out a tar-black thatch of uncombed hair that curled at his jawline. He bent his head forward, revealing a coin-sized albino patch at the crown. He regarded Keating with a hopeful smile, green eyes twinkling.

Keating squinted at him. 'It's customary to wait for an invitation before walking into a superior's office.'

'My apologies.' A pause. 'Sir.'

Keating sat back in his chair and beamed. 'Your apologies? You certainly have your father's charm, son. Shut the door. Sit down. Take your cap off if you like.'

The visitor closed the door and lowered himself into

the soft-backed chair facing Keating's desk. He took a moment to look around the room. Small window overlooking the main car park, corkboard with notes and a few photos, Macintosh laptop with blue gel wrist rest, wire tray of files. He leaned forward, elbows on knees, dangling the cap between his legs.

'I saw your father last week,' said Keating. 'At his new cottage. Well... He calls it his studio. Still keeps a flat in town, I think. He seems fairly settled. Couple of dogs. Nice view.'

'I preferred the pre-religious version.'

Keating frowned. 'Whatever gets you to the end of the day, eh?'

His visitor forced a smile.

Keating ran a palm across his tightly cropped hair, prematurely grey. 'How is your brother getting along?'

'He's had some problems.' Another pause. 'He'll be okay.'

Keating picked up a chunky ballpoint and tapped it on the desk as he spoke. 'Fresh out of probation. IPLD tutor commended you. First official day as a paid-up copper. Welcome to the fold, PC Sawyer. Sounds good, eh? Nervous?'

A shrug. 'Excited.'

'You studied psychology and criminology at Keele, along with our FLO, Maggie Spark.'

Sawyer nodded. 'Travelled a bit after getting the degree.'

Keating pulled a file out of his tray. 'Anywhere nice?'

'Nothing exotic. Canary Islands.'

Keating laughed. 'Well. That's practically Africa.' He browsed the file. 'So why did you join the force, Jake? Surely more than just following in your father's footsteps?'

'They fuck you up, your mum and dad.'

Keating raised his eyes from the file. 'Larkin.'

'But the man who killed my mother fucked me up a lot more.'

Keating took a deep breath. 'Marcus Klein.'

Sawyer bristled. 'That's the man who was convicted, yes.'

Keating set the pen down. 'But you don't think he did it.'

'He certainly doesn't.'

Keating eyed him, pulled a few papers out of the file. 'I see you've already applied for CID. Not too thrilled by the prospect of farmhouse domestics and fly tippers?'

Sawyer smiled, activating a dimple in his right cheek. 'Not crazy about the fashion.'

'That's how it works. You'll spend the first part of your career trying to get out of uniform, and the rest angling to get back into it. Let's see how you do. No promises. No fast track due to family connections.' He sprang to his feet, picked up the blue folder, screwed on his cap. 'I like the keenness, though. If you can make my job marginally less stressful, I'll get you on the carousel for consideration. It'll be a couple of years before you go before the board, though. At least.'

Sawyer stood up. 'Interview with a DI and DS. Six-week residential course. I'd prefer the Sheffield one if possible, sir. Easier for travel.'

Keating laughed. 'I'll see what I can do.' He walked around the desk and opened the door, turning to angle his head towards the corridor outside.

Sawyer followed him into a large meeting room with floor-to-ceiling windows. Buxton town centre bustled in silence down below. Three people sat at the far end of an oval conference table: two men, one woman. The men were almost comically contrasted: one was vast and bear-like, with a dense brown beard, thinning hair and semi-rimless spectacles; the other was slight, watchful, in a light blue suit that didn't suit him. The woman smiled at Sawyer as he entered, and tucked her rust red hair behind her ear.

He nodded at her. 'Mags.'

Keating slapped his hands palms-down on the table. 'Good morning, good morning. I'd like you to meet our latest recruit. This is Police Constable Jake Sawyer. I thought a bit of shadowing might be useful on his first day. See how the grown-ups do things.' He smiled at Sawyer and nodded to a chair, which Sawyer took. 'Jake, you know Maggie. This is our esteemed pathologist, Frazer Drummond.' The large man raised a hand. 'He's based at Sheffield Hospital but drops in from time to time.' Keating held an open hand out towards the other man. 'And this is Martin Pittman. Detective Inspector.' Pittman nodded at Sawyer. 'Martin is SIO, Senior Investigating Officer, on a complex and pretty nasty new case. Body found at an abandoned building up in the Hope Valley. Falls under our jurisdiction, but because of the nature of the crime, Martin is liaising with a specialist unit up in Sheffield.'

Sawyer took a seat. 'MIT?'

'Sorry?' said Pittman.

'Murder Investigation Team. The specialist unit.'

'Ah, yes. Local to South Yorkshire. We're learning a lot.'

Keating scoffed. 'We're hoping to establish some kind of MIT for Derbyshire soon. Possibly here.'

'Does the murder rate warrant it?' said Sawyer.

'It's rare, but it happens. And MITs also cover other serious crime.'

Sawyer nodded. 'But you suspect murder in this case?'

Drummond glanced at Keating. 'That much is barely in doubt.' He spoke with a Scotch growl, in sync with his stature. 'Victim's last moments wouldn't have been too pleasant. Judging by his injuries, he was tortured for a long time, and the killer flayed much of his flesh, I'm guessing while he was still alive. Rupture and bleeding in his vocal cord lining, probably from the screaming.'

'COD?' said Sawyer.

Drummond regarded Sawyer over the top of his spectacles. 'Looks like heart failure.'

'Obviously,' said Maggie, 'the family only have an impressionistic view of the details. So this conversation has to be private.'

'The investigation is drawing a blank,' said Pittman.

'Chicken farm owner,' said Keating. 'We're looking into possible connections to rival businesses. There have been issues of that nature recently in the livestock industry. It's competitive, and not always healthy. Maybe a feud of some kind. Something that's spilled over, got out of hand.' He slid the blue folder across the table to Sawyer. 'Crime scene photos. I'm assuming you're not squeamish?'

Sawyer opened the folder and sifted through the images: several angles of a hefty middle-aged man, beaten and bruised, slumped naked in the corner of a featureless outbuilding. Most of his torso was disfigured by bloody lacerations where oily patches of skin wilted away from his frame like peeling wallpaper.

'Your father is Harold, right?' said Drummond.

Sawyer nodded, keeping his eyes on the photos.

Keating walked to the window and looked up at the cloudless sky. 'Fine pedigree. PC Sawyer already has detective ambitions.'

Drummond nodded to the folder. 'Maybe build up to that slowly. Get a few stolen cars and local ratboys in the bank first.'

'It's not a feud,' said Sawyer, replacing the photos.

'Sorry?' said Pittman.

'It's personal, intimate. Hands-on.' He caught

Keating's eye. 'Emotional. This is more about pleasure than business.'

Pittman glanced at Drummond, smiled. 'Appreciate the input, PC Sawyer. We're following a few lines of enquiry, but we'll bear it in mind. You can maybe help me out with a few interviews here and there.'

Drummond drew a deep breath. 'You really want in on all this, Sawyer? Murder detectives are a bit like goalkeepers. You don't have to be mad, but it helps.'

'PC Sawyer isn't keen on the sartorial aspect of grunt work,' said Keating.

Maggie smirked. 'Women love a man in uniform, Jake.'

'Is there anything else you're not happy with?' said Pittman, yawning. 'There's a lot of paperwork, you know. And the canteen food is hardly *haute cuisine*.'

Sawyer thought for a second. 'I don't like the cars.'

2

PRESENT DAY

An orange-and-black Mini Convertible pulled up outside a stone-built detached house that looked down on the Victorian sprawl of Hall Leys Park. Music from within: a husky female vocal, something about talking with myself. The car lingered for a while, idling, then fell silent.

Jake Sawyer unfolded himself from the driver's seat and stepped out into the midday heat. He pushed a hand through his hair and walked down the path towards the front door. There was a slight tilt to his gait, but nothing you could confidently describe as a swagger.

Sawyer rang the doorbell and looked, down towards the picnickers gathered on the grass in front of the bandstand. A recent storm had taken the sting out of the record-breaking heatwave, but the air was still dense and sultry, and he plucked at his polo shirt.

A woman opened the door. She was late forties, short

and rounded, with long auburn hair tucked into a hasty ponytail.

Sawyer turned. 'Samantha Coleman?'

'Yes. Mr Sawyer. Thank you so much for taking the time to see me.' She shook his hand. 'Come in.'

Sawyer followed her down a narrow hallway, through an immaculate kitchen and out onto a modest back terrace with table and chairs set at the base of a small raised garden. An overweight tabby darted from under the table and disappeared into the house.

'Nice cat,' said Sawyer. 'Shame he didn't stick around for a bit of fuss.'

'She', said Samantha. 'And she rarely obliges with lap time.'

'Lowers your blood pressure, apparently. Stroking pets.'

Samantha set down a jug of iced water with two glasses and began to pour. 'I'll stick with my medication. More reliable. You got a cat then?'

Sawyer nodded and took a seat. 'Yes. As with all cats, though, he thinks he's got me.'

She smiled, sat down opposite. 'I heard your music. Electribe 101. I was a bit of a raver back then.'

'In the nineties?'

'Yeah. That was one of my comedown albums.'

Sawyer sipped his water. 'I love the electronic music from that time, but I don't dance. My body won't do it.'

Samantha leaned forward. 'Mr Sawyer, I really appreciate this. I know you've... had a busy time, lately. I want you to know that I think you did the right thing, stopping that bastard.'

Sawyer nodded. 'Which one?'

'David Bowman.'

He shrugged. 'I did a thing. My bosses are busy deciding how right it was.'

'So, this is okay? You're allowed to do other jobs?'

Sawyer held her gaze. 'I'm suspended from official police business. They wouldn't be crazy about me taking on investigative work, but I can get round it if I don't take payment.'

'Oh. Really. I can afford—'

'Tell me about Darren.'

She sat back, took a drink. 'He's lovely. Kind. Clever, in a good way. He's been gone for seven years now. He was fifteen at the time of his disappearance. Went out one night, said he was going to a party. Never came home.'

'Did he often go to parties?'

'Not much. He liked a lot of my old music, actually. But he didn't seem to fancy the idea of clubs or events or whatever. He seemed interested in my youthful excesses, the hedonistic lifestyle. But I don't think he was into the idea of pursuing it for himself.'

'How long have you lived in Matlock Bath?'

'Never lived anywhere else. My parents used to live five minutes from here. Bought this place with my husband twenty-odd years ago. We separated a couple of years after Darren's disappearance. As I said on the phone, I read a lot about you. About what you went through.' Samantha leaned forward again, and rested a hand on Sawyer's. 'I thought you would understand it. The pain.'

Sawyer slid his hand away and took another drink. 'Was Darren popular?'

She gave an awkward laugh. 'He was hardly a player, you know. But he seemed to have good mates, good relationships. He'd had a bit of a tough year, though.'

'In the run-up to his disappearance?'

She nodded. 'He had to move schools because there was a fire at his old place. Nothing suspicious but they couldn't keep it running.'

Sawyer's eyes drifted to a movement off to the side. The cat strutted out and slumped in a patch of sun at the foot of the garden. 'Why a tough year? Did he not adjust well to the new school?'

'No, he seemed to like it. He wanted to study business, and that wasn't an option at his old place. But they offered it at Cedar Mount, the new school. I think the general standard was higher than he was used to, though. I remember, I picked him up from an event late one evening, and he was a bit off with me. Withdrawn. There was a bruise around his cheek. He said it was nothing, just a "silly ritual" that all new pupils were supposed to go through. I was going to talk to the headmaster but he begged me not to pursue it.'

'How close was this to the date of the party?'

'Oh, a few months before.'

'What about the police investigation?'

She shook her head. 'Various appeals and "lines of enquiry". A few sightings, suspected hoaxes. Nothing concrete, though. They still call me in sometimes to identify an item they've found. I've never seen anything that I could link to Darren. The searches have turned up nothing. I have a case review file from a couple of months ago. You can take it if you like.'

'That would be perfect, thanks.' Sawyer sloshed his water around the glass and shifted his chair into the shade. 'I'll need to understand more about the period leading up to Darren's disappearance. All his friends, interests, places he went to, who he might have met there. Did you do the same for Virginia Mendez?'

'Yes. She contacted me late last year. Student journalist. Lovely girl. She wanted to make a podcast about the case. She lost her brother back in Venezuela a few years ago, so I think my case struck a chord with her. I helped as much as I could. She put out three episodes. They were very respectful, sensitive.'

'And now she hasn't been seen for just over two weeks.'

Samantha sighed. 'Awful. I hope it's a coincidence.'

Sawyer drained his glass. 'I want to help.' He stood up. 'And I don't want payment. But I can't promise you that I'll find Darren. Or that there will be a good outcome. You talk about your son in the present tense, but you have to be prepared—'

'—for the worst.' Samantha nodded. 'I'm ready to face whatever comes, Mr Sawyer. Anything would be better than this limbo. The not knowing either way.'

The cat eyed Sawyer as he moved back towards the kitchen. 'Could I take a look at Darren's old room? Have you kept his things?'

'Of course.' Samantha bustled in front of Sawyer and led him back through the house. 'I haven't kept his room like a shrine or anything, but I've held on to all his bits and pieces.'

Sawyer followed her up the uncarpeted staircase into a surprisingly small bedroom with a wide open sash window that looked down onto the back garden. *28 Days Later* poster, acoustic guitar propped in the corner, portable CD player, work desk with a chunky old Dell PC. Single bed with red-and-black Sheffield United duvet, modest TV and DVD player squeezed on top of a corner unit. Sawyer browsed the rack of books, CDs and DVDs on a wall shelf above the bed. Singles and albums from the early 2000s, horror films and action movies, graphic novels.

He turned to Samantha, perched in the doorway. 'Lots of *Walking Dead* stuff here.'

'Yes. He went through a big zombie phase.'

'DVDs and graphic novels. Bit of a fanboy.'

'I suppose so. We had a snow day the winter before he...

We watched my old DVD of *This Life*. Remember that? He tolerated it, but then when he saw that Andrew Lincoln was also the star of *The Walking Dead*, he made a connection.'

Sawyer leaned in to a framed photograph on the end of the wall shelf. A teenage boy in a red-and-black lumberjack-style shirt peered into the camera. Tapering, almond-shaped eyes; *Mona Lisa* smile; mane of thick, unstyled brown hair swept across his forehead in curls. His gaze was earnest, coltish; he was marooned in that awkward dead zone between child and young adult.

'That's one of the few pictures of himself Darren actually liked. I've got a few copies if you want to take one.'

'Thanks. That would be useful. He looks bright.'

'He was. Is.' She caught herself. 'Are you taking on any more... investigative work?'

Sawyer smiled. 'You have me exclusively. I've got my own limbo to deal with, while I wait to see what the brass are going to do with me.' He looked out of the window and was amused to see the cat staring up at him. 'So, yes. I'm all yours. Apart from a few personal affairs I need to tie up.'

———

Back at the Mini, Sawyer dialled a number and ducked into the driver's seat. He turned on the engine and opened the window.

The call connected. Male voice. 'The man of leisure!'

'No rest for the wicked, Dale. You should know.'

A pause. 'Business or pleasure?'

Sawyer sighed, swept his eyes across the park and the picnickers. 'We need to talk.'

3

The Koffee Pot was an upscale greasy spoon in Manchester's Northern Quarter: chequered floor, bright orange booths, walls splashed with art school murals. Sawyer and Maggie had eaten here regularly on city trips in their Keele days, and the place had barely changed, bar a few more options on the artisanal bread slate.

Sawyer arrived early, and dug into a plate of beans on toast while he sifted through the Coleman case review file and dipped into the three published episodes of the podcast. Virginia Mendez had used the first episode to introduce the case and outline the findings of the official enquiry so far: not much. Episode Two focused on Darren himself, as Virginia spoke to friends and family, while Episode Three was almost entirely devoted to an interview with Samantha that revealed little that Sawyer didn't already know, apart from further detail on Darren's father who had recently remarried. But his ear pricked at Virginia's sign-off, where she promised an exclusive interview with an 'interesting character' who was close to Darren. The interview was trailed with an audio clip: an unnamed male voice saying, 'There are rules. You're not supposed to say anything, reveal the location.'

Sawyer was deep into a second cup of tea when a short, grey-haired man in a fitted white shirt entered and slid into the opposite seat, followed by a much larger character in a sleeveless T-shirt who budged up next to Sawyer. The short man took off a pair of heavy-framed glasses and polished the lenses with his shirt cuff.

'It's never a good idea, is it?' said Sawyer.

Dale Strickland replaced the glasses. 'What isn't?'

'Two cups of tea. Sometimes, you really enjoy that first cup so much that you feel like you want another. But then the second just doesn't quite land and you lose interest halfway through.'

Strickland looked around. 'Nice place. Starbucks too grown-up for you, Sawyer? This is Jerome, by the way.'

The big man nodded but didn't lift his head up from his phone.

Sawyer smiled. 'Of course it is. You eating? They have an award-winning fry-up here. Maybe not quite right for your optics, though. Now you're in the political arena. Sorry to hear you didn't get the main gig.'

'Plenty of time for that. Hopped up a few rungs. The mayorship can wait. At least I'm still in gainful employment.'

'There's no need for spite.'

Strickland glanced at Jerome, then back at Sawyer. 'How's my wife?'

Sawyer slurped his tea. 'I would question the use of the possessive pronoun there.'

'Eva is still my wife.'

'Technically. But I'm not sure she sees you as her husband any more.'

Strickland scowled and studied Sawyer. 'Semantics.'

'Let's talk about guns instead of girls. The unfortunate business with Shaun Brooks. An ex-associate of your employer, Jerome. I assume you've been briefed. Dale, I'm going to speak frankly. Eva is technically your wife, I'm technically a civilian. The efforts you've put into recovering the Glock I took from our mutual friend, Mr Fletcher, suggest it must have had some involvement in Shaun's demise. I suspect you used him to set up your county lines operation, but since he wasn't the sharpest knife in the rack, he transgressed in some way and so you, or someone under your command, removed him from the picture.'

Strickland held up a hand and addressed Jerome. 'Get me a cup of coffee. Black, sugar.'

Jerome got up and approached the counter.

Sawyer continued. 'So, when Fletcher came after me, I took the gun off him and kept it in a safe place. Not safe enough, though. Whoever pulled the trigger on Shaun Brooks, it's all academic now. It looks like we share a problem.'

Strickland frowned. 'What do you mean?'

Sawyer took out his phone and navigated to a news story whose main image showed a burning house being doused by a team of firefighters. 'The former home of Hector Jurić. Another of your old associates whose life was tragically cut short before his time. This is a bit of a theme with you, Dale, isn't it? Does Jerome know what he's letting himself in for? Is everyone else in good health? How's the Scottish guy you sent to menace me last year? Marco, wasn't it?'

Strickland sighed. He took out his phone and turned the screen towards Sawyer. Grainy CCTV footage from an underground car park. A burly man with a short blond ponytail entered the back door of a parked car and the vehicle rocked as he struggled with the occupant. The car stopped moving and, shortly after, exited the car park.

Sawyer raised his eyes to Strickland. 'Any news?'

Strickland shook his head. 'That's from the hotel where Marco and I celebrated my appointment as drug tsar last week. Fletcher was obviously waiting for him.'

'The prospects aren't good.'

Strickland shrugged. 'I have other people.'

Sawyer sat back and squinted at him. 'Henchmen dot com? Like I say, we share a problem. Apart from Fletcher's attempts on my life, he was watching Eva and me recently, near the place where I hid the gun. It took him a while to find it, but it adds up. And I know he's also been watching my house. I get the sense that he's slipped your bonds, Dale. We have a common enemy. He's cleaning up your mess. Snipping off the loose ends. I know about Fletcher's dishonourable discharge from the SAS, but I wondered if you had any insight into what might be his next move.'

Strickland pocketed his phone. He picked up the glass salt cellar and turned it around in his fingers. 'Aside from my wife's peripheral involvement, I'm not really sure how this is my problem. There's plenty of time to square the Marco and Hector thing, discreetly. I don't want to get involved in any other business now, given my new role and status.' He nodded to Jerome as he queued for the coffee. 'Personally, I'm feeling pretty safe at the moment, Sawyer. But if I were you, I would draw a lesson from *The Art of War*. Take the initiative. Attack the undefended. Find the weak spot. As you've seen, it doesn't go well for those who wait for Fletcher to come to them.'

4

DCI Robin Farrell shuffled in the centre of the chintzy sofa: cream with a pattern of veiny green flower stems dotted with red petals. He took a small canister of breath mints from the inside pocket of his grey summer suit, tapped one out and flicked it into his mouth.

Jordan Burns sat opposite, perched on the edge of a matching armchair. He set down a bottle of mineral water before Farrell and leaned forward, elbows on knees. Burns was thickset and balding, grey at the temples, with a saggy white T-shirt that hung over a burgeoning belly.

A beat of silence, as Farrell broke the seal on the water bottle and took a slug.

Burns sat back. 'Steph's on her way down.'

'Thank you.' Farrell tried on a smile; he didn't wear it well. 'I'll keep it brief. Obviously, your wife has been through a terrible ordeal. Given the… circumstances, we're required to run an internal enquiry, overseen by the IOPC. Independent Office for Police Conduct.'

Burns nodded. 'You got your man, right?'

Farrell ran a hand across his forehead, then flattened his dyed-black hair. 'We're confident of that, yes. But as I'm sure Stephanie has told you, the circumstances of his apprehension were rather extraordinary, and we just have to be sure—'

Burns shook his head. 'As far as I'm concerned, Mr Sawyer saved my wife's life, and probably the lives of—'

Farrell raised a hand. 'I do understand that view. But Stephanie is the only independent witness to David Bowman's death, and we have to make sure the picture adds up.'

A young woman entered the room and made her way to a second armchair, next to her husband. She wore a dark purple dressing gown with the hood up. Strands of blonde hair seeped out over her shoulders, and her eyes were underscored with dark circles. She took each step slowly and carefully, feeling for footing. Farrell sprang to his feet; Burns walked over and steadied the woman into the chair. He crouched down beside her and draped an arm over her shoulders.

Farrell lowered himself back onto the sofa. 'Stephanie. I'm terribly sorry to disturb you. Just a few quick questions. Won't take long.'

'Do you want a drink, babe?' said Burns.

She shook her head. 'I'm okay.'

Farrell took out a notepad. 'As I was telling your husband, we're conducting an internal enquiry into the events surrounding the... resolution of your abduction. There's no implication of wrongdoing on anyone's part. It's all about establishing the objective facts of the matter. A formal procedure that we're required to pursue whenever there's a death following contact with police.'

Stephanie's faraway eyes hovered to the bay window and the sunlit back garden. She turned her head and faced Farrell. 'What more do you need to know? I've given my statement to your Liaison Officer.'

'Of course. This is purely a follow-up. I'm leading the enquiry, and there are a few points I wanted to be certain of. Firstly, before Detective Sawyer was brought into the house by David Bowman, did you hear a gunshot from outside at all? It might have been a distant sound, but I'm keen to know if you heard anything.'

Stephanie glanced at her husband. 'No. I was... asleep. Well. Barely awake. I'd been badly beaten. Dehydrated.'

Farrell made a note. 'Of course. I'm sorry.'

'And it was raining. Stormy.'

Farrell studied her. 'Ah, yes. This is a difficult one, but were you conscious when David Bowman murdered Julius Newton, the man who arrived with Detective Sawyer?'

Stephanie shook her head. 'I didn't see any of that.'

'Thank God,' said Burns, giving Stephanie a squeeze.

Farrell nodded. 'You didn't hear it?'

Stephanie coughed. 'The first time I was aware of anything was when I saw Detective Sawyer in the chair, hands behind his back.'

'And Detective Sawyer ultimately broke free and fought with Bowman. Is that correct?'

'As I've said, I wasn't fully aware of the whole thing. But I know that he managed to get the axe away from Bowman and then used it to defend himself.'

Farrell raised an eyebrow. 'What exactly was he defending himself against at the time he used the axe?'

Burns sighed. 'A psycho who'd murdered four women and was about to murder another.'

Farrell bristled. 'Mr Burns. Please. I need to hear Stephanie's view.'

Stephanie turned side-on to Farrell, facing the window. 'Bowman tried to strangle Detective Sawyer. He beat him. Punched him. Detective Sawyer broke free and struck Bowman. He then grabbed the axe, they struggled again...

And I looked away. Then I heard the impact, and saw Bowman with a wound in his neck. His throat.' She closed her eyes. 'I screamed when I saw it. There was so much blood.'

Farrell glanced at Jordan Burns. 'And did Detective Sawyer attempt to help David Bowman with the injury? Staunch the bleeding?'

Stephanie looked at her husband, then Farrell. 'I don't... No. He didn't. He came to me, checking I was okay. Comforting me. Bowman... He was done for. It was obvious.'

Farrell made a note. 'Why do you think Detective Sawyer struck Bowman with the axe, Stephanie? Why not try to subdue him with a non-lethal method?'

Stephanie glared at Farrell. 'Have you asked him? How would I know? Bowman was big and strong. I remember he said something about Detective Sawyer already being possibly concussed.'

Farrell nodded. 'He had been struck unconscious by Newton.'

'Yes,' said Stephanie. 'So, he had to put a stop to it. He wasn't strong enough to finish him off with fists. The axe was self-defence. I suppose he thought that Bowman would survive, with medical attention.'

'And yet Detective Sawyer made no effort to assist Bowman medically, in even the most basic manner.'

'He knew the other police were coming. He was checking on me.'

Farrell frowned. 'The innocent victim took precedence over the "psycho".'

'Yes,' said Stephanie. 'Look. Can I be honest with you? I was glad to see Bowman dying. I wish I could get the sight of him out of my head now, but at the time it's what I wanted. Detective Sawyer is a good man. He was defending himself against a... monster, and he saved my life.' She leaned forward. 'And I think it's a disgrace that you're treating him like some criminal.'

———

Jordan led Farrell out of the living room, down the hall. 'I'm sorry about the hostility.' He lowered his voice. 'Steph has suffered a lot. She has some... physical compromises, as a result of her captivity. And there's the psychological impact.' He opened the front door.

Farrell stepped forward, then paused. 'I imagine there's been an impact on your business. Quality Cottages, isn't it?'

'Yes. Steph runs the admin. It's all on hold. I can't see her getting back to it anytime soon.'

Farrell bowed his head, nodding. He kept his eyes on the floor. 'Is Stephanie receiving any treatment for the "physical compromises" and the emotional fallout?'

'She's been told she'll need physiotherapy. And counselling. The waiting lists are long, though. We can't afford private at the moment.'

Farrell looked up. 'From what you say about your business, it seems you can't afford not to.' He moved to the door and eased it shut. 'Jordan. You're both victims here. There is more to the story. And if you can get the full picture, then there may be an opportunity for you to right this terrible wrong. Stephanie is correct. Detective Sawyer is a good man. But he's the one who is free to carry on, financially secure, while you both suffer.' He stepped closer. 'It doesn't seem fair to me. Stephanie says that Detective Sawyer saved her life, but he's also risked your livelihood. Is that something you're willing to accept?'

When Farrell had left, Jordan made Stephanie a cup of tea and settled on the sofa with his laptop. He googled 'IOPC' and read about the processes for internal police investigations.

When he looked up, Stephanie was still staring out at the garden, tea untouched on the coffee table. 'Shall we head out later, babe? Bit of fresh air might help.'

She sighed and forced a smile. 'Yeah. I need to get back to work soon. Can't face it yet, though.'

Jordan nodded, turning back to his screen. 'Strange, isn't it? How they seem to be so keen on investigating what happened?'

She looked at him. 'I suppose they're getting all sides of the story.'

'I suppose. But there's only one true version. And only two people who really know for sure.' He glanced up. 'Did you really not hear this gunshot? What's that all about?'

Stephanie sipped her tea. 'No. I didn't hear anything like that. I was a mess.'

He closed the laptop. 'How long have we known each other?'

Stephanie raised her eyes to the ceiling, calculating. 'Almost ten years now. Why?'

'When you've been with someone for that long, you know them really well, don't you? It's almost like, what do you call it? Telepathy.'

'Like a connection.'

'Yeah. I think the policeman was satisfied with your account, don't you?'

She watched him over the top of the mug. 'My account?'

'But he only really spoke to you for ten minutes. And there's a big difference between ten minutes and ten years.'

Stephanie set the mug down. 'You're saying you don't believe me?'

Jordan shook his head. 'I'm not saying that. I'm just concerned that you're not giving... the full picture. I know you feel grateful towards Detective Sawyer, and so do I. But the police wouldn't be digging like this if they didn't think there was more to it.' He got up from the sofa and took her hand. 'Steph. For your own sake, for our sake, the truth is important. If you don't feel you can tell the police, you could at least share the full story with me. Make it three people who know the one true version.'

5

Sawyer dug his way out of central Manchester and settled into a crawl of early evening traffic on Wilmslow Road, heading south. He played the third episode of the Mendez podcast again, turning up the volume at the sign-off section and Virginia's teasing trailer for Episode Four.

Her voice flooded the Mini: soft, lightly accented. *'It's clear that Darren was a typical teenager, working out his friends, reassessing his family relationships, learning his place in the world. But all teenagers have secrets.'*

A male voice: young, local sounding. *'Yeah, you can't just share all the hot places. There are rules.'*

Virginia again. *'Next episode, in an exclusive interview, I'll be speaking to an interesting character who I believe was close to Darren.'*

The young male voice again. *'Some people are dumb, though. They stick up their hero shots. Bragging, yeah? But you're not supposed to say anything, reveal the location.'*

Virginia. *'Perhaps he can help us to... explore Darren's inner world.'* The music faded up. *'Join me next time on* Finding Darren Coleman.*'*

Sawyer jumped a red light and sped away, past the

budget barbershops of inner-city Rusholme. He set his phone on speaker and made a call. It connected immediately.

'Jake.' Male voice, London accent.

'Max. You well?'

The clunk of a Zippo lighter. 'Smalltalk answer? Fine. Detailed version? Broke my wrist playing squash.' He puffed out smoke. 'And, yes. It was squash. I hear you're teacher's pet again, then.'

Sawyer turned into a broad driveway and passed through a small estate of three-storey flat blocks. 'Just making new friends. Doing a bit of freelance while they make their case.'

DI Max Reeves laughed. 'PI Sawyer. So what do you need me to pretend I'm not doing?'

Sawyer parked by a neatly trimmed lawn at the base of one of the buildings: temporary accommodation serving the nearby university. A few students were sprawled out on the grass, drinking and chatting. 'Austin Fletcher.'

Reeves coughed. 'The geezer you called about last year? Ex-Marine.'

'Can you dig a bit deeper for me? I know about the SAS thing, the sexual assault allegations, the attack on his commanding officer. This time it's personal, though. Family connections, anything in his earlier background. Biography stuff.'

'I'll have a go. But this doesn't sound healthy, Jake.'

Sawyer looked up at the flat block. 'I'll survive. But I can't just sit on the naughty step while other people decide what to do with me.'

———

Lewis Vaughan led Sawyer past the yellow-and-white kitchenette and waved a hand at a grey sofa and armchair facing a wall-mounted TV. 'Have a seat. I could do you a tea?'

Sawyer took the sofa; it was skeletal and uncomfortable, with scratchy cushion fabric. 'I'm fine, thanks.' He looked around. 'This is a lot more luxurious than my old student digs.'

Vaughan smiled and flopped into the armchair. He wore a black-and-white Breton T-shirt, and was tall and angular, with quiffed blond hair. 'This is a "Deluxe Studio". My parents were pushy enough to get in early. It's not that different from the others. Just a bit more space. Don't have to share the kitchen.'

Sawyer watched Lewis as he fiddled with his phone. 'I'm investigating the Darren Coleman case, and obviously I'm also interested in Virginia, who was making a podcast about it. How long had you been seeing her?'

Lewis kept his eyes on the phone, typing a message as he spoke. 'A few months. We met towards the end of last year at a party. We were on the same media course.'

'Was her podcast part of a project?'

Lewis paused, finishing his message, then looked up. 'Project?'

'For the course.'

'Ah. Yeah. We all had to do something. She read about Darren Coleman and was planning to make it a one-off thing, focusing on media coverage. But she really got into it and it grew into a kind of investigation.'

Sawyer gazed out of the window at the ochre brickwork of the adjoining buildings, a sliver of blue sky between. 'When did you last see her?'

Lewis looked back down at his phone. 'I told the police all this. About a week before she...' He sighed. 'She lived in a shared house but spent a lot of time here as it's closer to the campus. I can show you the stuff she left if you like. She kept a few things here. Toiletries, a few clothes, bits and pieces. The police spoke to her housemates, but she only had clothes and books there. Do you think she might have gone back home? To Venezuela?'

'There's no record of her leaving the country. Her passport was retrieved by police from the shared house. Were you on good terms?'

Lewis scowled. 'Yeah. Never had a row or anything. She was normally pretty good at staying in touch so I was shocked when she went quiet. I have her mother's number in Venezuela. Called a couple of times but never got through. I can let you have the number, if you like.'

'Did she talk to you about the podcast project?'

'A bit. We were out a lot, though. Parties.'

'Clubs? Bars? Gigs?'

'Bars, yeah. I don't really go to clubs and I hate live music. Ginny dragged me out to some jazz thing once.' Lewis screwed up his face and shook his head.

'I've listened to the three published episodes of the podcast. Did she mention what she was working on for the other episodes? Someone she'd interviewed who might have been close to Darren? She calls him an "interesting character".'

'Not that I know. She was always well prepared. Meticulous. She recorded the episodes in the same way. Setting one in draft a week ahead of the broadcast date, and putting it live manually on the day.' He tapped something into his phone. 'The police checked the host, though. The next episode wasn't uploaded.'

'But it's possible she might have recorded and edited it?'

Lewis finished typing. 'Yeah. She kept a laptop here, edited on it. I gave it to the police.'

'And did she keep manual notes?'

'She used her phone for that. It hasn't been found. She did make some paper notes, though. There's some stuff in a folder here. The police looked at it but didn't take it away.' Lewis kept his eyes on his phone, scrolling.

Sawyer sat forward. 'Have you heard of the phrase "you protest too much"?'

He looked up. 'Sorry?'

'You helped the police a lot, didn't you, Lewis?'

'Yes.'

'You're keen to let me know that. You've told me several times.'

'Yes. It's true.'

'I'm sure it is. But you've told me about it so often it almost feels like you're telling yourself..'

Lewis set down the phone beside him. 'I don't know what—'

'You've cooperated with the police. I already know that. You know it. But you keep telling me. It doesn't sound like you're proud of the fact, though. Almost the opposite. You're protesting too much. It makes you sound guilty.'

Lewis scoffed. 'You think I had something to do with Ginny's disappearance?'

Sawyer sat back. 'No, I don't. I mean guilty in the sense that you haven't done enough. There's something more you think you could have done. There's something you're holding back. It's like a burden. You're thinking of offloading it onto me, but you probably don't know how to do that without making it look like you intentionally withheld it from the police, even if you didn't.'

Lewis raised his head and glared at Sawyer. 'I'm not holding anything back.'

Sawyer smiled. 'Yes, you are.'

Lewis sighed. 'Look. The only thing I didn't say was

that Ginny spoke to me about the podcast a few days before… She said she felt like it was getting a bit "heavy".'

'As in, serious?'

'Yeah. She said she was thinking of going to the police. She didn't say what about, though. I just got the feeling that she was—'

'Scared?'

'Not… Well, yeah, maybe. Just a bit freaked out.'

Sawyer ran the back of a hand across his brow. 'I'd like to see the folder you mentioned.'

6

Sawyer headed back to Edale with all the windows wide open, music pounding. Underworld, Leftfield, Aphex Twin. He stopped at the Peak View Tea Rooms and took a window seat, gazing out at the scorched moors as he sipped tea and demolished a hefty chunk of carrot cake.

He called the number for Virginia Mendez's mother, and got a generic-sounding answerphone message in Spanish. He hung up and opened Virginia's project folder. It was slim and tidy, with the structure for each of the three podcast episodes mapped out on separate sheets of custom paper, with handwritten sections of narration script marked "VO", voice-over. She had given each episode a production title: *1. The Case, 2. The Boy, 3. The Mother.* A piece of paper torn from a notepad had been tucked into a side pocket on the inside back cover. It was messy, with scrawled notes, connecting lines, and bullet-pointed lists that seemed to relate to the first three episodes.

On the back of the notepad sheet, Virginia had written a title: *4. The Explorer.* Beneath this, she had listed names, some with ticks next to them (*Samantha*), others with crosses (*Greg, Adam*).

At the bottom of the paper, she had written two names stacked above each other (*Price, Sutton*), with a curly bracket connecting them to the word *Urbex*. Beneath this, she had written a question mark next to a single underlined word.

Devil.

His phone rang; Sawyer sighed at the Caller ID: *LOGAN.*

He took it, waiting for the caller to speak first, listening to the wheeze in his breath.

'Is it a bad time?' Male, Estuary accent.

'Yes. But a call from you, Dean, it's always a tonic.'

Logan made a rattling noise, halfway between a laugh and a cough. 'So what are you doing with yourself, Sawyer? How loose have they cut you?'

'Forty-eight-hour notice. Full pay. Don't have to sign in.' Sawyer stirred his tea. 'I'm sure you know all this, Logan. You could probably argue it's in the public interest.'

'You are quite the star, Sawyer. A walking op-ed piece.'

'I can't imagine you working on those, these days. *The Derbyshire Times* is a long way from Wapping.'

Logan scoffed. 'I got out at the right time. The liquid lunches were out of favour. After the phone hacking business you couldn't scratch your balls without getting it signed off by a senior editor.'

'You want my take,' said Sawyer.

'Oh. Are we done with the pleasantries, then?'

'You want my side of the story. An exclusive. *JAKE SAWYER SPEAKS: HOW I TOOK DOWN THE RIPPER*. Your editor has told you to wait until the resolution of the investigation, but this is you getting your flag in the sand.'

'We've all got to eat.'

Sawyer slurped the tea. 'That hurts. First I'm a walking

op-ed, and then a lunch ticket. You're talking to a human being, you know.'

Logan let the moment hang. 'Got something for you.'

'In return for the exclusive?'

Logan sniffed. 'A bit of lubrication, maybe.'

'Be gentle with me.'

'You do have this habit of going off-grid just as interesting things start to happen.'

Sawyer mopped up some cake crumbs with a finger. 'Is this the part where I say, "meaning?"'

'A CI tells me—'

Sawyer spluttered. 'CI? Have you been watching *Chicago PD*?'

'Okay. A source tells me that your fine colleagues are looking into a nasty bit of litter found by a couple of wild campers in woodland. Just up the road from you. Near Hayfield.'

'Litter?'

'Body. Male. Found a couple of days ago.'

Sawyer sliced the cream cheese icing from the surface of his cake and pushed it to the side of the plate. 'How did he die?'

'Not well.'

———

Sawyer drove across the private driveway bridge and parked the Mini by the side of the cottage. Across the road, the fields that rose to form the lower slopes of Kinder Scout had been yellowed by weeks of pitiless sunshine, and the ditch beneath the bridge had long since dried up.

He slid his key into the front door lock. Fletcher was hardly likely to telegraph his presence with an obliging chair scrape or door slam, but he let himself in slowly and silently.

Bruce, his black-and-white cat, lay in a tight ball on the sofa, and raised an ear as Sawyer closed the door. 'Busy day, big man?'

He poured a glass of Diet Coke, scooped something unspeakable into the cat's bowl and set his laptop on the coffee table. There he logged in to his VPN software and navigated to the remote home screen of the police HOLMES database. His own access had been revoked, but he typed *edshepherd* into the User ID box and *Rideout95* as the password. Shepherd was an Everton FC fan and, since starting to work with him, Sawyer had tried several combinations of Shepherd's name and various passwords relating to his children and football. He had discovered Shepherd's obsession with Everton's last major trophy win —the FA Cup in 1995—and had hit on the correct combination of winning goal scorer and year.

Sawyer accessed the most recent case file, submitted by the MIT unit at Buxton Station early that morning. The body of a thirty-four-year-old male, Duncan Hardwick, had been discovered partially buried in woodland near the Mermaid's Pool area, near to Hayfield.

Frazer Drummond's pathology findings were preliminary, with toxicology pending. But there was enough detail to make Sawyer raise his head and gaze across at Bruce, his mind drifting, connecting.

7

MAY 2010

'Visitor for you, Mr Fenwick.'

The ward sister retreated back into the corridor, making way for Sawyer to enter the room. He approached the bed and brushed aside his orange tie, taking a warrant card from the inside pocket of his jacket. 'James Fenwick?'

Fenwick nodded. He sat up and studied the card with sunken eyes. '*Sawyer*. As in Tom?'

'As in Detective.'

Fenwick sat up, eventually. He was obese, with a clean-shaven head that glinted in the window light. Swirls of wiry ginger hair poked over the top of his hospital gown.

Sawyer pulled up a chair and sat down at his bedside.

Fenwick sniffed, winced with pain. 'No grapes?'

'Official visit. No budget.'

'Where's your uniform, then?'

Sawyer smiled. 'You've caught me between ranks. Just qualified for CID.'

'Congratulations. Good to know they think I'm that important.'

'You're not. I'm the lowest rank available. Well, rank in waiting. DC. My DI hogs the glamour gigs.'

Fenwick nodded. 'The criminals.'

'You're thinking of the saboteurs.'

'One of the cunts that put me in here, yeah. No doubt. I was contracted to do a job, Mr Sawyer. It's not a pleasant job, but if it's not done, then the results are even less pleasant. Diseased livestock. The animals we rely on for beef, dairy. In comparison, badgers are expendable.'

Sawyer nodded. 'I'm not here to debate the logic.'

Fenwick laughed. 'There's no debate. It's proven that culling reduces the spread of bovine TB. It's for the greater good, of all animals.'

'Apart from badgers.'

'I thought we weren't debating.'

'Tell me what happened on Tuesday night.'

Fenwick lifted his bedsheet, revealing a bandaged leg. 'This happened. While I was working.'

'I understand you stepped in a steel-jaw trap.'

'Yes. A leghold. Your lot found another five of the fucking things in the area where we were culling that night.'

'How's the leg?'

Fenwick scoffed. 'I get to keep it. Just. If I hadn't been wearing thick overalls... Broke my ankle, though.'

'And you think this was deliberate?'

'So someone dropped a few traps around there by accident?'

'I mean as a sabotage. The cull personnel were specifically targeted.'

Fenwick reached over and took a sip of water from a plastic cup. 'Course they fucking were. We had it before. They use all kinds of tactics. Harassing farmers and families, pestering the landowners. Boxes of shit posted to politicians and companies.'

Sawyer glanced at Fenwick's bandaged leg. 'Has it ever got violent?'

'The odd scuffle here and there. Protests. Nothing like this, though.'

'Talk me through what happened.'

Fenwick sighed. 'There were six of us, up near Padley. We had a couple of drinks in the Fox House pub nearby and went up to the area where we were contracted to do the job. I heard a clunk and felt this excruciating pain in my leg. I thought I'd twisted my ankle between a couple of rocks. Then I looked down and saw the trap. Blood pissing out into my overall turn-ups. It took two of the others to get the jaws open. Screamed the fucking place down.'

'And you know the others in the group well? They were the only people around?'

Fenwick covered his leg, widened his eyes in mock shock. 'You think someone might have infiltrated us? An undercover animal rights agent?' Sawyer indulged him with a smile. 'Yes. I know all the others. I've worked with them all before.'

'Have you encountered anyone recently who expressed an opposition to the cull? Anything that stands out?'

Fenwick frowned. 'No. Despite what the propaganda says, cullers do it because they love animals. And because they care about public health. The activists don't see the big picture. They only have eyes for the cute creatures. It's a childish, Disney view of the world. If it was worms or wasps, they wouldn't care.'

Sawyer held Fenwick's gaze. 'It's interesting, though, that somebody has taken this approach, rather than the non-violent methods of disruption you mentioned.'

'Interesting?'

'Yeah. I'm sorry this happened to you, but I'm trying to focus on the elements that stand out, that don't quite connect. I'm intrigued that someone has gone to a lot of trouble to potentially inflict pain and suffering when they could have taken a less direct route and still stopped the cull. Was there anyone in the pub who looked suspicious?'

Fenwick dropped his head. 'Place was busy. There were a few people being rowdy on the lane, as we headed up to the woods. Students, probably, out on the piss. By the time we got up there it was dark. My missus called as we were getting our gear on, so I was last to get kitted out. I had to catch up with them.' He looked up, glanced at Sawyer, dropped his gaze again. 'We passed alongside this field. I thought I saw a few cows on the edge under some trees, but it was too late for them to be out. Trick of the light.'

'A few cows?'

'Well, actually only one or two. You sometimes get them out late but most are taken in by farmers. It almost looked like... It was hard to tell. I was catching up to the others, rushing. So it was just a glimpse, really.'

Sawyer nodded, shifted forward in his seat. 'See, now this is what I mean by interesting. What do you think you saw? A few cows? One? Two?'

Fenwick scowled. 'Actually, it was more like... They sometimes wander around the edges of the fields later in the day, I think. They're a bit bolder.'

'Go on.'

Fenwick took another drink of water. 'Look, what has this got to do with whoever's been putting traps down?'

'Just tell me what you think you saw, Mr Fenwick.'

'Probably a bull. Like I said, I was catching up with the others and I only saw it in passing. Corner of my eye sort of thing. But it looked like it had horns.'

8

PRESENT DAY

A woozy guitar melody. Morning sunlight leaking in through a gap in the blinds, stirring Sawyer awake. He rolled away from a lukewarm patch of perspiration and lay on his back, eyes open, steadying his breathing, listening to the opening minute of his phone's wake-up song: 'Tender' by Blur.

It had been another endless night, jostled by the usual terrors: snapshots of his mother brushing her thick black hair in the hall mirror at the old family home. Long, slow strokes. The brush catching on a knot. Blood seeping over her bare shoulder as she wrestled to untangle the strands. Her eyes searched for Sawyer in the mirror, but he knew if he looked, her face would be replaced by something unbearable: bloodied and bulging, shattered nose and brow, the jaw collapsed and twisted.

At some point in the night he had groped his way to the toilet and back, and sunk into a dream memory of a caravan holiday somewhere in Wales, with a young Sawyer and his older brother Michael peeling strips of dead skin from each other's sunburned backs. They had competed over the lengths of uninterrupted single layers, and in the dream version, Sawyer dug his way down to his brother's flesh, prodding and prising it off the bone.

He hauled himself out of bed, showered, and stood before the shaving mirror. The shower screen behind caught the reflection of his tattoo, traced across both shoulders: Κατά τον δαίμονα εαυτού ('True to his own spirit'). He worked through a session on his 'wooden man' Wing Chun training dummy, rolling his palms into the thick struts, driving his forearms across their length, simulating the mechanics of close-quarter grappling.

Bruce strutted into the bedroom, squealing for his breakfast. Sawyer scooped the fishy mush into a dish and flopped back onto the bed, still in his underwear, unsure of the time. He liked to think of himself as loose and untethered, but since his suspension, he had found the lack of structure surprisingly unsettling. As he basked in the gathering heat, listening to the cat feeding, he hunted his mind for connections.

His phone showed two messages. One from Stephanie Burns's husband, Jordan.

Jake. This is Jordan Burns. Can we meet? It's about Steph.

The informality was odd. He had only met Burns once before, briefly, a few days after the conclusion of the case. He had told him that he would be willing to help if ever Sawyer needed anything.

The second message contained an image of a bright blue ocean stretching out to infinity from an unspoilt beach of white sand. The photographer had taken great care to include the calf-down section of her tanned legs. Long feet slotted into red-and-black Gucci sliders. Toenails painted cherry red.

Hard work here! Luka is enjoying himself, but I could use some adult company. ;) xx

He typed a reply.

Wish I was there. We'll get together when I'm all clear. X

Sawyer sent the message and lay still for a few more seconds, zoning out. He sprang to his feet, dressed, and walked through into the low-beamed, L-shaped living space where his laptop sat open on the coffee table. He dropped onto the sofa and navigated to the *Derbyshire Times* website.

INVESTIGATION AFTER MAN'S BODY FOUND

The details were sparse, but confirmed most of what Sawyer had seen on HOLMES: Duncan Hardwick, thirty-four, discovered partially buried near to the Mermaid's Pool area just outside Hayfield. According to the story, Hardwick had been the manager of a chain of local butcher's shops, and was a keen walker in the area.

Sawyer logged back in to HOLMES. No updates apart from role assignments. Drummond's initial assessment was unchanged. *Hands and feet secured... Lateral incisions around the knee and elbow joints... Top stratum of skin (thigh, calf, upper arm, forearm) scored and pulled back.*

His phone rang. Reeves.

Sawyer logged out and did a Google search for 'urbex'.

He set down his phone, tapped the answer icon, and set it to speaker.

'Max.'

'Jake. As requested, I've been digging. It's dirty work.'

'Someone's got to do it.' Sawyer browsed the search results, and navigated to a website: *Left Behind*. 'Anything interesting?'

The clunk-click of a Zippo lighter. 'Fuck, yes.' Reeves puffed out smoke. 'You've picked a colourful character to piss off here, Sawyer. A few highlights. Mr Fletcher had a daughter with a woman, Marla Jacob, originally from Middlesbrough. They moved back up there for a while. Didn't last, and he went off to the SAS jungle training.'

'This would be early 2000s, yes?'

Another puff of smoke. 'Yep. So, Marla gets herself a new partner, Seth Wagner. Social worker. Worked with ex-offenders. Turns out he's pretty fucking offensive himself. When the daughter was six, Wagner was arrested for sexually abusing her.'

The site loaded. Black background. Large white title text in a surprisingly classy font. Subline: *UK Urban Exploration. Decay, Abandonment, Dereliction.*

'Fletcher's daughter,' said Sawyer.

'Yeah. I'll spare you the detail. He took pictures. We're talking four on the SAP scale.'

'That's not sparing me the detail.'

On-screen, an image carousel cycled through a series of photographs: a deserted factory interior; a hospital ward with wilted separator curtains and floor littered with documents; a child's bedroom with flaked cartoon wallpaper, crib and a wheelchair angled towards a vast, multi-pane window.

Reeves continued. 'Now, Fletcher had a few sanctions for insubordination. Anger issues. But his commanding officer was accused of raping a young girl in a village in Brunei, where they were stationed.'

Sawyer sat back. 'You've told me this before. You said that Fletcher was the one accused.'

'Yeah. But it looks like they fudged it, after Fletcher found out and chinned the officer. Charges dropped against his commander, but he was forced out. He moved to Amsterdam. Dutch father, spent a lot of time there as a kid.'

Sawyer clicked around the site. Disused cinema in Port Talbot. Abandoned grain warehouse in Leith. 'So, what happened to Wagner?'

'He served three years, and they found him dead shortly after his release. Still unsolved. Are you sitting comfortably?'

'Go on.'

'Castrated. PM stomach contents showed that the killer had force-fed him his own cock.' Another puff of smoke. 'I've said it before, Sawyer. Whatever you've got going on with this geezer, you really should kiss and make up.'

9

'That's time.'

Maggie Spark smiled at the man perched on the edge of the chocolate-brown Heal's futon. He got up, walked to the window and looked out over the moor towards the rocks of the Staffordshire Roaches.

He sighed. 'It goes so quickly.'

Maggie patted down the back of her rust red hair, recently cut short for summer. 'You know what they say about time flying, Joel.'

The man's shoulders tremored with laughter. 'I'm not sure I'd call this fun. We're making progress, though, right?'

'I think so. Don't you?'

'Kathryn does.'

Maggie nodded. 'Your wife.'

'Yeah. We moved here for a bit of peace, after everything that happened. If anything, it's been even more turbulent.'

'I can't speak for your wife, or for your relationship, but I do think the work is helping you personally. And you're the common factor.'

'That's good to hear.' Joel angled his head. 'I should go. You have someone waiting.'

Maggie stood. Joel strode past her, squeezed out a smile without eye contact, and left the room, closing the door behind him.

Maggie walked over to the window. A tea-coloured Fiesta was the only vehicle in the small car park, with a blond man in the driver's seat, sitting perfectly still. He caught Maggie's eye and turned his head slightly, revealing a short ponytail dangled over the back of his thick neck.

She followed Joel out into the hall, where he stood at the base of a vast Kandinsky reprint, making a phone call.

Maggie opened the front door and stepped out onto the porch. As she walked round to the car park, an engine revved up, and she rounded the corner in time to see the Fiesta drive away.

10

Sawyer drove south through the centre of the National Park. The day was muggy but overcast, and a light rain speckled the windscreen as he pulled out of Bakewell. The road which passed the Tudor pile of Haddon Hall was flat and straight—a Roman runway—and he squeezed the accelerator, pushing eighty, before he was throttled to a crawl by temporary roadworks outside Matlock. He listened to Episode Three of the Virginia Mendez podcast again, focusing on the voice of the individual she had trailed as 'The Explorer'.

'But you're not supposed to say anything, reveal the location.'

His breathing quickened, and as he approached the spot outside Samantha Coleman's house, he touched a hand to his tightening chest.

Inhale slowly, five seconds.

Exhale slowly, five seconds.

Wait another five seconds, repeat three times.

The voices on the podcast swam behind a sheen of distortion. An insistent baritone rose out of the murk.

'Take care of your brother, Jake.' His father's final words before ending his own life.

Inhale.

Exhale.

Sawyer lifted his eyes to the rear-view mirror.

A young woman with long black hair sat in the back seat, forehead against the window pane, watching the raindrops.

Sawyer knew there was nothing supernatural about this. His mother could not have visited him in apparition form. But the urge to talk, to connect, was strong.

Inhale.

He opened his mouth to speak but then closed his eyes, forcing himself to disengage. The breathing had blunted his panic, and he knew from experience that he could rationalise his way through the worst. This would be distressing but brief, and at least he was alone.

Exhale.

Sawyer switched off the engine and sat in silence for a while, taking solace from the stifling confinement. He unhitched the phone from its windscreen dock and navigated to the Contact page of the *Left Behind* website. He wrote a short message to the site owner, requesting a meeting, then pushed his way out of the car, keeping his eyes forward, away from the mirror.

———

'Who's Greg?'

Sawyer took the same seat on the back terrace and looked down to the end of the garden, where a patch of indigo delphiniums teetered in the breeze.

Samantha Coleman set down two glasses of water. 'My

ex-husband. Didn't I mention his name last time you were here?'

Sawyer took a sip, shook his head. 'It was on Virginia's notes. Maybe she went to see him?'

Samantha retied her ponytail. 'He's an architect.'

Sawyer waited for more, but didn't get it. 'Are you still in contact?'

She scoffed. 'No. I can give you his number, though.'

'Were he and Darren close?'

'They were, in the early years. I hear that men usually get more interested in their sons as they get older. With Greg it was the opposite. He was good with nappies and nose-wiping. Not so sharp at the emotional stuff later on.'

The hefty tabby prowled past; Sawyer reached out a hand and ran his fingertips across her fur. 'Teenagers reach a point where they need to escape their parents' influence. I know I did.'

'Jesus. Me, too. And didn't they know it!'

Sawyer smiled. 'Do you know who Adam might be?'

Samantha shook her head. 'Could be Adam Grayson, Darren's form tutor at Cedar Mount. He was decent. Supportive when Darren started the school. Not sure if he's still there, though. Virginia asked about him, too.'

Sawyer checked the Notes app on his phone. 'Two more. Sutton?' Samantha frowned, shook her head. 'Price?'

She scowled. 'Probably Ricky Price. Darren hung round with him. Parents were loaded but I wasn't keen on him. Off with the fairies. In trouble with the police a lot. So, are we just playing a naming game today, Mr Sawyer?'

'One more thing.'

'You sound like Columbo.' She took a drink, forced a smile. 'Don't look like him, though.'

'You should see me when I'm on duty. I wanted to ask you about urbex.'

51

'Is that a cereal?'

'Urban exploration. A fascination with abandoned places, buildings. Usually factories, hospitals, that kind of thing. Places with a spook factor because of their past.'

Samantha brightened. 'Oh. I saw something on Channel Four about that. Don't they find old houses, too? Sometimes all the furniture is still there, and the owner's bits and pieces. Weird.'

'Was Darren into it?'

'Not as far as I know. I suppose all teenagers have secrets, though.'

Sawyer nodded. 'Virginia used that line. In the podcast.'

'Probably stole it from me. I repeat myself a lot, these days. Sometimes to myself.' She sighed. 'No. Don't remember him mentioning anything about the exploring thing. And I can't think of who Sutton might be.' She closed her eyes, tipped her head back. 'Can I ask you a personal question, Mr Sawyer?'

'Of course. But I might exercise the right to silence.'

'Do you talk to them?'

Sawyer placed his glass down on the table. 'Who?'

'Your parents. They've... gone, of course. But do you still...'

He blinked. 'I used to talk to my mum, when I was younger. Just out-loud stuff. Things I was confused about. I'd ask her about something and speak her imagined reply out loud.' He sat back. 'My dad... That wasn't so long ago. I imagine him commenting on my actions, though. Chiding me, usually.'

'Did you argue?'

Sawyer angled his head. 'We had our disagreements.'

'I talk to Darren all the time. I imagine his opinions on things. Music, TV shows. They say that missing someone is a way of spending time with them.'

'In the present, yes. I have a friend who wants me to spend more time in the present. My mum told me not to look back, too.' He picked up the glass, peered into it. 'I'm not so sure about that. You can't discard your past. You just have to find a way to carry it into the future without it weighing you down.'

Samantha reached across the table. For a moment, it seemed she was aiming to take Sawyer's hand, but she picked up her glass and took a drink. 'How can you spend time with someone "in the present" who isn't around any more?'

'There's a version of the... missing person in many different states, across their whole life. The present version might not be in good condition, but it's fine in the other moments. The difference is that those versions are frozen, unchanging. That's what makes grief so hard. You're denied the version that can still change, grow, develop.' Sawyer leaned forward, gathering himself to stand.

Samantha raised an eyebrow. 'Escape the parents' influence... I saw your mother's grave in the newspaper. What a beautiful inscription. Was that you?'

'*What will survive of us is love.* It's a Philip Larkin quote, yes. He's my favourite poet.'

Samantha laughed. 'I haven't met many men who confess their favourite poet.' She held her hand down low, beckoning the cat, who slunk over and turned a circle as Samantha stroked her back. 'I'm sure you know this, but Darren will soon be considered legally dead. I got an email from a digital artist who said she could do an e-fit to see what he might look like now.'

'Aged progression.'

'Yes. I don't want it, though. I don't want another version of him that's frozen, that won't change.' Tears welled at the base of her eyes. 'Where's my boy, Mr Sawyer? Why isn't he with me?'

Sawyer kept his eyes on the cat. 'You shouldn't assume the worst. Young people go missing for lots of reasons. Problems at school, mental health, relationship breakdowns, outside influences like gang affiliation.'

'Let's assume my son is still alive. Do you think I'll see him again?'

He looked up. 'Do you want me to tell you what I think or tell you what I think you want to hear?'

'Give it to me straight.'

Sawyer pushed his hair out of his eyes. 'If he's still alive after seven years, either he doesn't want to be found or someone else doesn't want him to be found.'

———

Sawyer slotted the phone back in its cradle and set it on speaker. He tapped in a number and drove out of the town centre. Almost half a minute later, as he crossed the bridge over the River Derwent, the call connected.

Throat clearance from the other end. 'DI Sawyer.'

'DS Shepherd.'

'Should we be talking?'

'You tell me. Spoken to Farrell?'

Deep sigh. 'Ears burning, are they? Of course I've spoken to Farrell. Well. He's spoken at me.'

'He knows you were with me. On the Bowman raid.'

'No. He doesn't.'

Sawyer steered onto the Bakewell Road and veered around a cyclist, a little too close. 'Did you deny it?'

'He didn't ask.'

'And what would you say if he did ask?'

Another sigh. 'Sir...'

Sawyer screwed his eyes shut for a moment, glanced up towards the mirror, but didn't look into it. 'How's the head?'

'What?'

'Still above water?'

'Are you enquiring about my mental health?'

'We can get it out of the way quickly, then I'll change the subject.'

Shepherd laughed. 'It's better than it was last year.'

'I think I have a touch of what you had.'

'I'd be more worried if you weren't feeling any effects. You mean panic attacks?'

'Sort of.' Sawyer slowed to ease past a farm truck at the entrance to a single-track road. The engine was quiet enough for him to hear Shepherd's breathing.

'Sir, if he asks—'

'Ricky Price.'

'What?'

'Had any dealings with him? Anything recent? Before I came back from the Met?'

'He's a minor name. Nothing big, though. Possession. Public order. Parents sell farm machinery and vehicles, don't they? Big house up near Padley. So what's this? Bit of extra-curricular? I can't imagine the likes of Ricky Price as a candidate for your social circle.'

Sawyer smiled. 'You know me. I'm more about acquaintances than friends.'

A flare of sunlight rolled across the windscreen. The angle and intensity seemed familiar, oddly caustic. Sawyer caught his breath and raised his eyes to the rear-view mirror.

The back seat was empty.

11

Sawyer parked up alongside Fairfield golf course and strolled through the Buxton side streets. The portable sign for Dale Strickland's Players club was still propped up outside its retrofitted pub premises. He ducked inside and nodded to the quiffed thirtysomething behind the raised desk at the entrance.

'Clem, isn't it?'

A musky, back-bedroom fug hung in the air. Cliques of young men crowded around wall-mounted consoles and old-school arcade games. At the back of the room, a group wearing headphones sat around a connected hub of laptops near a serving hatch and café area. An abrasive techno track segued awkwardly into hectoring trap hip-hop, and Clem looked up from his laptop DJ software, squinting at Sawyer.

'Yeah,' said Sawyer. 'It's the copper. Don't worry. I'm off duty. Just wanted to check my Robotron high score was still standing.'

Clem nodded, blank faced. He turned his attention back to his laptop. 'Tenner for all you can play. No food or drink of your own.'

He paid and headed for the retro arcade section, with a rack of ten bulky cabinets, restored with original bezel artwork and control panels. A portly teenager in top-to-toe branded sportswear stood before the Missile Command machine, swiping and rolling the giant trackball, painting the digital sky with explosions that neutralised a cascade of incoming rockets. As his final base was destroyed, the screen filled with a fiery sign-off: *THE END*, and he lurched away from the cabinet in theatrical disgust, grubby dreadlocks whipping back over his shoulders.

'*Fuck* this shit!'

'Ashley Becker,' said Sawyer.

The teenager turned, rolled his eyes.

'You were shooting *at* the targets. You have to aim ahead, at where they're going to be.'

'*Ash*, yeah? Even my nan don't call me Ashley. The fuck are you doing here again?'

'Depends.'

'On what's in my bag? Sorry, Miami Vice. Just a few eggs. Temazepam.'

Sawyer stepped up to the machine and started a new game. 'Not sleeping?'

'Brain won't turn off, you get me?' Ash watched as Sawyer took out the first attack wave with precise and efficient rolls of the trackball, each shot timed to destroy multiple enemies.

Sawyer eyed him. 'More than you can imagine. Are you still working with the upstanding Mr Strickland?'

Ash gave an exaggerated shake of the head. 'Nah. I'm done with all that shit. Taking a course. Computers.' Sawyer raised an eyebrow. 'Hey. I'm *decent* at maths. And I know games.'

'Dale's moved into politics anyway, now.'

'True that.'

Sawyer tore into the second wave. 'I'm working on something. I hoped you might help.'

Ash laughed, wheezy. 'If you need me to go and say hello to some old woman again, I'm down. For a fee, yeah?'

'Have you heard of a lad called Ricky Price?'

Ash ran a hand across the folds in the back of his neck. 'Too right. Scary. Not as scary as he thinks, but still scary. Workout freak. Went to a party at his place once. Saw his gym. Crazy. He's well got Budgie Syndrome. Y'know, strutting around, preening and chirping at his own reflection. Thinks he's on Muscle fucking Beach.'

'Did you have any dealings with him?' Sawyer glanced over. 'Off the record.'

Ash scoffed. 'I told Shaun to tell Dale that he might be an issue, like. Dale wasn't bothered, though.'

Sawyer finished the wave and stepped back from the machine. He nodded, and Ash took over. Sawyer held up his phone. 'Do you recognise this voice?'

As Ash struggled to fend off the faster rockets in the second wave, Sawyer played a bookmarked section of Episode Three of the Virginia Mendez podcast.

'*Some people are dumb, though. They stick up their hero shots. Bragging, yeah? But you're not supposed to say anything, reveal the location.*'

Ash shook his head. 'No way. This guy is rougher. Price is proper posh. For this dump, anyway.' He sighed, as the missiles overwhelmed his bases, again ending the level, and the game.

'Tell me more about the party.'

Ash snatched up an open bottle of Tango Tropical from a nearby table and took a long swig. 'Dunno. Just... a party. Lots of dope. Shit music. I think his folks are away a lot. The house is well massive, up by the gorge. He usually opens the place up every Friday and Saturday. I heard there's a thing tonight.'

'How do I get an invite?'

Ash waved a hand. 'Ain't no invites. You go, and you either get in or you don't. And let me tell you now. No offence, yeah, but you are at least ten years over the age limit. They'll think you're a friend of his parents or something.' He smirked, took another drink.

Sawyer stared him out. 'I'll dress young. Borrow one of your hoodies.'

Ash spluttered and wiped his mouth.

'Not really. I am going, though. And you're coming with me.'

12

Sawyer strode along the corridor and stopped outside the last door on the right. While the lower levels of Buxton's Cavendish Hospital were NHS only, the Benedict Ward was a private patient aftercare unit, designed for comfort not crisis: tinted windows, wood panelling, the acidic tang of frequently used cleaning products.

He tapped twice on the ajar door and entered. The occupant was a hefty man sitting on the edge of his bed, facing a wide but narrow window that looked out across the sun-baked heather of the Goyt Valley. He cast a look over his shoulder as Sawyer took a seat on a cushioned chair near the door.

'Mike.'

The man nodded but didn't turn. 'Hello'.

Sawyer leaned to the left and saw that his brother was peering down into the screen of his handheld gaming device. His grey hair had grown out, emphasising a broad bald patch at the back of his scalp. He wore a standard hospital gown, which looked fresh and laundered, but Sawyer's nostrils wrinkled at the waft of stale sweat.

'What's the game?'

'Zelda.'

Michael angled his body away from the window and found Sawyer's green eyes with his own. The scars along his arm seemed redder, angrier, and he looked drawn and distant: drooping eyelids, callow skin.

'How are they treating you?'

Sawyer held the gaze, but Michael flinched and shifted back to his screen. He shrugged. 'Alright.'

'Trying to find a young lad. Fifteen. He's been gone for a long time, though. Seven years. Do you remember being fifteen?'

'No.'

'We went to a place in Wales. Saundersfoot. Caravan park. Dad let us have our own caravan.' Michael turned and peered at Sawyer, before returning to the game. 'It was the nineties. You were in a Pink Floyd phase. I was listening to Britpop. Lots of Underworld, too. Tricky, Massive Attack.'

A musical fanfare from the game. Michael lifted his head and looked out of the window. 'I don't remember.'

'You know why you're here, right?'

Head down again. 'Yeah. I shouldn't be here at all.'

'One of the attendants found you, saved you. Victoria. Do you know her?' Michael nodded. 'I'm glad you're still here. If you don't want to go back to Rosemary House, you could stay with me.'

A fortysomething man with a staff badge on his lapel entered the room and hovered near the door.

Sawyer leaned forward towards Michael. 'Life can be good again, Mike. I promised you I'd help you get it back. Do you remember?'

Michael looked up again and thought for a second. 'No.'

———

The hospital branch of Costa was busy with staff and patients, but Sawyer found a spare corner and huddled in with an unseasonal hot chocolate. He dialled a number; the call connected instantly.

'The Kraken awakes.'

'Mags.'

'Where are you?'

He sipped the froth from his drink. 'Coffee shop. Cavendish.'

A pause. 'Michael?'

'He's better. Sort of. Conscious, at least.'

'He'll need time.'

Sawyer exhaled. 'He'll need more than that.'

'What does his doctor say?'

'That he'll need time.'

Keyboard clatter. 'He's the patient—'

'But I need to have patience.'

She sighed. 'Yes. Are you paying for the care?'

'Out of my late father's trust fund, yes. I don't...' He took a drink. 'I'm not sure he knew who I was.'

'Mike? Of course he did, Jake. Be careful not to catastrophise. I'm sure that came up with Alex.'

'Not really.'

More keyboard. 'Well, you know how I feel about you dropping out of therapy. Are you staying busy? Did you take the missing boy case?'

'Yes. What are you typing?'

'Emails. You're on speaker. It's called multitasking. Mia says that demanding undivided attention is "old-fashioned". I'm sure I wasn't that precocious at her age.'

'I'm sure you were. Has Keating got you on FLO with the Hardwick case?'

A deeper sigh. 'Dare I ask, why do you ask?'

'It's ringing bells.'

'I'm sure you're not supposed to know, but yes. Not a nice way to go.'

'Is there a "nice" way?'

'Drowning in chocolate?'

He took a slug of his drink, checked the time. 'Me and Mike had this thing we used to say to each other, in the bad old days when Dad was struggling, after Mum had gone. "There's always death to fall back on."'

She laughed. 'How lovely. Jake...'

Here it comes.

'You should resume your therapy. Take the opportunity, now the day job has calmed down. It's a bad idea to just walk away. It's a form of self-medication.'

Sawyer slipped a hand into his pocket and tweaked the wrap he'd lifted from Ash as he'd played the videogame. 'I've already had my head examined.'

'You had another scan?'

'About to head in for a follow-up. Alex recommended the neurosurgeon. Kevin Tsong.'

'That's good to hear. I'm sure it'll be interesting. But you should get back to talking therapy, too.'

'I'm focused on Michael for now.' He stood up, walked through the doors, past a large sign, white on grey.

THE NUFFIELD HOSPITAL FOR NEUROLOGY & NEUROSURGERY

'You have to work on yourself, Jake. It's like a plane safety check, when they tell you to put your own oxygen mask on first in the event of an emergency. You can't help others when you need help yourself.'

———

Sawyer leaned forward and squinted at the computer monitor. An oval outline, glowing blue on a black background, corralled a complex but symmetrical array of branches and channels.

'So, this is you.' Kevin Tsong rolled his wheeled chair closer and aimed a pen at the screen. He hitched up his silver-rimmed glasses for focus. 'Transverse segmentation, top-down. We used the contrast dye to get a good look at the section highlighted in the scans you had many years ago. This leafy vegetable-looking part here is the cerebellum. All the white matter is nerve axons. This area here, in the temporal lobe,' he hovered the pen over a brighter section, left of centre, 'is the caudate nucleus. Basically, the housing for your amygdala, which is the almond-shaped structure here, just at the front of the hippocampus. Now look, there is a lesion, just over a centimetre.'

'Is that big?'

'Relatively, no. It's a focal bilateral lesion, and I don't see any evidence of malignancy. I'm confident of that because I see no other tissue damage in the area. It's likely to be a trigeminal schwannoma—a benign tumour at the base of the skull. They rarely cause any problems, and if they do grow, they grow very slowly. You've probably had it for a long time. It is in an awkward place, though. I suggest we monitor with another scan in six months. It's unlikely to cause any trouble, but if it does we can hit it with a bit of radiotherapy.' Tsong sat back and turned his chair towards Sawyer.

Sawyer's expression remained steady. 'What could have caused it?'

Tsong swept his thick brown hair across his head, tidying the side parting. 'Who knows? I understand you suffered some physical trauma as a child.'

The sun poking through Tsong's window.

His dog barking, barking, barking.
Blood on grass, shining red.

'My mother was murdered. With a hammer. The killer also used it on me and my older brother. I was six, he was nine.'

Tsong nodded. 'I'm sorry to hear that, Mr Sawyer. Life must have been... complicated. So this will have taken place around thirty years ago. And you're thinking the assault might have caused the lesion?'

Sawyer shrugged.

'Any other issues? Dizziness? Nausea? Weight loss?'

'No. I sometimes have a strange tingling feeling at the base of my neck. But it's hard to connect with—'

'What it's telling you?' Tsong gave a vigorous nod. 'And this sensation usually occurs in situations of stress?'

'Yes, and it's often when there's a lack of oxygen.'

'It could be that your amygdala has been damaged to the degree where you can only interpret, or detect, its signals in extreme situations.' Tsong pushed his chair back and stroked his chin. 'My brother-in-law is a free climber. I'm astonished by the risks he takes, but he says it's the only thing that makes him feel alive. It may be that some people's brain function means they need that intensity just to hit their baseline. Are you depressed? Do you take any medication?'

The catch in his mother's voice.
'Run, my darling. Don't look back!'

'No medication. And, yes, sort of. But I wouldn't call it depression. It's more anxiety. Flashes, memories. Almost like the event is playing out again and I'm feeling the same things, only the adult version.'

Tsong shifted in his seat. 'We may be straying outside the boundaries of my expertise, Mr Sawyer. It sounds like there may be emotional or behavioural issues you need to address. But physiologically, my concern is minor.'

'How about functional MRI? A go/no-go test?'

Tsong raised an eyebrow. 'To measure behavioural inhibition? What's your specific concern?'

Sawyer inhaled, held the breath for a few seconds. 'My decision making, motivations. Compulsions. I sometimes have this sense of detachment from my surroundings.'

Tsong wheeled his chair closer. 'Could you close your eyes for me?'

Sawyer did so. He caught a whiff of coffee on Tsong's breath as he leaned in.

'That's fine. You can open them again.'

Sawyer blinked. 'What are you looking for?'

Tsong backed away. 'There's a genetic condition called Urbach-Wiethe disease that can be related to amygdala damage, and it's possible that physical trauma could exacerbate symptoms. It often comes with skin lesions around the eyelids and elsewhere. You have a little dryness, but nothing severe. Urbach patients often have unusual fear conditioning. Faulty startle response, difficulty in recognising fear in others. This is why it's sometimes confused with a lack of empathy.'

'And how does it progress?'

'The prognosis is good. It's not a life-threatening condition. It can present with minor respiratory issues, and there's usually a progressive issue with episodic memory.'

Sawyer squinted. 'Long-term.'

'Yes. Events. Emotions associated with those events. But Urbach-Wiethe is exceptionally rare. Only a few hundred cases have ever been recorded.' Tsong drew in a deep breath, pondering. 'As I say, I deal with the hardware. We could run some tests for galvanic skin response, but otherwise I see no reason to clinically assess your response to stimuli, unless you're concerned about the effect it's having on your job, or vice versa. From what you're telling me, I would suggest you seek assessment from a trauma consultant. I have several colleagues—'

'Have you read Henry Marsh's book? The brain surgeon.'

Tsong cast his eyes up to the ceiling. '*Do No Harm*?'

'Yeah.' Sawyer ran a palm across the stubble on his chin. 'The part where he says he has an "internal graveyard" of the people he lost in surgery. Do you have that?'

Tsong sighed. 'Of course. I operated on a chap a couple of years ago. Late fifties. Glioblastoma. The most aggressive tumour we know. I removed half but then I nicked a perforating branch of the basilar, an artery that carries blood to the brain stem and regulates the rest of the brain. Bright red blood shot upward, like a mini geyser. I stopped it, but it was too late. Oxygen deprivation damaged the stem irreparably and the poor man never regained consciousness. Marsh is actually referring to a French doctor, René Leriche, who said that every surgeon carries within himself a small cemetery, where he goes to pray from time to time.' Tsong tilted his head forward and regarded Sawyer over the top of his glasses. 'I'm sure you experience something similar. As a policeman.'

Sawyer gazed at the image on the monitor. 'It's not really a cemetery for me. More like faces. Voices. Events. An internal projection that runs when I least expect it.'

Tsong nodded. 'We give our very best, Mr Sawyer. That's all we can do. Sometimes it isn't enough, or we're just not capable. But we can't save everyone.'

13

Sawyer parked the Mini on a verge at the end of a narrow track, near Grindleford Station. The early evening sunset cast a honeyed glow across the dense woodland of the Longshaw Estate, as it dipped towards the moorland trails and waterfalls of Padley Gorge.

'Decent spot,' said Ash, glancing up from his phone.

'Decent?'

'Yeah. Y'know. Pretty, like.'

'I used to come here a lot when I was a kid.'

They got out of the car and stepped over a stile onto a walking track that wound its way up to a ridge at the top of the valley.

Ash took the lead. He turned and shuffled backwards, smirking. 'It's weird. I can imagine you as a kid. Most coppers, they're like, *old*. Get me? Like they were fucking born old.'

Sawyer smiled. 'I'm not exactly young.'

Ash turned and pushed on. 'No, but... I ain't ever seen a five-o doing the business on *Missile Command*, yeah?'

Sawyer stumbled on a tree root. 'Couldn't we have parked any closer?'

'Nah. I think there's a private road round the other side of the estate. Too much hassle, though. I've always got in this way. Tradesman's entrance, like.' Ash looked over his shoulder, caught a raised eyebrow from Sawyer, turned back. 'See what I mean? *Mature*.'

A distant thrum of music drifted down from a large stone-built house that stood alone just beyond the estate boundary.

'Is that the place?' said Sawyer, waving a hand.

'There's no fooling you. And I meant to ask. The fuck do you want with Price, anyway?'

'I'm trying to find someone he might have known. A lad who's been missing for a while.'

Ash turned and gave Sawyer a grave look. 'So, what's the story tonight?'

'Like I said. Use the money I've given you, find Ricky Price, buy some dope.'

Ash clicked his tongue through his teeth. 'He won't be happy about dealing at his crib.'

'He doesn't have to be happy. You just have to make sure he sells you the drugs.'

'Isn't this, like, entanglement or whatever?'

'Entrapment. And no. It isn't. I just want to loosen him up, not arrest him.'

They passed a vast outdoor storage facility secured by high fencing. Tractors, harvesting machinery, trailed fertiliser spreaders, hay rakes, bale wrappers. Further ahead, two men at the front door of the house welcomed a couple and waved them inside.

Sawyer kept low. 'I'll hang back. Stay in touch. Text me.'

Ash laughed. '*Text*. So you're not that young.'

Sawyer watched as Ash approached the men and, after a brief conversation, entered the house. He propped himself up against a tree and killed half an hour with a few games on his phone.

As he guided a skier down a complex slalom course with subtle flicks of his thumb, an email alert led him to quit the game and navigate to the *Left Behind* website, where he'd received a reply from the site owner, PaulX.

Could talk tomorrow. Let me know when/where is good.

He looked up. Ash had exited the house and was making his way across the surrounding scrubland onto the walking track, towards Sawyer's position.

'Forty sheets.' He handed over a cellophane wrap of marijuana resin. 'This can't be for real. Buying drugs for police.'

Sawyer sniffed the contents of the wrap. A little tainted but the resin was solid and malleable, not brittle. 'Did he ask who it was for?'

'Like he gives a shit.'

Sawyer looked at him. 'How much was it, really?'

Ash hissed through his teeth again. 'I told you. Forty.'

'I know you told me that. But you're lying.'

Ash sighed and dug into his pocket. 'Twenty-five. C'mon, man. I'm fucking *polo*. I still owe him for some speed I bought last week, which has now gone walkabout. FML.' He caught himself, looked away.

'Keep the change.' Sawyer walked past him and headed towards the house. 'Wait by the car. I won't be long.'

―――――

'Fellas'. Sawyer nodded to the men standing either side of the vaulted front door. Close-up, the music sounded like it was coming from a large one-storey outbuilding around the side of the house.

The taller of the two stepped into Sawyer's path. 'You going inside?'

Sawyer smiled, giving him the dimple. 'That's the plan.'

The man was slight, and stood only an inch or two above Sawyer, but he looked agile, and his stance was confident; slightly side-on, semi-braced. He scrubbed at his chin. 'And can you give me a bit more on this "plan" of yours?'

The second man gave a mean little laugh, but stayed back in the shadow of the porch.

'I'm a professional assassin,' said Sawyer. 'I've been hired to murder Ricky Price and torch the place, leaving no evidence and no witnesses. I can take you guys out first if you like. I promise to make it quick.'

The tall man laughed. He turned to his colleague, then back to Sawyer. 'Haven't seen you before. How d'you know Rick?'

Sawyer held up his hands. 'It's a fair cop. I'm actually his Grindr date.'

The second man took out a phone and typed something. 'Rick's inside, in the main house. Let's try one more time, shall we?'

Sawyer walked around the tall man and approached the porch. The first man let him pass, but the second looked up from his phone and stepped in front of the door. 'Tell him I'm a detective investigating the disappearance of two people. I'm here because I think that Rick can help me with my enquiry.' He gave a broad smile. 'You do know that's a euphemism, right?'

———

The inside of the house was an ugly mix of original features and gaudy refurbishments. Sawyer crossed the marble-floored hallway, and tapped on a rustic, barn-style oak door beside a wide staircase. A short but stocky man in a good suit leaned over the balustrade on the landing above, sipping a drink, watching.

'Yeah!' A voice from inside.

Sawyer stepped into the room. It was still just about light outside, but the blinds had been drawn, and a vast TV mounted on the near wall flashed its imagery onto a rakish individual propped on the edge of a bright yellow velvet sofa. Barefoot, denim shorts, faded pink hoodie. The room smelt of zesty detergent, tainted by marijuana.

The man handed his game controller to a young girl in a bathrobe perched on the arm of the sofa and raised his head to look at Sawyer, face obscured inside his hood.

'What can I do for you, chief?' He slipped back the hood. Piggy eyes; bushy black neck beard; thatch of turquoise hair on top, shaved around the sides.

Sawyer walked forward and flopped into an armchair angled towards the screen. 'You're Ricky Price, right?'

Price exchanged a glance with the girl. 'I'm not aware we had a meeting scheduled.'

'Hardly looks like your diary is packed, Ricky. Is this the new *Call of Duty*?'

'You a fan, yeah?'

'Haven't played it. I like the older games. There's a purity about them. I loved the original *Modern Warfare*, though.'

Price recoiled in mock shock. 'That's fucking ancient, man.'

'I'd say it's still the peak of the series, before the money started to direct the art.'

Price scoffed. 'Okay, boomer.'

'You're about twenty years out. Are your mum and dad around?'

'What are you, neighbourhood watch or something? We had a complaint about the noise?'

'I'm a detective. Lloyd Robbins.' Sawyer had named his alias after his favourite stage pickpocket, Apollo Robbins.

The girl looked over at Price, who kept his eyes on Sawyer. 'My mum and dad aren't the "around" types, Detective Robbins. They sell farm gear, to farmers.'

'Online?'

He nodded. 'Auctions too, sometimes.'

'And you're hoping to follow in their footsteps? Take over the business?'

Price winced. 'Nah. I do e-sports. Bit of producing. Not into shit-spreading.'

'You recently spoke to a young woman called Virginia Mendez.'

'Did I?' Price took back the controller from the girl and re-engaged with the game. Crashes, shouts, gunfire.

Sawyer raised his voice. 'You did. She was investigating the disappearance of a lad called Darren Coleman, from Matlock. Went missing seven years ago. You knew him, didn't you?'

'Vaguely. He was alright. Long time ago, man. Seven years.'

'Particularly for his mother.'

Price's eyes flicked to Sawyer. He hitched up his hood and went back to the game. 'This Virginia his mum?'

'No. She's a journalist, looking into his disappearance. You would have spoken to her just over two weeks ago.'

He shrugged. 'Don't remember.'

'Yes, you do.'

Price played for a few more seconds, then paused the game. He let the controller fall to the floor and sat back in the sofa. 'Oh, yeah. Spoke on the phone. I didn't have much to say to her about Darren, though. We were supposed to meet for a proper interview but she didn't turn up.'

'You say you knew Darren. In what way?'

'He was a mate of a mate, I think. School connection, maybe.'

'Did you sell him drugs, Ricky?'

Price spluttered and leaned forward. '*Drugs*? No, I did not sell him drugs.'

'But you do sell drugs, don't you?'

Price gaped at Sawyer and laughed. 'Can you make your mind up? Are you gonna arrest me for kidnapping or drug dealing?'

'Well, I have evidence for one of those.' Sawyer took out the wrap of marijuana and held it up.

'Where did you get that?'

'We've been watching one of your clients. He just left here with it.'

Price shook his head, smiling. 'Strike One for the war on fucking drugs. Do you really think anyone gives two shits about a bit of dope, these days?'

'By "anyone", do you mean your parents? This is still their house, right? Am I going to find more of your product on the people in that outbuilding?'

Price called out. '*Taylor*.' He picked up the joypad and resumed play. 'Look, Mr Robbins. It was nice to meet you. But unless you've got a warrant or something, I'm so over this conversation.'

Taylor—the suited man from the landing—entered and approached Sawyer. 'Let's have you, cowboy. Time for bed.'

He reached out with his left arm, but Sawyer stepped to the side and gripped the forearm, holding it firm. Taylor attempted a right punch but Sawyer checked it with an elbow strike to the crook of his arm. As they stood for a moment, frozen in the grapple, Sawyer kicked Taylor's forward foot to the side, unbalancing him, and moved in close, holding his arm firm at the elbow joint and stepping behind him, denying the angle for any counterattack. Taylor roared in pain as Sawyer twisted and applied pressure on the back side of the joint.

The girl cried out, and sprang to her feet. Price dropped the joypad and scurried over the back of the sofa, using it as a barrier. He flipped back his hood and gaped at the scene, laughing. 'Holy shit. It's Johnny Fucking Cage.'

Sawyer eased the pressure on Taylor's elbow joint, but held him firm. 'I'm not quite ready to leave yet, Ricky. I was hoping for some insight into your relationship with Darren. I think it was a bit more than a "mate of a mate".'

Price scowled and held up his hands, palms up. 'What the fuck, Taylor? Where's your black-belt shit?'

Taylor groaned and tried to jerk himself forward, but Sawyer twisted at the joint and applied more pressure, causing him to howl.

Price took a wary step around the sofa. 'You know what, Mr Robbins? Looks like you've got the idea that Missing Boy was some kind of angel.' He shook his head. 'I did sell him some gear, yeah. None of that shit you showed me, though. He was into something stronger.'

14

Sawyer woke way too early. He lay in bed for a while, gazing up at the ceiling, tuning in to the dawn chorus. He made coffee and forced himself to work out with overladen hand weights, grunting through each lift and curl. He showered, dressed and flopped onto the sofa. The wrap of speed he'd lifted from Ash at the Players club sat on the coffee table; he pocketed it, and fired up his favourite PS4 game, *Bullet Symphony*, a comically hostile 2D shoot-'em-up.

Sawyer jinked his way through a torrential onslaught of glowing, pellet-like missiles, and paused the game, freezing the mayhem into a flickering, static image. He caught a flavour of something, a distant nag of memory. He closed his eyes and let his mind drift, but it would only latch onto the usual terrors: the wrinkles in his father's neck as he dug the shotgun barrel under his chin; his mother's pulverised face; his brother, looking over his shoulder, looking back but seeing nothing.

He dialled Shepherd's number, set the phone to speaker and continued with the game at a low volume. The call connected, to silence.

'Ed?'

'Jake. We're going informal now, then?'

'Sorry, it's a bit early.'

A clunk as Shepherd closed his office door, reminding Sawyer of the open-plan MIT floor with its side offices and central conference room. Shepherd sighed but said nothing.

'You've spoken to Farrell,' prompted Sawyer.

'Briefly. We're due for a formal debrief later with the IOPC goon.'

'It's taken him a while to get round to you.'

A tinkling teaspoon from Shepherd's end. 'Probably his idea of sweating me.'

'He's letting you know he's giving you time to prepare your story. It's a domination thing. Showing that he's all set to pick holes in it.'

'He told me not to discuss it with you.'

'So that's going well.'

Shepherd laughed. 'Did you catch up with Mr Price?'

Sawyer paused the game again, suddenly irritated by the chaos, and turned off the console. 'Yeah. Quite a charmer. Any leads on the Hardwick murder?'

'No. But I couldn't tell you, anyway.'

'You just did.' Sawyer switched the phone off speaker and picked it up. He found his car keys and headed for the door. 'It's... pinging something.'

Shepherd slurped at a drink. 'Pinging?'

'The body. The method.'

'And how, dare I ask, do you know about the method?'

'I couldn't possibly reveal my sources.'

'Logan.'

Sawyer opened the front door and cradled the phone in his shoulder as he locked up. 'Butcher's shops. Hardwick owned a chain of them.'

'You think he overcharged someone for their sausages?'

Sawyer climbed into the Mini. 'Any toxicology yet?'

'Yet?'

'I take it Drummond didn't fast-track it. Hardwick was thirty-four, male. Not young enough or female enough.'

'Partially buried.'

Sawyer turned the ignition. 'Yeah, that's interesting. It's an outlier. But I'd be keen to know if his killer drugged him before peeling off his skin.'

———

The noise of the car engine sounded an alert on a tracking device by the side of a man in a dilapidated farm outbuilding, in a grazing field close to Sawyer's house. He took a few lungfuls of morning air and sat up in his sleeping blanket. He opened a bottle of pills marked with a green logo—three concentric *C* symbols—and tossed two into his mouth, then washed them down with water.

He scraped his loose blond hair back, tied it into a ponytail, and reached for his boots.

15

'PaulX, I presume?'

Sawyer offered a hand to the timid-looking man stirring the straw around his milkshake. He took far too long to accept the hand, and, after shaking, lathered his hands together as if he were washing them.

'Sorry. I don't mean to be rude. I don't normally...'

Sawyer ordered tea, and browsed the cake selection. 'Do you want anything else, Paul?'

'Uh, no. Thanks.'

Insomnia was a popular indie coffee shop on a busy crossroads in the Hope Valley. It was packed to capacity with morning locals and tourists, and they had to raise their voices over the chatter. Sawyer bought an apple pastry: browned and frosted with sugar. 'Why the X?'

'Oh.' He coughed out a laugh. 'It's not my surname. I'm Paul Barton. Just... an online alias, I suppose.'

'Is it a fairly secretive thing, the urbex world?'

'God, yeah. There's all kinds of politics.'

Sawyer brought his tea and cake over to the table.

Barton smiled. 'Is that breakfast?'

Sawyer dug in with a mini-fork. 'Well. It's sort of fruit. With a bit of carbs for dessert.'

Barton sucked on his straw. He was scrawny and sallow, mid-to-late twenties, shaven-headed, in a saggy blue T-shirt with a bright yellow legend rendered like a graffiti tag: *BILLIE EILISH.*

Sawyer munched on his cake, watching Barton as his eyes flitted around: anywhere but at Sawyer. 'Thanks for meeting. My name's Jake Sawyer.'

Barton nodded. 'As in Tom.'

'The Mark Twain character or the Rush song?'

'What's Rush?'

'An old band. Three Canadians.' He nodded at Barton's T-shirt. 'You wouldn't like them. I'm investigating the disappearance of a local lad, Darren Coleman. Have you heard of him?'

Barton shook his head and put down his straw.

'He went out to a party in Matlock seven years ago. Never came home. I think he might have been into urbex, and I wanted to find out a bit more about how it all works. Can I just play you something?'

Sawyer took out his phone and navigated to the bookmarked section of the audio snippet taken from Episode Three of the Mendez podcast. Barton replaced the headphones with his own and Sawyer pressed play.

He listened for a few seconds, then removed his headphones and lathered his hands together again, swiping his palms over each other.

Sawyer stirred his tea. 'What do you think?'

Barton caught Sawyer's eye for a moment then looked down at his writhing hands. 'Sounds like an urbexer. I don't recognise the voice, though.'

'He talks about "hot places", "hero shots".'

'Yeah. A hero shot is a pic of an explorer looking smug

or happy about something he's discovered. Like a trophy. A brag. You get people shots, action shots. Dirty shots are where the light is low but they've bumped up the gain, so it's rough and grainy. A hot place is somewhere that's either a new explore or it hasn't been rinsed yet. Y'know, over-exposed, fully investigated. No surprises.'

Sawyer nodded. 'Virgin territory.'

'Sort of. People do it for different reasons. Some love the ruin porn aspect; some like the danger of sneaking into forbidden places. Then you get all the Goon Tubers who do it for likes and attention.'

Sawyer sloshed his tea around and took a sip. 'How about you?'

Barton made fleeting eye contact before looking out of the window. 'I'm all about the ruin porn. I love the darker places like asylums and mortuaries. Hospitals. I grew up near an abandoned hospital, near Sheffield. I wandered around it a lot when I was a kid and it got under my skin. Sometimes I don't even take pictures. I just wander around and breathe it in. The hospitals and mortuaries are wonderful. You get artefacts still lying around, and there's something quite beautiful about an old porcelain mortuary slab.' He looked back at Sawyer, holding his gaze this time. 'I know what you're thinking. Weirdo. But you'd be surprised. It's a social community. We have parties, meet-ups.'

Sawyer smiled. 'I wasn't thinking that. Are there still plenty of hot places or have most of them been... rinsed?' He sliced off a crusty corner of cake and forked it into his mouth.

'Oh, there are loads of places only a few people know about. There's a public forum on *Left Behind* where you're expected to reveal the locations. That's usually reserved for the obvious places. But there are other levels. A section called "non-public", which is for the inner circle, and there are regional groups within that, and then a small group of super elites who keep the really good stuff to themselves.'

'Are there tensions? Fallings out?'

'All the time, yeah.'

'And what about the people who own the buildings? Landowners, security?'

Barton shook his head. 'Depends. They're normally okay with standard urbexers, but you also get metal buries.' He winced. 'Sorry to say the word, but... pikeys, basically. You know what I mean. They get in and steal copper. Some of them make a living out of it. And, obviously, the listed buildings tend to be secure. There are plenty of old cotton mills in Huddersfield and Halifax, but they're listed and you can't get near them.'

'What use are abandoned buildings to the landowners?'

Barton laughed. 'Well, exactly. Not much. Some of them, though... They mysteriously catch fire. Then the owner can flatten the land and rebuild on it. The bloke who owned the Derby Hippodrome drove a JCB in there and said the roof collapsed. You get tension between the locals who want to restore, and the owners who want to raze everything and build more lucrative businesses on top.'

'Do you ever clash with security, police?'

'We do our best to avoid that. Some owners hire people to watch over the building, give them keyholder status. They can get aggressive. North Wales hospital in Denbigh had a notorious security guy who looked after the site. He was bipolar. Sometimes he'd be nice and other times he'd set his dog on you.'

'And you set up the website yourself, yes? Where are you based?'

Barton smiled. 'I couldn't possibly reveal the location.' He held the moment a bit too long. 'I've got a flat just outside Monyash. I work for a local IT company.' Barton finished his drink. He dropped his gaze and placed his hands in his lap, folding them over and into each other.

Sawyer kept his eyes on the hands. 'Have you heard of anyone called Sutton who may be involved in the urbex world?'

Barton shook his head; the hand movement continued.

'How about locations near to Matlock that could be interesting, or might have been hot places a few years ago?'

'There'll be one or two. Can't think of any off-hand. I'll check and let you know.'

Sawyer drained his cup and clunked the mug back down on the table. 'Thanks again for taking the time to meet, Paul. Last question, I promise. Well. More of a word.'

Barton raised his head, looked around, anywhere but Sawyer.

Sawyer leaned back in his chair. '*Devil*.'

The hands froze in place. Barton gave a slow nod. 'What about it?'

'Does the word ping anything for you? Association with a place? Person? A nickname?'

With effort, Barton turned to face Sawyer. He held eye contact for a moment, then looked back down at his hands, got them moving again. 'No. I can't think of anything, sorry.'

―――――

Sawyer drove to Buxton Police Station and took his usual spot in the car park, surprised that Farrell hadn't rented it out during his suspension. He sat there for a while, scrolling through the public forum of the *Left Behind* website on his phone. Photo galleries of recent explores, access advice, a long thread about clothing and safety during exploring. He tried a few searches: *Sutton, Darren, Coleman, Price, Matlock, Mendez, Devil.*

Nothing.

He navigated to his account page, which informed him that his posts would be moderated for a while as an anti-spam measure, and that he had access to 'most' of the forum features.

Sawyer looked up. Karl Rhodes, the station's digital media adviser, approached a white BMW parked in the far corner. Sawyer wound down his window.

Rhodes caught the movement and walked over, stooping to peer into the Mini. 'Look who it fucking well is! This your idea of a discreet spot for a shady meeting?'

Sawyer angled his head towards the passenger side and Rhodes climbed in and closed the door. He was short and square-headed, with a neat moustache. As he settled into his seat, Sawyer caught a whiff of whisky on his breath.

Rhodes turned to Sawyer and grinned. 'What can I do for you?'

'I need some digital media advice. So I thought I'd ask our digital media adviser.'

'Our? Let's see your warrant card, then.'

Sawyer sighed. 'Okay. *A* digital media adviser.' He opened the glovebox, took out a crumpled packet of lemon bonbons and offered it to Rhodes, who smiled, took one, popped it in his mouth. Sawyer replaced the packet.

'You not dining with me?'

'Already eaten. How are things?'

Rhodes rolled the sweet around his mouth. 'Hectic. Nasty new case. I'm sure you know more than I do, though.' He chewed, regarding Sawyer with a smirk. 'Keeping your hand in, I assume?'

'Working on something extra-curricular. Could you have a look at a website for me?'

'By "have a look" you mean—'

'I mean illegally hack the back end and don't tell anyone.'

Rhodes laughed. 'I could be wearing a wire, you know.'

'It's a victimless crime. In fact, it's a crime that might help to prevent someone becoming a victim of a more serious crime.'

Rhodes looked out of the windscreen and took a few seconds to enjoy his sweet. 'Here we sit, two police officers, in the car park of a police station, plotting criminal activity.'

Sawyer gave a slow nod. 'How ironic.'

'What's the site?'

'It's called *Left Behind*. Urban exploration. People who get off on abandoned buildings, factories, that kind of thing. I'm trying to find someone, and I think they might have contributed to one of the site's hidden areas. There's a public forum but other levels are only accessible to members with specific status.'

Rhodes looked at him. 'That's it? Fucking hell, Sawyer. You could do this yourself with a bit of googling.'

'Maybe. But you could do it without the googling. Saves time. I'm looking for references to three things. The word "Devil", and two names. "Sutton" and "Darren Coleman".'

Rhodes took out a pad and made a note. 'Isn't Coleman that kid who went missing a few years ago?'

'Seven, yeah. Do you remember the case?'

'A bit.' He grimaced and held Sawyer's gaze. 'Seven years. Going back a bit. I'm sorry for him and his folks but you're not going to find him now. Is there really any point in raking over dead ground?'

Sawyer opened the glovebox and took out a sweet, slipped it into his mouth. He looked out at the station building. 'A great philosopher once wrote, "The past is never dead. It's not even past."'

Rhodes angled his head. 'Deep. Who said that, then?'

'Faulkner. He meant that we tend to dismiss the past because we say that we're always changing and need to look to the future and the present. But the present is constantly moving into the past. So, in a way, it's inescapable.'

Rhodes shoved the pad back into his pocket and opened the door. 'See, this is why you don't get invited to parties.'

16

AUGUST 2010

Sawyer had to duck slightly to enter the main door of The Nut Tree, a compact café on the corner of a patch of detached houses just outside the village of Hartington. Maggie Spark sat in one of two facing brown leather sofas, browsing the newspaper sections on a coffee table. She tucked her hair behind one ear and looked up, pointing to the cups on the table.

Sawyer headed over, sidestepping through a lively lunch crowd gathered around the counter. Maggie greeted him with a hug and he sank into the sofa.

'Got you a coffee.' She smiled, watching him take in the place. 'And a thing.'

He smiled and plucked a corner section off the slice of cake on a plate beside a tall mug of coffee. He posted it into his mouth and raised his eyebrows in approval. 'A coconut thing.'

Maggie nodded, sipped her coffee. 'Nice new place.'

Sawyer brushed a crumb from the corner of his mouth. 'Good to see someone addressing the shortage of coffee and cream tea options round these parts.'

'Been to see your mum?'

He managed a strained grin. 'Yeah. She's doing well. Certainly no worse.'

'I tried to get you some flowers for the grave but the shop was shut. They had a flood or something.'

He sipped his coffee. 'Great anecdote.'

She laughed. 'So, how does it feel?'

'Velvety. Good blend. Little bit bitter. I'll add some more sugar.'

'I mean the new role. Your new status. Detective Constable.'

'My bobby days are behind me.' He ate some more cake, looked at her, held off for a few seconds but then returned her smile. 'So far, so good. A monumental change. DC from PC.'

'You can finally wear your own clothes.'

'And I'm so made for the catwalk.' He glanced at her wedding ring. 'You've changed, too. From Miss to Mrs. How's *your* new role?'

Maggie looked away. 'It's good. Exciting. Justin is lovely. Very clever.'

'*A wrangle for the ring.* You're looking sun-kissed. Where did you go? Caribbean?'

'Jamaica. Bit too hot for me.'

He laughed. 'Did nobody tell you it's tropical?'

She sipped her herbal tea. 'My God, Jake. I couldn't believe it when we got off the plane. It was like a sauna outside. I was so glad for the air-conditioned hotel. We didn't travel around much, apart from a fishing trip with a few locals. I feel a bit guilty—'

'That you didn't see the real Jamaica?'

Maggie gave Sawyer a look.

'Does he want more kids?'

'Justin? What about me?'

'I know you do.' He looked over the *Observer* Travel section. 'We should probably have got married.'

She gaped. 'After uni?'

'Yeah. In an alternate reality, we went travelling. Europe, Africa, Canaries.'

'Uhuh. And did we have kids?'

'No. We stayed itinerant, exploring the world.'

Maggie shook her head. 'See, there's an old romantic in you somewhere. Beneath those defences.'

He held her eye. 'I'm glad you didn't change your name. It's too good. What's he? Jenkins or something?'

'Perkins.'

'I rest my case.'

She took a long drink. 'You don't rest anything. Least of all yourself.'

'Does Justin know you're meeting me?'

A sigh. 'Of course he does.'

'Thinking of heading south.' He dug back into the cake.

'Where? London?'

He nodded. 'Still a bit early for a transfer to the Met, but it's an idea. I need to get away.'

'Jake. We talked about this at the wedding. You need to look after yourself. You can't just run away from your—'

'Demons. I know. I wouldn't be running away from anything. Just... embracing possibility. Mum told me to run, don't look back.'

'I'm going to buy you a book on Stoicism. The classical type. It's a philosophy I think you'll get behind.'

Sawyer browsed the newspaper. 'Is this the basis for your therapy thing?'

'I want to wind down the FLO work and start my own counselling business. It's just too emotionally draining, propping up the poor people whose lives have turned into nightmares. I can't cope with all the horrors. At least therapy would feel like I was—'

'Helping to prevent things? Maybe heading off some of the horrors?'

'Well, yes.'

He pushed the paper away. 'Did you ever get anywhere with that case you showed me on my first day? Remember? The guy who was tortured and skinned.'

She winced. 'I don't think so. Ask DI Pittman. It was one of his. Hideous, but in a weird way. The open-ended cases are worse. The ones with no bodies, no resolution. Yesterday, I was with the wife of a professor who's gone missing. Totally out of character. No sign. Just awful.' She caught herself. 'Are you sure detective work will be good for you?'

'I think so. I don't seem to...' He lubricated the thought with a sip of coffee. 'I don't really feel the danger. The threat, the fear. It keeps my head clear to... see the angles others don't see, maybe. Through the fog of emotion. But I also find it hard to project, extrapolate for—'

'Consequences?'

Sawyer shrugged.

'Maybe it's because you feel there's nothing that can happen that will be worse than the trauma you've already experienced.'

'I wouldn't be running away if I go to London. I'm not planning ahead.'

She leaned forward. 'Jake, what happened to you as a child... It taught you that things can change at any moment. It's made you wary of everything. Second-guessing. Expecting terrible reversal at any moment. Of course you have to go forward with some kind of hope. But it's okay not to plan too far ahead. It's one of the pleasures of life, the not knowing. Not knowing what's going to happen, not knowing how it's going to end.'

Sawyer sat back. 'Spoiler. Everybody dies.'

17

PRESENT DAY

Dale Strickland entered the carpeted office and fell into the revolving chair by the wide glass-topped desk. He pushed the chair away and spun round to face the view down to Deansgate far below.

'Movies!' He took off his glasses and laid them on the desk, but didn't turn to face Jerome, standing in the corner.

Jerome produced a digital tablet and approached the desk. He accessed a video file and propped the tablet on its cover stand.

Strickland leaned forward and flopped his arms onto the desk. 'First item on the agenda. I've been offered a new office in the mayor building. Broadhurst House. It'll be a shame to abandon the glamour of this place, but I simply can't face another summer with faulty air-conditioning.' He looked at Jerome. 'So I'll need someone to run the clubs for me.'

Jerome nodded, solemn.

'Now. Movies.'

Strickland cleaned his glasses with his shirt cuff and set them on the end of his nose. Jerome stood over the tablet in silence, watching. Dale nodded at him, and he played the video.

'This is an edit of two weeks' worth of drone footage taken over Fletcher's position.' His voice was accented—Eastern Europe—and surprisingly high-pitched for such a hefty man, but there was a colourless chill to his tone.

Dale watched the video: a bird's-eye view of the farmland around Edale. The image zoomed in to a dilapidated building as a man resembling Fletcher emerged and walked to a path at the edge of the field, where he disappeared beneath tree cover. The background switched to gritstone moorland on a rainy day. A brown Fiesta driving along the track by Ramshaw Rocks. Jump-cut to the vehicle in a small car park beside a smart-looking detached house that overlooked the Roaches.

'Is he still living in a fucking field?'

'He is. And he's an early riser. I stayed at some pub hotel for a few days. Flew the drone from my car parked nearby. He's tracking Sawyer still, but sometimes goes to check on Sawyer's friend, Maggie Spark, at her house.'

Dale took a bottle of Glenfiddich off a shelf and splashed a little into a weighty glass. He pointed to the bottle and looked at Jerome, who shook his head. 'Has he been to the house? Is he watching Eva?'

'No. She's away at the moment. Greece.'

Dale sipped his whisky and peered into the tablet screen. 'Why?'

Jerome stepped forward, giving himself a view of the screen. 'Why what?'

'He's cleaned house. Taken out two of my employees. Why doesn't he just do Sawyer and disappear?'

'The gun?'

Dale grimaced, shook his head. 'I don't think he cares. He knows he's on my shitlist.'

'Maybe because of the previous run-ins with Sawyer, he's taking his time, assessing his angles. Making sure he gets it right this time.'

The screen showed Fletcher's Fiesta in the car park outside Maggie's house.

'I know Fletcher. He's lateral. I think he's stalking Maggie as an option to get Sawyer away from home, draw him out, engineer a moment of weakness.'

'Or maybe he's just having second thoughts about taking out a copper.'

Dale laughed. 'Fletcher wouldn't care either way. I might have an angle with Sawyer, anyway.'

Jerome retrieved the tablet and switched it off. 'How about my idea?'

Dale took off his glasses again, fiddled with the arms.

Jerome stepped closer. 'It would keep you out of the picture and could deal with two problems in one go.' He held up a packet of Fatima brand Turkish cigarettes. 'We use Sawyer's skills against him. Get him to do the dirty work for us. Even if he doesn't make the direct connection, Sawyer will already suspect that Fletcher has been watching him, and Maggie.'

Dale pivoted his chair and opened the window a few inches. The chug of traffic slipped into the room. A Metrolink tram squealed as it braked for the station. He nodded. 'Make it unpleasant, but not permanent.'

18

A bell jangled as Sawyer opened the door of Scrivener's, a second-hand bookshop in the centre of Buxton. He inhaled the oaky fragrance of ageing paper and browsed a shelf of custom-bound hardbacks on local history, positioned, bizarrely, beside a doorstopper biography of the band Queen. The room was small and narrow, and every available surface was wedged tight with books; mostly collectable and antiquarian on the ground floor.

The elderly owner watched him from a cushioned rocking chair, writing in a logbook. 'New arrivals.' He took off his flat cap and nodded at a pile of paperbacks at his side.

Sawyer smiled. 'I've never been in here. Always meant to.'

'Most people default to the High Peak Bookstore. Coffee and cakes and all that. We're more old-fashioned, I suppose. I do bookbinding demonstrations. We have five floors of books, though. Over forty thousand, at last count.'

'Feels like a place you could get lost in.'

The man laughed. 'Oh, people do! We've had three shut-ins over the twenty-three years we've been here. They became so engrossed, in a dark corner somewhere. We just leave a key now, so they can let themselves out. I find if you trust people then they tend to live up to expectations. Can I help you with anything in particular? I'm Alistair, by the way.'

'Jake. I'm interested in urban exploration.'

Alistair pushed himself to his feet. 'I saw something on that the other day. It's the chaps who nose around abandoned hospitals and factories and what-not, yes?'

'It is. "Chaps" being the operative word.'

He laughed. 'Well, we men do like our pointless pursuits. The women have more important things to do. Let me just find that book for you.'

Alistair hobbled through to a back room. Sawyer walked over to the till where the impulse buys sat in a line across the main counter: bookmarks, local guides, reading lights, and a box of Cadbury's Dairy Milk chocolate bars.

'Here it is!' Alistair called through. '*Beauty in Decay: The Art of Urban Exploration*. More of a photo book, really, but there's plenty in here about how it all works. £16.99.'

'Sounds perfect, thanks.' Sawyer took a chocolate bar and slipped it into his pocket.

Alistair reappeared with the book and made his way over to Sawyer at the counter. 'Yes, we re-bind old titles. Mostly restorations for the owners but some go to auction. We had an old botany book from 1540 recently. It sold for several thousand pounds.'

He reached the counter and thunked the book down next to the till. It was a coffee-table book, and not really what Sawyer was looking for, but he browsed the pages for a few seconds and looked up into Alistair's expectant eyes. 'Sold.'

———

Jordan Burns waved Sawyer over to a far corner of The Source coffee shop, a standard breakfast and lunch joint close to the station. He slid the urbex book onto the table and shook Burns's hand.

'Thanks for agreeing to meet, Jake. Can I get you a coffee or—'

'I'm fine. How is Stephanie?'

'Not too bad.' They sat. Burns slurped at his cappuccino; the handle of the cup and saucer looked child-sized in his chubby fingers. He had clipped his greying hair at the temples and shaved his head to a cue ball polish. Battle-ready. He read the cover of Sawyer's book. '*Beauty in Decay*. Bit of light reading while you're on hiatus?''

Sawyer watched him. Deflection. Darting eyes. 'What's this about, Jordan?'

Burns wiped his mouth. 'I know what you did.'

Sawyer nodded. 'Earlier this summer?'

Burns locked eyes on Sawyer. 'Yes. Steph gave me the full picture.'

Sawyer sighed, sat back. 'Are you sure you've thought this through?'

Burns stared into his cup. 'You fought with Bowman, overpowered him. But then when he was basically helpless, you murdered him in cold blood.'

'You'll forgive me if I don't respond to this accusation without a lawyer present.'

Burns kept his head down. 'We spoke to Mr Farrell. DCI Farrell. Steph told him you acted in self-defence. But she admitted to me that it was nothing like that.' He took another steady sip of his coffee. 'She's obviously conflicted. We're both grateful to you for saving her life. But we can't be part of this lie.'

'So this is a moral issue for you? You've come to me for advice because the ethics are keeping you awake?'

Burns lowered his voice. 'We've suffered emotionally. It's put an immense strain on our relationship. The business has struggled, with Stephanie being out of action. I... read about your father. I'm sorry for what happened, but this is about survival.'

'What's it got to do with my father?'

'I read the *Derbyshire Times* piece. He was an artist. I looked him up. His work was commanding decent prices. I'm guessing you benefited from that.'

Sawyer closed his eyes.

His father's face. Shotgun blast.

A bright flash. Brain matter on the ceiling.

He opened his eyes, glanced at the coffee shop owner: out of earshot. 'Like I say, Jordan. Are you sure you've thought this through? We have a word for it, you know. It can get you up to fourteen years in prison. How would Stephanie cope then?'

Burns looked up, leaned forward and bared his teeth. 'It's not...' He dropped his voice to a whisper. '*Blackmail*. I'm just asking you to help us out. Now I know what actually happened. You saved Steph's life, but your actions contributed to her... her trauma. They're part of the reason why she can't work.'

'Just to be clear on what's happening here. What will you do if I say no to *helping you out*? Your answer to that question will make it nice and clear if it's blackmail or not. Whatever you've told yourself it is.'

Burns stayed silent, drummed his fingers on the table.

Now Sawyer leaned forward. 'I would imagine, since you've mentioned DCI Farrell, your plan would be to threaten to tell him what you know, unless you get what you want from me. Yes?'

Burns raised his eyebrows, looked back down at the

table. 'Are you willing to risk a manslaughter charge? Maybe even murder?'

Sawyer smiled. 'There it is. At least we understand each other now. Definitely blackmail. You do realise that if I refuse this, and you go to DCI Farrell with Stephanie's information, then I could still prosecute you for blackmail. We might even end up sharing a cell.'

Burns gave a strained laugh.

'Does Stephanie know about this?'

Burns looked up sharply. 'No, she doesn't. And she'd better not find out.'

'Or what? You're going to blackmail me twice?'

Burns's face flushed, and he drummed with both hands. 'We keep it strictly between the two of us, and it ends well for everyone. I know this isn't pleasant, but look at it from my perspective. Our life, and our business, has fallen apart. Steph wants to work, but she simply isn't capable. We just need something to get us back on our feet. I'm not...' He glanced at the owner, who finished tidying a stack of mugs and moved off into a back room. 'I'm not greedy. I'm just seizing an opportunity. It's simply numbers. I used to work for Citibank, Jake. The world moves on money, and the bedrock of money is debt.'

Sawyer folded his arms. 'So, I'm in *your* debt?'

Burns pushed on. 'Debt enters the economy in the form of loans, and those loans are based on interest rates, and interest rates are based on risk.'

Sawyer nodded. 'Will there be a test on this? Do I need to make notes?'

'So, risk is measured in probability. The probability of getting a loan paid back. And how do we measure probability?'

'Odds.'

'Exactly. So it's all just gambling. Which means that

gambling is the bedrock of society. The people with money are just better gamblers than the people without it.' He held out his hands, palms up. 'I'm willing to take the gamble that you're not prepared to risk your freedom for the sake of a few thousand pounds.'

19

Sawyer stripped down to his underwear and stood in front of the full-length bedroom mirror. He cued up an ambient album—*Sakura* by Susumu Yakota—and switched to horse stance before easing into the third Wing Chun form: *biu gee*. Darting fingers.

He was feeling too spiky for the flow and calm of the first two forms, and craved the elbow and finger strikes of *biu gee,* with its emphasis on attack and counterattack. His execution was smooth and direct, embedded in muscle memory. Nothing extraneous or showy or telegraphed: optimum efficiency.

He showered, dressed and served up a bowlful of meaty mush for a grateful Bruce. The dope from Ash sat on the coffee table next to the chocolate bar he'd stolen from the bookshop. He opened the drawer beneath the sink and took out a small metal tin embossed with the Jack Daniel's whiskey logo: a keepsake from his student years. He sifted through the stale tobacco and torn cardboard, and pulled out a packet of Rizla cigarette papers: brittle but still functional. He rolled a scruffy joint and lit it on the oven hob gas burner. Bruce turned his head as the dark smoke curled into the air, then returned to his food.

Sawyer took a puff, inhaled, piped the smoke out through his nostrils. It was surprisingly smooth on his throat for cheap marijuana. He spluttered, took another drag.

A numbness stole over him, easing his aching muscles, fuzzing the edges. For a moment, the world receded; his pain was still close, always ready to pounce. But the tension in his strings had loosened, and the thought of the memory flashes was no longer so troubling.

His phone rang, jolting him back to reality: a muggy summer afternoon, the familiar heightened sense of self-consciousness. Bruce had cleaned his dish and was busy washing himself. He paused and glared at Sawyer, as if willing him to silence the ringtone.

He checked the Caller ID.

Rhodes.

He tapped the answer button and set the phone to speaker.

'Sawyer. Got some goodies for you. Not much, but it might be interesting.'

Sawyer snuffed out the joint in a Diet Coke can. 'Go on.'

'I had a root around the urbex website back end. Couldn't find anything related to "Darren Coleman" or "Devil", but I did find a profile, "ST60", connected to a "Stuart Sutton". Your lad might have used the site but not under his real name. Maybe he was savvier than Sutton.'

Sawyer pulled over his laptop and navigated to the *Left Behind* site. 'ST60'?

'Yeah. Before you bother, I couldn't find any posts. Maybe he never actually posted, maybe he deleted them all.'

Sawyer's head swam. 'Thanks, Karl.'

'Pleasure.'

He rang off. Sawyer browsed through the *Beauty in Decay* book, letting his mind drift. He googled 'Stuart Sutton' with variations of 'urbex' and 'urban exploring'. No likely hits in the main search results. He switched to the Videos tab and followed a YouTube result. The video was shaky, handheld POV and labelled *Abandoned Children's Asylum*. Empty staircases, crumbled plaster and exposed brickwork, collapsed ceilings. No voice-over, just occasional captions for context. It had been posted by 'The Great Explorer', whose avatar image showed a pair of eyes glaring out from behind a balaclava-style face covering. Sawyer clicked on the name and browsed The Great Explorer's channel. The About section made Sawyer's stomach flip.

Welcome to my undiscovered world. My name is Stuart Sutton and I travel around finding derelict and abandoned locations to film and take pictures of. NO LOCATION DETAILS. I DO NOT FORCE ENTRY OR VANDALISE!

The channel had few followers and contained only videos: *Abandoned Cement Factory, Messed-up old hospital, We found an old chapel in the woods!* The most recent post was almost five years old. Sawyer scrolled through and watched some of the footage: all in the same shaky handheld POV, all captions.

He clicked on a video labelled *Security Incident!* It had been filmed at night, and showed a torchlit POV approach to a perimeter fence.

Voices. Laughter. Two males. Judging by the volume and distortion, one voice came from the person filming. As the camera reached the mesh of the fence, the screen went blank and filled with a clumsy caption.

NO YOU DON'T GET TO SEE HOW WE GOT IN!

The video switched to the interior of an industrial building: decrepit but with intact fittings and arcane-looking piping and equipment that seemed in relatively good shape. The person holding the camera swung to the side occasionally, catching sight of the second explorer: male, with a dark hoodie and a scarf covering his face. He pointed up.

'*Rails, man!*'

The camera followed his lead and briefly captured an intricate network of ceiling-mounted track runners.

Voice behind the camera. '*Fucking hell. Imagine being up there.*'

A clumsy jump-cut to a sign.

USE BOOT WASH BEFORE ENTERING OR LEAVING PRODUCTION AREA

The camera panned across a large open-plan area of metallic troughs and sinks.

'*Has that been cleaned?*'

'*No way.*'

A high-pitched alarm sounded. The camera shook and lurched to the side, resting for a split second on the boy in the hoodie. His eyes were wide, terrified.

Shaky images. Sounds of running and panting.

The screen faded to black. Caption.

TO BE CONTINUED!

But that was it. None of the other videos seemed to connect or follow on.

Sawyer scrolled down to the comments beneath the

video. A couple from The Great Explorer himself, mostly replying to random praise.

'Slydad' claimed to 'work in a similar place up in Scotland boot wash stunk sometimes we started at 5 lol.'

'Mike Finlay' had seen an opportunity to make a political point. 'This is because of Blair misunderstanding EU rules. The damage he did lives on.'

'Daryl97' was more succinct ('awesome day'). His comment had been blessed with an old-school smiley emoticon from The Great Explorer.

Sawyer looked up from the screen and watched Bruce, curled into a tight ball on the armchair, his torso rising and falling as he snoozed.

97. Darren's birth year.

If it were him, why not Darren97?

He googled 'Daryl'. The first hit was the Wikipedia entry for *D. A. R. Y. L.*, an inoffensive sci-fi movie from the mid-eighties.

The second hit was another Wikipedia page, this time on Daryl Dixon, a character from *The Walking Dead* TV series. He thought of Darren's graphic novels and DVDs, and Samantha's story about how he got into the show after she had shown him *This Life*.

Sawyer replayed the video and frame-skipped to the moment where the boy in the hoodie looked startled by the alarm. He took Samantha's photograph of Darren out of his jacket pocket and compared the two. The on-screen image was dark and blurry, but the eyes were the same shape and it looked like he wore a similar red-and-black shirt beneath his hoodie.

He navigated back to the *Left Behind* site and searched for posts from Daryl97. There were two or three, all fairly bland replies in other threads.

Sawyer replayed the section of the video where the boys looked at the ceiling rails.

'*Fucking hell. Imagine being up there.*'

He took out his phone and played the trail from Episode Three of the Mendez podcast.

'*Some people are dumb, though. They stick up their hero shots. Bragging, yeah? But you're not supposed to say anything, reveal the location.*'

The voices were a match: the rhythm, pitch, intonation.

Sawyer lifted his eyes back to the sleeping cat.

A shudder ran through him.

He was following the same trail as Virginia Mendez.

20

Sawyer bypassed Bakewell and followed the spindly back roads down through Youlgreave. He bounced the Mini over a rough track and stopped at a bridge to let a tractor pass by; a long line of traffic trailed it like imprinted ducklings.

He bowed his head and waited, braced.

Metal on bone.

He looked up, focused on the tractor, the cars.

Michael, lying still in the grass. The dog's barks fading to yelps.

'You had Dad's memory.'

His mother's voice, from the back seat. He looked up to the rear-view mirror. This time she sat smiling, upright. Sawyer closed his eyes, opened them again. No change. For a moment, he wondered if he might actually be seeing a ghost.

'He could always remember the day, the details.'

Jessica kept her smile, but her gaze passed through him.

'Michael got more of my genes, though. Head like a sieve.'

Holes.

The hammer. Metal on bone. Her face; the flesh pulped.

Sawyer's breathing quickened as he spoke. 'You said not to look back.'

Her smile faded. 'It'll come to you.'

Inhale.

Exhale.

He wanted to reach out, but the rational part of his mind told him this was all illusory, impossible.

One of the cars behind the tractor sounded its horn and Sawyer startled. He jerked his head to the side and glared at the driver. When he refocused on the Mini interior, the back seat was empty.

His phone rattled against the plastic of the dashboard compartment. He checked the Caller ID, slotted it into the mount, set it to speaker.

'You do pick your moments.'

Shepherd sniffed. 'Can you talk?'

The traffic cleared and Sawyer drove onto the bridge and crossed over the still, shining surface of the River Lathkill. 'Is it good or bad?'

'Well. It's not good. Speaking to Farrell and friends later.'

'By this time, he's probably got ballistics on the bullet that hit the axe. He might even connect it with Cross.'

Silence from Shepherd.

'If he asks, I know you have to tell him.'

'It would be worse for both of us if I didn't tell him and he found out.'

Sawyer checked the rear-view mirror. Back seat still empty. 'No point you making it bad for yourself, no.'

'Sir.' A creak as Shepherd sat down. 'I don't think that's fair.'

'It's divide and conquer. Classic. If he can prove Cross was there as our—*my*—guest, then it strengthens his case about undermining his jurisdiction.'

'Why?'

'It looks intentional.'

'It was intentional. You called him in as back-up. You do realise that if Farrell can make gross misconduct stick, he might be able to push Bowman's death as unlawful.'

Sawyer joined a wider A road and squeezed the accelerator. 'Let's change the subject. Are you looking into a misper? Virginia Mendez. Manchester student.'

'That would be a GMP gig, but I overheard Moran mention it, too.'

'And how are you doing with the Hardwick murder? Is Walker helping?'

Shepherd paused. 'He is. And we're nowhere with it. Any progress on this "ping" you mentioned?'

'I've been busy. I'll try to get it to ping louder.' Sawyer pulled into the driveway of a handsome detached house surrounded by a low dry-stone wall. He parked the car and gazed out across the trimmed garden: three widely spaced saplings wavered in the afternoon breeze. 'Hardwick wasn't drugged.'

Shepherd sighed. 'No. Drummond says the killer took off most of the skin on his limbs, some around his torso.'

'Was he gagged?'

'I don't think Drummond's report mentioned that.'

'Find out. It might tell us more about the scene of death. You're going to scream pretty loud if someone is peeling off your skin.'

Shepherd groaned. 'What about the partial burial?'

'Someone interrupted him? Something spooked him? Maybe it's the first one he's messed up and there are others he buried properly. Look at serious crime or unsolved murders involving people connected to the meat industry. Could be a connection to Hardwick and his business.

Follow the inevitable tabloid headline once they find out how he died.'

'Which is?'

'*BUTCHER BUTCHERED.*'

———

Adam Grayson brought over two glasses of water with lemon slices. 'You'll have to excuse my heightened state of excitement, Mr Sawyer. We've had a bearded vulture sighting, near Bleaklow.'

Grayson was mid-fifties, bottom heavy, with a wide, ruddy nose and a bald head that tapered slightly at the top. He blinked too frequently, giving the impression he was trying to get something out of his eyes.

'Is that rare?' Sawyer poked the lemon slice deeper into the water and set the glass down on the black steel bistro table. A putting mat and golf balls were laid out along the side of the small back garden.

Grayson laughed and took a slug of water. 'It is indeed rare, Mr Sawyer. Bearded vultures are larger than golden eagles and it's highly unusual to get a visit from one in the UK. I was just talking to my birders on Facebook Live. The consensus is that it's flown over from the Alps where it's being reintroduced at the moment.' He sat opposite and set down his glass. 'Of course, the bloody twitchers are all over it.'

'Like vultures.'

'Well, quite.'

'So there's a difference between birders and twitchers? I thought—'

'That twitcher is slang for birder? No, no, no.' He shook his head and took another drink. 'Twitchers are box-tickers. They travel to sighting areas, bag their spot, make a note, and go home. Birders are more watchful and appreciative.'

'Do you still teach?'

'Part-time, yes. I left Cedar Mount a couple of years after Darren Coleman's disappearance. I now work at Langley Park School for Boys, teaching English, a little History. I also do some private tutoring, which can be immensely rewarding.'

'My mum was a teacher.'

Grayson frowned. 'Has she passed?'

'I'm not fond of that euphemism. She still feels present for me. She died when I was very young.'

'Ah, I'm sorry. My own mother is still with us, but only in body. Dementia. Such an awful business. Like being both alive and dead simultaneously. There's nothing worse than seeing someone you care for in that state.'

Beads of red in the grass.

Smears of gore across Michael's face; the perfect powder blue of his T-shirt.

Sawyer squeezed his eyes shut then opened them again, clearing his head. 'What are your memories of Darren?'

Grayson rubbed his hands together in a circle, pondering. 'Shy lad. But then fifteen-year-olds are rarely effusive creatures.'

'A lot going on inside, though.'

'Well, of course. The veritable swan. Calm on the surface but furiously paddling away beneath. I thought he had a lot going for him. Obviously bright. But that's not enough, these days. You need to work, make good choices.'

'He had to move from another school. Do you remember him struggling to settle in?'

Grayson puffed out his cheeks. 'This is many years ago, Mr Sawyer. I recall that he mentioned studying business, which was something his previous school didn't offer.'

'His mother described an incident where she picked him up from a school event, late one evening. He had a bruise on his face. He said it was a "silly ritual thing". Do you know what that might have been about?'

Grayson narrowed his eyes and looked out to the garden. 'Not really. There were one or two cliques and the like. The odd hazing tradition. It's all fine banter. It's good for them.'

'What is?'

'Ego deflation. A little humbling. It's good for them to be aware of the peer hierarchy. It's part of school life, and those who react against it are the ones who have trouble. No?'

Sawyer shifted in his seat. 'It's a two-way thing, though, surely? It's only "banter" if both parties are complicit, in on the joke. Otherwise, that sounds like good old-fashioned bullying to me. No?'

'I don't know, Mr Sawyer. I wasn't aware of a bullying culture. I'm obviously hopeful that you find Darren safe and well, although it has been quite a few years now.'

'Did you speak to a woman named Virginia Mendez?'

'I did. Briefly, on the telephone. We were due to meet and record an interview for a podcast but nothing ever came of it. Are you working directly for Mrs Coleman? Or is there some official police involvement?'

Sawyer took a drink. 'I'm a Detective, up at Buxton Station. But this isn't official, no.'

Grayson nodded, frowned.

A silence persisted.

Sawyer leaned forward. 'Did you know of a boy named Stuart Sutton?'

Grayson raised his eyebrows. 'I did. He was excluded the year before Darren's disappearance, I believe. He wasn't in my form, though. I think he was in the year above. So, about to leave, anyway.' He toyed with his glass. 'Tell me, Mr Sawyer. Given your official status, I trust we're not drifting into an area where I'm under suspicion.' He forced a chuckle. 'After all, we're discussing a serious matter and if there's any implication of accusation—'

'I could shine a bright light in your face if that would clarify things?' Grayson looked suddenly unhappy; Sawyer smiled. 'Joke. No. Not at all. I'm looking into the possibilities, and as someone who had regular contact with Darren before his disappearance, I hoped you might be able to point me in the right direction.'

'And how am I doing?'

'You've helped me in more ways than you know.'

Grayson nodded, uncertain.

'One more question, then you can get back to your vulture. Do you remember why Stuart Sutton was excluded from the school?'

Grayson held Sawyer's eye. 'I don't recall the exact details. We weren't told everything. He was caught in possession of contraband. Drugs.'

———

Outside, Sawyer lingered by the Mini, basking in the low afternoon sunshine. He took a lemon boiled sweet from his pocket, unwrapped it, popped it in his mouth.

He took out his phone and angled his face to the screen while slowly raising his eyes to the house. Grayson stood at the window, watching.

He turned away and dialled a number; it connected immediately.

'Sir.'

Sawyer glanced through the window into the back seat. 'DS Walker.'

'How are you, sir?'

'Rosy. Apart from the career-threatening investigation into unlawful killing. Shepherd tells me you're working on the Hardwick case.'

Walker paused. 'Not that there's much to work on.'

'Anything around the deposition scene?'

'Sally's team came up blank. Nothing on the body.'

Sawyer looked back at the house; Grayson had gone. 'I was hoping you could help me with something. Just a bit of rummaging. Background stuff. No need to make it official.'

'All legal, though?'

Sawyer rolled the sweet around his mouth. 'Naturally. Can you have a look for a character called Stuart Sutton? I'm helping the mother of a missing teenager, Darren Coleman. I want to find out more about Sutton. They were friends, but there might be more there. Some kind of drug connection. Sutton was excluded from Cedar Mount School near Matlock in the early 2010s. Possession. I assume he was cautioned by local plod at the time.'

'So, what do you need? A recent address?'

'Anything would do. Detail on the charge would be good, too. I'd like Mr Sutton to help me with my enquiry, but I'd prefer someone else to do the initial enquiring, and I'll cover anything face to face. Also, can you see if there's any history of officer attendance or complaints about hazing rituals or initiation ceremonies at Cedar Mount?'

Walker cleared his throat. 'I'm on it.'

'Thank you, Matt.'

'So what are your thoughts on the Hardwick murder?'

Sawyer climbed into the car and shut the door. 'Somebody wanted him to suffer.'

'Uhuh.'

He adjusted the rear-view mirror. 'Somebody wanted to see him suffer.'

21

Maggie snuck up behind Mia as she admired herself in the hall mirror beside the enormous Kandinsky reprint. She slipped a ten-pound note into her daughter's pocket, leaned down and whispered, 'Get popcorn.'

Mia smiled and whispered back, 'Dad doesn't like us eating popcorn.'

'Sit on the end seat. Pretend you're going for a wee when he's engrossed in the film, get it then. He won't notice.'

Mia swished her bright blonde hair out of her face. 'Mum! You're bad.'

Maggie hugged her. 'It's a minor crime, darling.' She lowered her voice. 'Enjoy yourself, and make sure you share it with Freddy.'

Mia rolled her eyes. 'Oh, yeah. Like I'm going to eat a whole bucket of popcorn by myself.'

'Plenty of people could.'

'Uncle Jake.'

Maggie laughed. 'Oh, definitely.'

'And my friend Emma can eat a Creme Egg in two bites.'

'Let's go!' Freddy's voice from the car outside.

Mia hugged her mother and ran out onto the porch and down to Justin's Mercedes. Dusk had settled over the Roaches, and the rocks squatted on the horizon in violet silhouette.

Maggie waved them off and headed back inside, into the vast kitchen with its centrepiece table. Handmade oak. She and Justin had bought it bespoke, at crippling cost.

She gathered the ingredients for tomato pasta sauce and set a pan of water to boil.

Garlic clove on the chopping board. Peel it.

Thin slices with the heavy Wüsthof knife. Cutting with a rocking motion. Maggie preferred clean, sliced garlic to the mess of the crusher.

Goat's cheese from the fridge. Fresh basil.

Later this evening she could get through a few episodes of the second season of *Doctor Foster* on iPlayer. Only three years late for it.

She took out her phone and set an album playing through the Sonos speaker. A-ha. *Scoundrel Days*. A mildly guilty pleasure for cooking.

Squat down to the low cupboard. Pan for the sauce.

Stand up again.

She startled, and released the pan. It made an almighty clang as it fell to the floor.

A tall, broad man stood at the open kitchen door. He wore a sleeveless T-shirt and a black-and-white New York Yankees baseball cap, and his features were obscured behind a dark balaclava.

Maggie's stomach lurched; she yelped in alarm.

The man covered the distance across the kitchen with long, flowing strides.

Maggie snatched up the knife, but he grabbed her forearm with a gloved hand, held her firm.

They stood there for a second, suspended, the man dwarfing her in size.

He raised a meaty fist.

Maggie jerked back, and cracked her head against the hood of the cooker.

The man held her firm, kept still, staring.

The house was remote, on the edge of the Roaches. Only the sheep would hear her scream.

The man uncurled the fingers of Maggie's hand, forcing her to release the knife. It skittered across the stone-tiled floor.

He held her at arm's length, out of range of a kick or knee to his groin. She kept her eyes away from him, tried to calm her breathing. 'You don't have to hurt me. My handbag is on the table in the hall. There's money. I'll give you plenty of time to...'

Maggie raised her head slowly; the man averted his gaze as he rested his other hand at the top of her chest, then pushed it up, closing his fingers around her neck, squeezing.

22

APRIL 2011

DI Martin Pittman parked his royal blue Subaru Outback in a lay-by on the edge of woodland at the south-eastern tip of the National Park.

Sawyer dipped his head and peered out of the passenger side window into the gathering dusk. 'Looking stormy.'

Pittman laughed. 'With foresight like that, you'll be a DCI in no time.'

'Who's this again?' Sawyer nodded to the stereo. Music played at a low volume.

'Twelfth Night. Prog rock titans. Not your thing?'

Sawyer screwed up his face. 'Is that their name or a reference to how long the songs last?'

Pittman opened the door. 'We can have your Underground on the way back.'

'Underworld. Prog techno titans. Sort of.'

'I don't get how you can listen to that shit when you're not on drugs.'

Pittman stepped out of the car, straight into a puddle of sludge. 'Fan-fucking-tastic.' He edged round onto the road, scraping his shoes against the tarmac.

Sawyer got out, avoiding the sludge. 'Should have brought your wellies.'

'Haven't got any. I wasn't planning to walk through open fields.'

'We might have to. It's a bit out of the way, for obvious reasons.'

They set off, up a steep track, and cut into the trees as the road bent round, beginning its descent into Ashbourne. Pittman took the lead. They swished away the soggy branches and joined an underused walking track.

Pittman pointed to an overgrown gate with a lurid sign (*KEEP OUT*). 'Used to be a private road up there.' He swiped at his light blue suit. 'Fucking hell. We should have sent a couple of DCs on this.'

'Couldn't trust 'em.'

Pittman looked over his shoulder at Sawyer, smiling. 'You've only been a DC yourself for a year.'

'Eight months.'

'You going for DS soon?'

'Of course. It's no fun, just bossing the bobbies around.'

Pittman shook his head. 'There's serious talk of Buxton becoming a Major Crime Unit.'

'Are there enough major crimes to cover?'

'Spoken like a true DC. You'll find you get access to the darker corners the higher you go up the chain. You're down with that, right?'

Sawyer smiled. 'I like it dark. But I'm not sure how long I can stick around here.'

'Fuck me. A couple of promotions and he thinks he's Morse. Where are you off to, then?'

'Probably London. Test myself in the urban jungle.'

Pittman scoffed. 'It's such a myth, you know, that the Met are the fucking elite and the regional forces are hicks or whatever. If anything, it's the other way round. They've got all the big-city resources, while we have to rely on instinct. And the criminality is more insidious. Easier to hide.' Pittman looked over his shoulder again, frowning. 'No other reason why you want to head to London?'

'I met someone. She's gorgeous and her dad is loaded.'

'Fuck off! So that's your idea of testing yourself?'

Light up ahead. Sawyer moved around Pittman and pushed through into a clearing. A large, squat industrial building sat at the centre of a patch of open ground, surrounded by high fencing topped with barbed wire. Most of its windows had been smashed, and it was smothered by weeds and climbing ivy. Several derelict brick outbuildings lay on the far edge of the site, with a larger barn-sized structure connected to the main building by a covered passageway. Tall, low-grade floodlighting shone down on the main building, but most of the other structures were unloved and unlit.

'Cameras?' said Sawyer.

'No. There's security, but I don't think there's anything worth stealing. All the copper went ages ago.'

'So what would Professor Pope be doing up here?'

Pittman crouched down by Sawyer, out of breath. 'No idea. He hasn't been seen for almost a year now. The tech people screwed up on the data and so we ran it all again, using this new guy.'

'Rhodes.'

Pittman nodded. 'Yeah. The Manc. Knows his stuff. The other guys missed a lot of the passive data but he recovered it all. Even so, the only thing that might be significant is the prof's phone.'

'It pinged the mast near here, yes? On the day he disappeared.'

'Yeah. At 10:30pm.'

'Hard to imagine an esteemed Professor of Cognitive Neuroscience skulking around a place like this at a time like that.'

They waited for a few seconds in silence, listening.

Shuffling trees, drowsy birdsong.

'Let's have a look around.' Sawyer headed out of the trees and walked onto the site, heading for the barn-sized building.

Pittman hesitated, then followed. 'Slow down. This could all be unsafe.'

'Anything in Pope's background?'

Pittman caught up. 'Not really. He was cautioned for a run-in with some protesters last year. They were camped outside his house.'

'What kind of protesters?'

'Animal rights. His department was involved in animal research or something. They usually go more for disruption, though. Indirect action. He'd had a few nasty deliveries. No specific threats.'

They stood before the barn. The brickwork was grey and mottled, but still solid. Sawyer moved around to the covered passageway that connected it to the large central building and pushed his face against a small window. No light inside; just the outline of a few shelves and fittings.

'Can't get in,' said Pittman. He rattled the padlock on a sturdy iron bolt covering the barn's sliding metal door.

Sawyer studied the lock. 'I disagree, sir.'

'What do you mean?'

'It's locked. But that doesn't mean we can't get in.' He pulled an oblong black case from his pocket and took out kirby grip hairpins.

Pittman laughed. 'Oh, fuck right off. We're not doing that, Sawyer. Keating will have my bollocks.'

Sawyer ignored him and got to work on the lock. 'Strong case for a Section 17, sir. Danger to life and limb. We have evidence that the professor was in this location, and there's a locked building with a door that doesn't match. Looks like it was installed fairly recently.'

Pittman crouched and watched Sawyer work one of the pins into the padlock and bend it, while he slotted in the second pin straight. 'This isn't actually going to work, is it?'

Sawyer grinned. 'The padlock is strong but it's a standard Abloy. First pin is a tension wrench, and the second is used as a pick to feel your way into the pins that hold the lock closed. If I can get in and we find something, we're clear.'

'And if we don't find anything?'

'Put the padlock back in place. Nothing broken. No harm done.'

The padlock clicked and Sawyer pulled the shackle free. He dropped the lock onto the ground and pulled away the metal covering, freeing the bolt. He turned to Pittman, smiling. 'Do you want to do the honours, sir?'

Pittman shook his head. 'Fuck me, Sawyer. Aren't you full of tricks?'

'Only the practical stuff.'

Pittman stepped forward and pulled the bolt to the side. The grinding cut through the stillness of the surroundings and made them both wince.

Pittman turned on the light from his phone and edged inside.

Sawyer followed, and turned towards the connecting passage that led to the main building. He shone his phone light on the solid wooden door, secured by a cluster of grimy chains and padlocks. 'They're a bit more serious about this door.'

'I suppose it gives access to the main building. Although why anyone would want to get in there...'

Their voices seemed to die in the air, almost without echo.

The barn was large and tall, but empty apart from a few workbenches and rusted pipes that ran around the base of the stone walls. A rail structure had been fitted into the ceiling; it ran to the passageway and looked like it might pass through into the main building. Sawyer poked around one of the workbenches; they were mostly dusty and disused, apart from one with recent-looking notches gouged into the wood. He stood up and sniffed the air; damp and sulphurous, with a hint of coal tar.

Pittman shone a light at the far wall. 'What's that?'

Sawyer walked over and crouched down. He pushed his head in close to examine a metal base link fixed into the stone around the lower part of the wall. 'Don't know. Did you ever resolve the attack on the guy from the badger-culling group?'

Pittman frowned in recall. 'Fenwick? The one who got caught in the man trap? No. He tried to make a fuss about lack of protection for a legitimate environmental operation. Blah, blah, blah. Blew over, though.'

Sawyer stood up. 'How about the guy you found in the chicken broiler farm, a few years ago?'

Pittman held his light towards Sawyer, keeping it low, casting himself in silhouette in the final slivers of daylight at the open door. 'Broiler farm?'

'Yeah. He owned it, I think. Drummond showed me on my first day. Someone had peeled off chunks of the poor bastard's skin.'

'Different MOs.'

Sawyer smiled. 'There's a link, though, sir. Animals. Animal cruelty or industry. Pope's work fits.'

Pittman turned away. 'Bit of a reach, young grasshopper.'

'Was that ever solved?'

'No.' He hitched his suit up over his shoulders and shuddered.

'Let's get out of here before the walls start bleeding. Give forensics a call and get them to have a nose around. Replace the lock first, though. Legitimate entry. See if we can find any evidence of the good professor.'

Sawyer ran his finger along the notches in the workbench. 'He could be refining. Escalating. Maybe the kick of killing isn't enough. The broiler farm guy was up close, hands on. If he's also the one responsible for the man traps, then that was a bit more distanced. Maybe the professor got it worse.' He followed Pittman out of the door. 'Or he's tailoring the punishment to the severity of the crime. As he sees it.'

Pittman closed the door and slid the bolt back in place. 'So, we're after someone from the militant wing of the vegetarian society.' They walked back to the track, towards the car. 'See, I'm a bit more of a romantic than you, Detective. Phone mast pings can be unreliable. What if our professor met a secret lover somewhere around here?'

'Somewhere a bit more bucolic.' Pittman looked at him, confused. 'Prettier.'

'Yes. And they did a runner. Not everyone who disappears wants to be found, you know.'

Sawyer ducked under a branch, following Pittman, and they headed into the trees. If he'd chosen that moment to look back, he would have seen an observer, looking down from one of the few intact windows on the first floor of the large central building, his outline defined by the room's low electric light: muscular upper torso, unnaturally large head with a protruding horn shape pointing up at either side.

23

PRESENT DAY

Sawyer shouted. A distress call, into the indifferent dark at the side of his bed. Again, it came: a wailing, dredged up from the deep. The second shout startled him, woke him. There was outrage in there, some panic. But no fear. Just anguish, desolation. It was a child's call for comfort, unfulfilled.

He rolled onto his back, away from the patch of night sweat, and unspooled the last few minutes of the dream. Always his mother, walking off the sand and into the sea, her Bible-black hair trailing through the water behind. He looked back, far up the beach, where his father scored a moat around a sandcastle with a plastic shovel, while his brother placed pebbles along its rim. When he turned again, his mother was too far out, but still moving away. Sinking, fading.

And he called and called to her, in his six-year-old voice. And the shouting skimmed across the water, whipped away by the wind, until it found the adult Sawyer in his bed.

Clock.

6:15am.

He tumbled out onto the floor and stripped the covers, piling them into the corner for washing later. He pulled open the blind and squinted at the flare of morning sun.

Sawyer closed his eyes; he knew what was coming. The sounds, approaching and roaring up like cresting waves.

His dog, barking and barking.

His mother. Screaming, sobbing.

There was nothing abstract about this. As he opened his eyes, he was planted right back there in the field, in the heat of the sun; an impotent observer to his mother's slaughter. It was like a waking nightmare; if he reached out, he would surely feel the swish of the bloodstained grass.

He pulled himself away from the window and stumbled into the bathroom, turned on the shower, trying to drown the sounds.

The water was too hot, but he endured it, wallowing in the way it diverted his senses, muffling the chaos.

After dressing, he fed Bruce, then shook out a bowl of Corn Flakes for himself and ate them standing on the front porch, gazing up at the lower slopes of Kinder Scout, warming in the dawn light, emerging from the long shadows of the imperious ash trees.

Sawyer opened his laptop on the coffee table. He logged in to his VPN and navigated to the HOLMES remote screen.

Login: *edshepherd*.

Password: *Rideout95*.

The Hardwick case files showed little progress: interviews logged without follow-up; dead ends with victimology, camera data. DC Moran had interviewed an ex-business partner, with no lead. Sally O'Callaghan had submitted a standard forensic report based on scene searches, with inconclusive outcomes for trace evidence. Multiple tyre tracks and footprints.

He closed HOLMES and began cross-referencing local searches for 'dogs', 'puppies', 'kittens' with 'animal cruelty', 'animal welfare', 'arrested', 'illegal'.

A local BBC News article reported on the case of Jon Reed, missing since 2006. Reed had recently been released from prison after serving nine months for causing unnecessary suffering to puppies, rabbits and ferrets bred for sale on his farm in Hayfield.

'Dogs' and 'animal cruelty' led to a piece on the League Against Cruel Sports website, which covered the break-up of a dog-fighting network in Gradbach. The leader, Jason Donaghy, had boasted of breeding 'the ultimate dog'.

Sawyer logged into the PND—pleased to find that his access hadn't been revoked—and discovered that Donaghy was still the subject of an arrest warrant since he'd failed to turn up at a court hearing, way back in 2007. More digging revealed that Donaghy had lived with his now-deceased mother who had officially reported him missing two weeks after his no-show.

His phone rang.

Shepherd.

Sawyer connected the call and set the phone on speaker, waiting for Shepherd to speak first.

'Sir?'

'Did you look into the Hardwick thing? Unresolveds connected to animals and the meat industry?'

'Got a DC on it.'

Sawyer took a sip from a glass of yesterday's Diet Coke. 'Is it Farrell?'

'Sorry?'

'It's something bad. Farrell is my first guess.'

Shepherd drew in a shaky breath. 'It's Maggie.'

———

Sawyer hurried down the corridor of Buxton's Cavendish Hospital. A large man in a short-sleeved shirt sat by the entrance to the acute care ward. He stood as Sawyer approached and nodded to the nurse at the station.

Sawyer stopped. 'Ed.'

'Sir.' DS Ed Shepherd bowed his head and brushed his plump fingers over his goatee beard. 'She's okay. I spoke to the doctor.'

'Where?'

'He said she has to rest. I wanted to tell you, because—'

'Where?'

Sawyer glanced at the wall, freshly decorated with icons showing human figures connecting and caring.

We are actively respectful.

'Minor concussion. Broken nose, two ribs. X-ray shows no internal damage. Not good, but she's okay.'

We work positively together.

Sawyer slowed his breathing, looked Shepherd in the eye. '*Where?*'

Shepherd sighed. 'Room 5.'

A fortysomething man in a crumpled suit emerged from the double doors by the nurse's station. He eyed Sawyer and approached the nurse. 'I'm going to get a cup of tea and make a couple of calls.'

The nurse smiled and nodded, and the man walked past Sawyer and Shepherd and entered the lift.

Sawyer strode past the station and pushed through the double doors. The lighting back here was muted, and he kept a slow pace past a small open recovery ward to a series of individual rooms at the back side of the hospital. The door to Room 5 was half-open, and he stepped inside.

Maggie sat slumped in a bed near the window. A facial bandage covered the bridge and base of her nose, keeping her nostrils free. Both eyes were underscored with angry red bruising. As Sawyer entered, she shuffled herself upright and brushed her hair aside, wincing.

Sawyer hovered by the door.

Maggie held his gaze for a moment. 'It's okay. I'm not contagious.'

He moved around the bed and stood by the window, looking out to the surrounding hills, with the two-storey stone folly of Grinlow Tower just visible in the distance. 'Nice view.'

'Have you ever been up there?'

'That's one for the tourists. It was built by a man called Solomon Mycock.' He glanced at her; she raised an eyebrow. 'Sounds like a prank call name.'

Maggie took a shaky sip from a plastic cup of tea. 'Did you see Justin leave?'

'Yeah. And he saw me.'

She sighed. 'He's demanding justice.'

'Well, he is a lawyer.'

'Barrister.'

Sawyer pulled up a chair and sat down. 'How are you feeling?'

'Sore nose, sore body. A bit groggy. I suppose it could have been worse.'

Sawyer frowned, and placed a hand on her arm. 'Did you get anything on him? A scratch? Anything we could take as DNA?'

'We?'

He smiled. 'Figuratively speaking.'

Maggie looked away. 'Is Michael still here?'

'In the private ward.'

'How is he?'

'He'll live. Much to his annoyance. I'm not sure he recognises me.'

She scoffed. 'Like I said before, that's ridiculous. Of course he does.'

Sawyer withdrew his arm, took out a boiled sweet and tossed it into his mouth. He waggled the packet at Maggie; she shook her head carefully. 'But enough about other people.'

'Shall we talk about you? Did you have the brain scan results?'

Sawyer nodded. 'Inconclusive. Benign lesion. Stable. Near my amygdala, though. He said that might explain—'

'Your choices.'

'I was going to say, the way I laugh at danger.'

'And drop ice cubes down the vest of fear.'

Sawyer smiled. 'Haven't seen *Blackadder* in a while. Maybe since college.' He rolled the sweet around his mouth. 'What did he look like?'

'Who?'

'The guy who attacked you.'

Maggie adjusted her position, wincing again. 'Are you going to get him for me?'

'He does need getting.'

'He wore a balaclava. Big guy. It was strange, Jake. I don't know what he wanted. It didn't seem like he was in a hurry, either. Justin had just left for the cinema with Freddy and Mia. He must have been watching and waiting because...' She gathered herself. 'He was there so quickly.'

'Where were you when you first saw him?'

'In the kitchen. I was cooking.'

'Did he take anything?'

She shook her head. 'It doesn't look like it. Justin said

he left a mess in my consulting room. Drawers were pulled open, but nothing seems to be missing. He even left my purse by the computer. DC Myers is at the house.'

'Does Keating know?'

'Yes. He's in Manchester, though.'

'Did he say anything? Did he smell of anything?'

'No, and no.'

Sawyer looked out towards Solomon's Temple. 'Any strange clients lately? Anyone spooked you or expressed outrage at their progress?'

'Or stormed out, vowing vengeance? No.' Maggie took a breath.

Sawyer turned to look at her. 'But...'

'But what?'

'You're thinking of something that might be significant. But you're not sure you want to tell me, because of my suspension, and maybe you don't want me to be personally involved because you want me back in therapy.'

She rolled her eyes. 'Stop.'

'Can I have a look around the house?'

'Promise you won't snoop through my underwear?'

'I promise I'll try not to.'

Maggie turned onto her side, facing Sawyer. 'There was a car outside the other day. The driver was just sitting there. My client noticed, but when I came out to check, he drove away.'

'Brand?'

She scowled. 'I don't know. I don't do cars. Not a posh one. Sort of light brown.'

'And the driver was blond. Ponytail.'

She gaped. 'Yes.'

24

Sawyer drove out of Buxton and climbed through the open moorland of the western Peak. Up here, the sky was vast and brooding, and as he entered the pastured valleys on the approach to the Roaches, he played the first Black Sabbath album: a favourite of his mother's. The weather mirrored the ominous mood of the music, and a blush of grey clouds peppered the Mini windscreen with hailstones.

He parked in front of Maggie's house, took a second to check the rear-view mirror—back seat empty—and climbed out of the car, inhaling the post-storm petrichor.

He approached the main door, crunching over the gravel. The house sat on high ground at the edge of the Roaches' gritstone ridge, and a carpet of purple heather rippled out to the climbing hotspot of Ramshaw Rocks.

A hefty man with tall, slicked-back hair stepped forward from the door and smiled at Sawyer. 'I can't let you in, sir. Sorry.'

'You don't have to, DC Myers.' He held up a door key. 'From the owner.'

Myers frowned. 'Sally O'Callaghan's team have done an initial sweep, but Sally will be here in person any minute.'

'She'll understand. We're close.'

He shuffled in place. 'You're... I should—'

'No, you shouldn't.' Sawyer held up a pair of latex gloves and a pair of disposable shoe covers. 'I won't contaminate, I have permission from the house owner to go inside, and Keating would need to really step on it to get down from Manchester and stop me.'

Myers forced a grin.

Sawyer stepped closer and slapped on the gloves. 'Five minutes.'

————

Inside, Sawyer fitted the shoe covers and swept each room, checking the window locks, looking for potential hiding spots. Had Maggie's attacker been in the house waiting, or had he broken in once he saw the coast was clear?

He stood at the door of the main consulting room and looked out across the moor through the huge bay window. He examined the open drawer in Maggie's work desk. Notepads, a spare box of tissues, pens, a block of multicoloured Post-it notes. He turned and gazed down at the shiny parquet floor, inhaling.

The leathery aroma of the chocolate-brown futon.

Sickly-sweet tang from the vase of lilies on the coffee table.

Fingerprint chemicals: iodine, silver nitrate.

Sawyer walked into the kitchen and opened the back door. Tiny dents and scuff marks decorated the centre of the outside keyhole; a few fresh-looking nicks around the edge. Nothing forced.

He crouched down and scanned the edges of the wooden decking, stepping along and shining his phone light over the surface. Something caught his attention and he reached out to investigate.

'DI Sawyer.'

He looked up. A tall woman in her mid-fifties stood in the doorway. She peeled back the hood of a turquoise Tyvek suit and puffed her peroxide blonde hair off her face. 'Sally.'

'What. The fuck. Are you doing stomping all over my crime scene?'

He held up the door key. 'Owner's orders. Just trying to help. I didn't touch anything.'

'Oh. That's good of you. I also appreciate the shoe covers and gloves. Did you recover any boot prints? That'll save me a bit of time.'

Sawyer stood up. He held Sally's gaze, unsmiling.

Sally sighed. 'Is she okay?'

'Bloodied but unbowed.'

'Who would do that to Maggie?'

He nodded to the back door. 'Someone with a bump key, judging by the state of the lock. Not an internal pick. Not exactly a pro, but hardly an amateur, or an opportunist.'

Sally folded her arms. 'Noted. And any other elements to the profile?'

'Smoker.' Sawyer held up a half-smoked filterless cigarette with *L&M* printed in gold near the tip.

———

On the drive back to Buxton, the sun cracked through the cloud, and Sawyer played his favourite album—*Loveless* by My Bloody Valentine—and immersed himself in the mind-clearing wash of overlapping guitars. He let his thoughts drift, hoping the music would hook whatever was nagging him and drag it out into the open.

Unknown to his mother, Darren Coleman had been into urban exploration. The YouTube video showed him visiting an unknown building with Stuart Sutton, who had been excluded for heroin possession. Virginia Mendez must have seen the same video and interviewed Sutton for the fourth episode of the *Finding Darren Coleman* podcast. He needed to find Sutton and discover what he had discussed with Virginia Mendez, which could give him a lead on her movements after the interview.

Was Price correct in his jibe about Darren being into 'something stronger'? The association with Sutton made it plausible. Had he crossed the wrong dealer? Made a fatally poor choice in a desperate attempt to feed his habit? He needed more names, more potential threads that might connect to Darren.

The Hardwick murder was, officially, out of his hands, but there was something there. Did his tabloid crack to Shepherd—*BUTCHER BUTCHERED*—carry more meaning than he expected? Was the killing a personal act of sexual sadism or did it relate to something wider, perhaps related to the unresolved cases involving animal abuse? If the killer was basing his actions on a twisted ethical basis, he'd hardly be short of potential victims.

'What about yourself, Jake?'

His mother's voice again.

He kept his eyes on the road, ignoring the flash of movement in the rear-view mirror.

His breathing quickened. The burning rose in his chest.

Let it come.

You've seen it before.

Wait for it to pass.

Keep breathing.

It was a National Speed Limit road. He should find a lay-by, pull over, take a break.

'I know Dad said to look after Michael. But you should also look after yourself.'

His eyes flicked to the mirror.

Again, Jessica Sawyer rested her forehead against the back window, eyes closed this time. She wore her burnt orange bathrobe, her black hair fallen over one shoulder.

Inhale slowly, five seconds.

Exhale slowly, five seconds.

Wait another five seconds, repeat three times.

Sawyer turned into a side lane and parked up in a tight passing place. He switched off the engine.

Inhale.

Exhale.

'Mum.' No answer, of course. His voice sounded choked and distant. 'I can look after myself.'

He looked to the mirror. Jessica smiled, but didn't open her eyes. 'All shall be well, Jake.'

Inhale.

Exhale.

Her smile was tender, but doubtful.

Sawyer balled his hands into fists, clenching away the hot flush of panic. 'What am I missing?'

He opened his mouth to speak again, and, remembering the last time, closed his eyes, forcing himself back to reality.

He got out of the car and walked along the edge of the lane. He stopped and looked out across the moor, the wind whipping his jacket up like a cape.

After a moment's pause, as his breathing settled, he dialled a number and waited for the familiar male voice.

'Greetings, fellow pariah.'

'I was hoping you could help me out.'

Tony Cross laughed, too loud. 'Because that went so well last time.'

'I asked you to surveil my house, a couple of weeks ago. Remember?'

Cross sighed. 'What do think I am, Sawyer? Eighty? Of course I remember. I saw the guy in the light brown Fiesta sitting nearby.'

'And you said there were bothies and farm sheds. Places where he might be holed up.'

'Yeah, but they are seriously not your Rural Retreats cottage rental-type places.'

Sawyer turned and walked back to the car. 'Have another look. See if you can find out where Mr Fiesta is hiding.'

'Dare I ask why?'

'I'd like a word with him.'

25

Sawyer hammered both buttons on the control panel alternately in quick succession. On-screen, his pixelated athlete kept pace with another runner, eventually dipping through a finishing tape as the 100m Dash timing flashed beneath his score.

A fuzzy digital voice confirmed the result. '*Nine point five two seconds.*'

'Didn't make the top three.' A voice from behind. Sawyer turned to see Ash licking the edge of a rolling paper he'd filled with tobacco. 'What's your best?'

'I've done under nine seconds.'

Ash whistled his approval and walked away, taking a seat in the café area at the back of the Players club. Sawyer followed, and slumped down onto the low cushioned bench opposite.

Ash eyed him as he finished his roll-up. 'What now? Am I scoring for you again?'

'I need more on Price. But I don't want to go up there myself.'

Ash grinned. 'Didn't hit it off, yeah?'

'He didn't accept my Facebook friend request.'

Ash pocketed the roll-up, shoulders heaving in silent laughter. 'Ricky Price does not use Facebook, my friend. Just like nobody under the age of, like, thirty.'

'He mentioned something about the lad I'm looking for. He said he was into "something stronger". I want to know more about that.'

Ash stuck out his bottom lip, nodded. 'He's not talking about skunk or whatever. You know that, right?'

'I know that. I'd like a bit more detail. What did he sell him? How often? When did it start and stop?'

Ash laughed. 'You think your boy might have been jacking Ricky's supply?'

'I'll know more about what I think once you shake out some details.' Sawyer took three twenty-pound notes from his wallet and laid them on the table. Ash looked at them, raised his eyes to Sawyer, who added another.

Ash snatched up the money. 'Why don't you get the feds on this, man?'

'I don't want anyone to know that I want to know.'

'So, I'm your undercover boy, yeah? Your sidekick?'

'More like my Huggy Bear.'

Ash smiled, nodded. 'You think that one's lost on me, right? I watch *Starsky & Hutch*. Classic.'

'I'd have thought you'd still be bingeing your way through the third series of *Love Island*.'

Ash clicked his tongue through his teeth. 'You boomers, man. You're so bait. You think we're all stuck in our phones, but we get more than you think we do. YouTube, innit? I like seventies stuff. *Sapphire and Steel. The Tomorrow People.* It's the internet. It's, like, made everything up for grabs now, y'get me? Ain't no such thing as the past on there, really. It's like, we've got access to everything now, all across history. It's like we're always in the present.'

Sawyer took a coffee out to his car and sat inside, watching the video from Stuart Sutton's 'Great Explorer' channel. He screenshotted a few images featuring the boy in the dark hoodie, then leaned in close, squinting, studying the boy's eyes, again comparing the pictures to Samantha's photograph of Darren.

His phone screen was interrupted by an incoming call message. Walker.

'Sir. How are you?' The voice was echoey.

'Another day in paradise, Matt. Are you really calling me from the station toilet?'

Walker sighed. 'It's busy today. I've got to be quick. Stuart Sutton. Excluded eight years ago, from Cedar Mount School. Teacher caught him with heroin.'

'Possession?'

'He only had a small amount. Invited for interview but didn't attend. Doesn't look like it was followed up.' Clattering noises as Walker moved elsewhere. 'I've got you an address, though. Not far from here. I'll send it.'

'Any whiff of the hazing rituals I mentioned? Assault complaints? Officer attendance record?'

'Not that I could find. Sir. Listen...' He dropped his voice. 'I've been reading up on the Coleman case, and also Virginia Mendez. I listened to her podcast.'

Sawyer smiled. 'Thoughts?'

'This "interesting character" she talks about. Sutton?'

'I'm sure it is, yes.'

'Well. I was wondering how she found Sutton, to record the interview. And what she might have found out. Could be something to do with her disappearance.'

Sawyer's phone pinged with a message from Walker.

He checked the address, started the engine.

Sawyer took a five-minute drive to an estate of identical three-storey council houses in the Northern part of Buxton. He parked near a corner building and pushed the buzzer for the ground-floor flat.

He turned to face the street as he waited, tilting back his head and inhaling the clammy air. A group of teens eyed him from the gateway to a small playing field opposite. They muttered to each other and one cackled with laughter, as he held a bright red inflated balloon out of reach of another.

The sound of a chain sliding away. Sawyer turned as the door opened on a man with dark, tanned skin and a dense monobrow perched above heavy-lidded eyes. He was middle-aged, but well-muscled and paunch-free. He hung back in the doorway and tugged at the neck of his wifebeater vest.

Sawyer smiled. 'Mr Zengana?'

The man gave a slow nod and folded his arms. 'Yeah. What's up?'

'My name is Lloyd Robbins. I'm a private investigator, looking into the case of a missing young boy. I've been told that a close friend of his lives at this address.'

'I can't disclose any information about my tenants without their permission.'

'Of course not. Have you been the landlord here for long?'

Zengana paused. 'Yeah. Going on ten years. I look after the properties. My brother is the actual owner. He lives in Turkey.'

'I see.' Sawyer looked over his shoulder; the teenagers were crouched in a group, facing into the gate, backs to the road. The boom and click of hip-hop drifted over from a portable speaker. 'Did you know of a lad called Stuart Sutton who used to live here?'

Zengana scowled and cast his gaze to the ground in front of Sawyer. 'Yeah. Long time ago. And no, I don't know where he is. I told the woman the same thing.'

'The woman?'

'Yeah. She came looking for him a few weeks back. Vanessa or something.'

'Virginia.'

He looked up. 'That's the one.'

'Did Stuart leave on good terms, Mr Zengana? Was he a good tenant?'

Zengana gave a bitter laugh. 'Not really. Always having parties, too many people over. Upsetting the other tenants.'

'Any problems with illegal activities?'

'What kind of illegal activities?'

Sawyer managed a smile. 'The kind we're both thinking of.'

'Alright, then. Yeah. Needles. Drugs. Plenty of that round here.'

'Was that why you ended the tenancy?'

Zengana sniffed, pondered. 'It was periodic. Rolling. Six months. I gave him plenty of notice. He didn't seem that bothered. Left the place in a state, though. Listen, I'm very busy. I've got to get on.'

Sawyer took out his phone. He glanced back at the teenagers; they had begun to shuffle away, across the playing field. 'One last thing. Do you recognise this boy? I know it was a few years ago. Take a close look.'

Zengana crouched forward and peered into Sawyer's screen, at the image of Darren in the red-and-black lumberjack shirt. He gazed for a few seconds, then stood upright. 'Yeah. He's been here.' He shook his head. 'Long time ago.'

Sawyer headed back towards the car. He raised the transponder fob, paused, then crossed the road to the park entrance. The teenagers had disappeared into trees at the far side of the field, leaving a scattering of litter at the foot of the gate. Deflated balloons, energy drink cans, a Styrofoam takeaway carton, and a pile of silver nitrous oxide canisters.

He crouched and sifted through them. All spent, apart from one, with an unpierced cap. He slid it into his pocket.

26

DCI Farrell opened the interview room and stepped to the side. Sawyer entered and hovered by a chair opposite a central desk. DSI Keating sat in the facing chair, in full uniform with his cap on the desk, writing with a stout ballpoint. Two other men, suited, sat at a temporary desk by the window. One was around Sawyer's age, slim and bearded with rimless glasses; the other was thickset with unkempt grey hair.

Farrell took a seat at an open laptop next to Keating. Sawyer lowered himself onto the chair.

Farrell looked up. 'Do sit down, Detective Sawyer. No need to stand on ceremony.'

Sawyer smiled. 'Are you being sarcastic, sir? It's hard to tell.'

Keating sighed and looked up from the paperwork. His white hair had been shorn down to stubble, and his eyes betrayed a moment's tiredness, before he snapped into character and fixed Sawyer with his standard patrician glare. 'Let's keep it cordial. Nobody is enjoying this process.'

Sawyer caught a tiny smile on Farrell. He nodded at Keating. 'Sir.'

'You know our fellow inquisitors,' said Farrell, indicating the other two men. 'Federation rep DC Simon Gail and IOPC Lead Investigator Callum Whitehead. Since our last meeting, I've interviewed Stephanie Burns and her husband Jordan. Stephanie is sticking to her story.' Keating eyed him. 'By that, I mean she is adamant that, although your actions were responsible for the death of David Bowman AKA Malcolm Powell, you acted in self-defence and used acceptable force—'

'Against a man who had committed five murders at that point, and had kidnapped Stephanie Burns.'

Farrell nodded, squeezed out a smirk. 'Indeed. But, in my professional opinion, I got the impression that she was rather...' He glanced at Keating. 'Well briefed. Maybe even coached.'

The bearded man spoke up. 'DCI Farrell. Baseless allegation helps nobody.'

'Absolutely, DC Gail.' Farrell turned his gaze to Sawyer. 'I just wanted to get my impression on record, and to report that Jordan Burns has recently contacted me and seems rather keen to privately discuss his wife's account.'

Whitehead cleared his throat. 'With respect, Jordan Burns was not present at the incident. Let's not lose focus.'

Keating scribbled something, murmured a note of assent.

Farrell ignored him and typed into the laptop. 'The last time we spoke, we mentioned the axe used by Detective Sawyer, and a damaged section of the blade that held traces of a metal alloy consistent with that used in the manufacture of bullets. I have a final report from an independent forensic firearms team, with a spectroscopy analysis, which confirms that the axe was indeed struck by a high-calibre bullet, suggesting a long-range weapon. A rifle. I trust the Federation and IOPC will share my curiosity on this matter.' He ran his fingers through his waxy hair. 'Detective Sawyer, could you explain the origin of this firearm discharge? Did you see anything? Hear anything?'

'Not that I recall. Bowman was threatening me with the axe, and I was attempting to control the man we now know was his unwitting accomplice, Julius Newton. It was a chaotic scene. I saw him drop the axe, and then Newton hit me from behind.'

Farrell tipped his head back, grinned. As the corners of his mouth upturned, the skin on his face seemed to transform into liquid and sloshed upward, sealing over his eyes.

Sawyer looked down at his shoes, trying to shut out the emerging scene.

Voices. Imploring, echoing.

Sawyer calling. 'No!'

He braced, but still flinched at the shotgun blast, as plain and present as if Farrell himself had fired it into his own head across the desk.

Sawyer jerked his head up to the room's low ceiling. White, polystyrene tiles with a square pattern of alternating horizontal and vertical lines. The tile above Farrell's head was smothered in gore; blood and brain matter coaxed by gravity, oozing into a stalactite shape.

'DI Sawyer?' Keating's familiar, fatherly tone cut through the reverie.

Sawyer touched a hand to his shoulder. 'Sorry. Put my arm out, training. Bit of pain.'

'*There is nothing in darkness that will not be disclosed.*' His father's voice. '*Nothing concealed that will not be brought to light.*'

Keating studied Sawyer for a moment, then nodded to Farrell, who angled his head. 'If you need to take a moment, Detective Sawyer.'

Sawyer leaned forward and filled a paper cup of water from a jug on the desk. 'No. Carry on.'

Farrell typed into the laptop, taking his time. He kept his eyes on the screen as he spoke. 'I believe you've worked on cases with DS Shepherd. Is that correct?'

'Yes.'

Inhale.

Exhale.

'I wonder...' Farrell clasped his hands together. 'Might DS Shepherd have been aware of your impromptu operation? Might he even have been present at the scene?'

'DS Shepherd isn't an AFO.'

'Oh, I'm not suggesting he might have pulled the trigger. But if he was in attendance, then perhaps he'll be able to enlighten us as to the source of the gunshot. Seeing as you don't "recall" it.' Farrell raised his eyebrows. 'Because, Detective Sawyer, if you attended the scene with armed back-up, then that rather changes the narrative. Wouldn't you agree?'

DC Gail shifted in his seat. 'In what way, DCI Farrell?'

Farrell took out a canister of breath mints and flicked one into his mouth. 'It raises the issue of premeditation.'

'Why,' said Sawyer, forcing himself to keep his voice steady, 'would I have any intention of killing a suspect before he's been arrested and put to trial?'

Keating bowed his head.

Farrell continued. 'David Bowman was responsible for unspeakable crimes against young women. He displayed extreme misogynistic tendencies.' Keating glanced at him; he pushed on. 'It occurs to me that there were parallels between his actions and philosophy, and that of William Caldwell, the man responsible for the murder of your mother, Jessica.'

'Run, my darling. Don't look back!'

Sawyer raised his eyes and locked eye contact with Farrell.

'And,' Farrell continued, 'I wonder if you saw Bowman as some kind of proxy. If I've read the account of your apprehension of Caldwell correctly, you were in the position to take revenge on him but, rightly, chose to hand him in to custody. Perhaps you weren't able to take revenge on Caldwell, and so you vented that anger on Bowman.'

Whitehead waved a hand. 'DCI Farrell. This is not a courtroom. DI Sawyer is not on trial. I'm as eager to get the full picture of what happened as you are, but we're in danger of descending into cod psychology.'

Farrell sat back in his seat and rolled the mint around his mouth, maintaining eye contact with Sawyer. 'Nothing to say, Detective?'

'It's not even worth ignoring.'

Farrell smiled, nodded. 'I'm not denying that Detective Sawyer is a competent officer. But we must all be seen as above reproach in our methods. This isn't *Life on Mars*. We have a strict code of conduct to follow, and in order to carry it out, we have to leave our subjective opinion, our personal emotions, to one side. I'm sure you agree, Mr Whitehead. But, of late, Detective Sawyer's... choices seem to suggest an individual not quite in full control of his emotions. Just because you're good at something doesn't mean it's good for you.'

27

Sawyer drove out of town and joined the undulating Snake Pass A road across the Pennines, aiming for Hollow Meadows and the point where the National Park blended into the scruffy suburbs of north-western Sheffield. He rolled up and over the road's blind summits at speed, imagining Maggie's protests over his driving.

He filled up at a petrol station in Hope, and bought a pack of six multicoloured balloons. On the way back to the car, his phone rang.

Cross.

'Three words for you, Sawyer: Well, well, well.'

Sawyer climbed into the Mini and shut the door. 'Can you give me a few more?'

'Mr Fiesta has taken residence in a delightful maisonette with hardly any roof, on the outskirts of a farm not too far from your place.'

'Have you got a postcode?'

'No, but I can show you the way. I'm not sure he'll be in the market for guests, though. Are you sure it's a good idea to show up there all by yourself?'

'Of course not.'

Greg Coleman led Sawyer down a side path to the end of a back garden that could have easily grazed a small herd of livestock. He was short and slender, with a neat corona of blond hair and a manicured beard.

Coleman unlocked the door to a recently built one-storey brick building, turned on the light, and stood aside, allowing Sawyer to enter first.

The building housed an office with a wooden floor and a central glass-topped desk that looked out across the Hope Valley. The room was sterile and uncluttered, with a calendar wall chart, corner filing cabinet and a neatly stocked bookshelf.

'Have a seat.' Coleman gestured to a metal-framed chair that faced the desk, and the rear of an enormous iMac monitor. Sawyer sat, and Coleman did likewise, falling into a tall-backed padded chair and wheeling it to the side to give Sawyer a direct eyeline. 'Sorry to quarantine you out here. But Emily has friends over in the house. The boys are home, too. Bit crowded over there.'

Sawyer noted the accent: local but clearly upscaled for effect. 'I appreciate your time.'

Coleman drummed on the desk with both palms. 'So. You saw Sam?'

'Samantha, yes. She's asked me to help.'

'And you used to be a detective, right?'

'Still am. Just taking a break.'

Coleman offered a doubtful smile. 'Well. I'm sure you have Sam's perspective and there's little point in me raking over things. But the facts are there. We separated shortly after Darren's disappearance. But to be honest, the cracks began to show a few years before.'

'And you live with your new partner now.'

Coleman waved a hand. 'No reason to be coy. There was a bit of overlap. Sam and I had a lot in common, at the start.' He frowned, and trailed off.

'What do you remember about Darren's disappearance?'

'The panic. The feeling that he was going to walk in the door at any moment. Or the phone would ring and it would be him. And the way Samantha became so single-minded, with no time for anything else.'

'Including you.'

Coleman gave a theatrical shrug. 'It's not always easy to keep all your emotional columns in the black. We all have our flaws. I suppose I just wasn't a very natural father. I still find children a little tedious, to be honest. I'm sure that's true for many adults. It's just not something most people are comfortable admitting.'

'Samantha said you were good with Darren in the early years.'

'Did she? That's gratifying. I suppose I lost interest when he started to get hormonal and surly. I was getting enough of that from his mother.' He paused, clearly hoping for a laugh, but didn't get one. 'At first I was trying to make it all add up, make it work. Failure is a part of life, but if you can fail on your own terms, confident that you at least did everything in your power to succeed, then it becomes the kind of failure you can learn from, rather than the kind you regret. Wouldn't you agree?' He didn't wait for an answer. 'Can I get you a drink? I have a mini fridge in the cabinet. Coke?'

'No, thanks. Was there anything about Darren's behaviour in his teenage years that concerned you? Did he confide anything in you?'

Coleman's eyes flitted to the wall chart. 'Girls?'

'Possibly.'

'No. He showed some interest in my work. I'm an architect. Mainly domestic projects. We're sitting in one of them right now.'

'In what way was Darren interested in your work?'

Coleman studied his fingernails. 'I remember he asked me about exploring buildings. Abandoned places. He wanted to know what happens to places when they're not used. Who owns them, who decides what happens to them. That sort of thing.'

'It's called urbex. Urban exploration.'

Coleman typed into the computer. 'Yes. In many ways, buildings are like people. They retain a certain essence of their history.'

'I suppose that's because we love stories. We like to attach stories to everything.'

Coleman looked up from the monitor. 'Absolutely. Myths, shared rumours. Tales that grow taller in the telling. And there are places that become synonymous with events, usually emotional or negative. Rillington Place, Cromwell Street. Hungerford, Lockerbie. It's the places with grim histories that seem to be favoured by the explorer crowd. Asylums, hospitals, slaughterhouses. Darren said he knew his mother wouldn't approve and would worry about him.' He turned the monitor to face Sawyer. 'He got interested in it through a boy he met at school.'

'Stuart Sutton.'

He smiled. 'I believe so. A young woman came to see me a few weeks ago.'

'Virginia.'

'That's right. I showed her this video. It's from a trip that Darren took with Stuart, a few months before he disappeared. I loaned him my old camcorder. It was an ancient thing that used those micro cassettes. He took away the cassette, but the camcorder was set to transfer video to the hard drive.' Coleman switched the video window to full screen. 'I transferred the video a couple of years ago before I sold the camcorder. Didn't even know it was there.'

The footage had been filmed at night. It showed a brief shot of a wire fence, then flashes of brickwork. Distorted crunches of audio.

The image stabilised to reveal a teenage boy standing in front of a wall in a dark room. He held a torch at his side, pointing the beam up to the ceiling, casting his features in a pale, flickering light. Shadows fluttered on the wall behind.

'Right. Yeah. We're here again. There's me, The Great Explorer. And my colleague, who has promised not to *shit out* this time when he hears a little noise.'

A voice from behind the camera. 'Fuck off, Stu.' Darren's voice. Sawyer glanced at Coleman, who raised an eyebrow.

'We're going to have a look round the main building here. But before we go in, I thought you might want to know a bit about me.'

An awkward pause. Sutton nodded to the camera.

'Oh, sorry.' Darren again. 'So, where are we at the moment?'

Sutton dipped his head, revealing a shaven head with scars from razor nicks at the peak of his scalp. He looked up again. 'This is what we call a hot place.'

'And so you don't want to tell us the location, right?'

'Yeah, you can't just share all the hot places. There are rules. They'll get taken over. You get reported.'

Sawyer looked at Coleman. 'Do you know where this was filmed?'

Coleman shook his head. 'We never spoke about it. And it's too dark to tell from any features or fittings.'

Sawyer leaned forward as Darren laughed from behind the camera. 'Must be loads who know about this place.'

'Nah.' Sutton gave a slow, robotic shake of his head. As the left side of his face passed through the light, the camera caught a glint from a stud in his right earlobe. 'This is not well known, which is why it takes a great explorer—'

'Like you.'

Sutton laughed. 'Like me. To find it.'

'And that's pretty much the code of urbexers, yeah?'

'That's right.' Sutton gave a simian pout. 'Some people are dumb, though. They stick up their hero shots. Bragging, yeah? But you're not supposed to say anything, reveal the location. And also, this place is hardcore. Nobody would want to come here.'

'Why not?'

Sutton pushed the torch into his chin and shone the beam up over his face. 'Because it's haunted.'

The movement of the torch made Sawyer shudder.

His father. Shotgun under the chin.

'Fuck off, Stu.'

Clustered gore on the ceiling, dripping.

Sutton collapsed in laughter. 'No, man. It's true. I know a few people who've been here. There's some creepy shit going on. People have seen a weird guy who haunts the place. A demon.' He shifted the torch up so the beam highlighted his staring eyes. 'Some say it's the Devil himself.'

The video cut out.

Coleman smiled. 'Boys will be boys.'

155

28

Sawyer closed the blind on the deepening dusk and stood in front of the bedroom mirror, topless. He slowed his breathing, watching his shoulders rise and fall, then slipped into the first movements of the second Wing Chun form, *Chum Kiu* ('Searching for the Bridge'). Precise turning, synchronicity in movement to generate power for strikes and blocks.

He had replayed the trail from Episode Three of the Virginia Mendez podcast. The words spoken by Stuart Sutton were a match to the video he had seen at Greg Coleman's.

You can't just share all the hot places. There are rules.

Some people are dumb, though. They stick up their hero shots. Bragging, yeah? But you're not supposed to say anything, reveal the location.

He was stepping into Virginia Mendez's footprints now. So close behind he felt he could reach out and touch her.

She hadn't interviewed Stuart Sutton at the time of recording Episode Three. She had seen this video and recorded the audio, perhaps without Greg Coleman's knowledge.

Had she gone on to track Sutton for the trailed interview, or was it just bluster? Her boyfriend had said she was meticulous, well prepared. It was hard to believe that she would have trailed a new interview without securing it first.

He showered, fed Bruce and himself—Fish Selection in Jelly; pasta with pesto and courgettes—and sat on the sofa, gazing at his muted reflection in the TV screen. He stared ahead as he ate, tuning in to his churning thoughts, reaching for something close to meditation.

He startled, almost dropping his fork.

The scene unspooled in front of him: an overlay of agony. The shouts, the sounds, the barking dog.

And lately, always a new detail. As if his mind was growing weary of protecting him from the worst of it.

Caldwell, cold and efficient, looming over his mother as she held out her hands, trying to fight him off.

Before, Sawyer had felt a sensation close to a fast-acting headache. But now there was no warning, and the past fused with the present instantaneously, with no distinction.

Jessica swiped at the hammer, as Caldwell brought it down, over and over.

It was happening there in front of him, on the living room carpet, as real as rain.

With each blow, her cries grew shorter and more strained; terror and pain replaced by distress and confusion.

She called out to him. '*Why?*'

She tried to speak again, but Caldwell silenced her with a hammer blow to her mouth, crushing her jaw.

The intensity was increasing. Each episode seemed to engrave the horrors deeper into his mind. Sawyer not only feared the next flashback: he knew that each one would serve to amplify the next.

He screwed his eyes shut and leapt up from the sofa.

He squinted, keeping his gaze from the scene and opened a kitchen drawer. He took out the packet of balloons, canister of nitrous oxide, and a stainless steel whipped-cream dispenser, bought as part of his attempt to step up his culinary game earlier in the summer. He stumbled into the bedroom, where the bed seemed to hover in the centre, with the rest of the room a shimmering aura. Sawyer fell onto it, knees first, and inflated the red balloon with shaky breaths. He unscrewed the cap on the dispenser, locked in the canister and fitted the balloon over the end. He squeezed the pump trigger, filling the balloon with nitrous oxide, and pinched tight.

He fed the balloon into his mouth, wrapped his lips around the end, eased up the pinch, and inhaled, allowing the gas to surge into his lungs. He fell back onto the bed, tasting the sickly sweetness.

The room around seemed to solidify again, as Sawyer smiled to himself at the blissful rush of dissociation. He was numb, weightless; he let himself drift away from the vision, his eyes darting around the bedding and furniture, marvelling at the shifting visual geometry: glowing outlines, interlocking circles, liquid colour. And he felt it all lifting: the leaden sense of being tethered to events long gone, to the pain from the past. All of that existed now in a place impossibly distant, as he wallowed, without a care, in amniotic serenity.

After a couple of minutes, the effect faded, and Sawyer found himself back in the real world, on his bed, in a cloud of his earthy aroma, his training dummy in the corner.

He lay there for a while, breathing deep and slow, waiting for a tickle of nausea to subside.

He stood up, checked his pockets, peered through the window blind.

The fields across the road were blackened by night, their thresholds now grey outlines at the base of Kinder Scout.

Sawyer threw cold water onto his face and headed outside onto the porch. He stared up the road towards the Hayfield crossroads, and checked his watch.

29

Sawyer vaulted a dry-stone wall and ducked through a gap in the boundary fence. The moon lurked behind the clouds, but he kept low and stayed in tree cover until the field dipped to an open expanse of pasture with a cluster of outbuildings and a distant farmhouse, windows unlit.

He glanced back up the ridge, turned on his torch, then followed another stone wall down to a scrubby edgeland near a long, flat-roofed building with fractured machinery poking through an open entrance. He scurried past and veered off left, wading through the dense grass towards the trees and a rotting old shed with a hole in the roof.

Sawyer stopped, crouched, and observed the shed.

Glowing from within. Probably a small fire.

He shuffled through the grass, keeping eyes on the shed, trying to make an angle for a look inside.

A figure—large, male—stepped out and tended to a small woodpile, his back to Sawyer. He crouched, seemingly absorbed in whatever he was doing. Sawyer edged towards him, taking slow and silent steps.

The figure paused for a second before standing up and

turning towards Sawyer. The light from the fire glinted off something metal in his hand.

Knife.

Sawyer rose to his full height and shone his torch towards Austin Fletcher. 'There's a perfectly good Travelodge up in Glossop, you know. Twenty minutes' drive.'

Fletcher looked to Sawyer's left, then right, scanning the fields.

'Where's the Fiesta?'

Nothing from Fletcher.

Sawyer took a couple of steps forward. 'We should talk. One or two issues to resolve.'

Fletcher turned his gaze back to Sawyer. 'Closer.'

Sawyer nodded. 'Really? Isn't this where you say, "That's far enough"? Or is that too chatty for you?' He held Fletcher's gaze, locked in on his pinhole eyes. 'Got something to show you.'

Fletcher raised his weapon—an evil-looking hunting knife with a serrated blade—and walked towards Sawyer. They were less than ten metres apart.

Sawyer raised a hand, looked over his shoulder.

A vivid green point of light appeared on Fletcher's white T-shirt, hovering over the heart area. He stopped walking and looked down, then followed the beam up to the ridge behind.

'Laser sight,' said Sawyer. 'Sniper rifle. Military grade. Semi-automatic. You probably know it from your adventures in the SAS.'

Fletcher turned his gaze back to Sawyer.

'Keep the knife if you like. That's okay. This won't take long.' He pulled out his phone and navigated to an image of Maggie, bandaged and bruised in her hospital bed. He raised the device in the air and turned the screen to face

Fletcher. 'This is my friend. You've been watching her. I've seen your pills, Austin. Creatine, yes? Maybe they're giving you a few issues with impulse control? Anger?'

Fletcher narrowed his eyes and studied the screen.

Sawyer dropped his voice, sounded a grave tone. 'Did you do this?'

Fletcher shook his head. He looked past Sawyer, squinting towards the source of the light.

Sawyer pocketed the phone. '*Why?*'

Fletcher stared at him.

'Why are you still here? Stalking me, spying on Maggie? You won. You took away my leverage over our mutual acquaintance. You got the gun. Strickland's gone up a few floors now, though. I don't think he's that interested in me, or you, any more.' Sawyer took a couple more steps towards Fletcher. 'There's been substantial mission creep since he first set you on me. So. Why don't you just fuck off?'

Fletcher's granite features crumpled into something resembling a smile. 'No gun.'

A rush of epiphany. 'You didn't find it?'

Fletcher fixed him with those empty eyes. 'No. Gun.'

'Well.' Sawyer inhaled the muggy air, catching a sour whiff of silage. 'This is awkward. Have you got a cigarette?'

Fletcher frowned. He reached into his pocket and pulled out a packet of L&M cigarettes.

Sawyer took the stub from Maggie's house out of his pocket and held it up. 'Here's one I prepared earlier. Same brand. Except...' He flicked the stub to the ground. 'There's no DNA. Nothing. Someone let it burn down, snuffed it and left it outside my friend's house.' His phone vibrated in his pocket. 'Someone who is pretty keen to put you at the scene of a serious assault, and who would be sure I'd find out about it.' He took out the phone. The Caller ID was withheld. 'I think we both know who this someone was. An old friend of yours.'

Fletcher dropped his gaze. 'Dale.'

'Who needs enemies, eh?' Sawyer took the call. Sharp, rapid breathing at the other end. Muttering. Self-soothing. 'Hello?'

'Oh! Mr Sawyer. Sorry. Detective Sawyer. This is Lewis Vaughan.' He paused, caught his breath. 'It's Ginny. Virginia. She… She came back.'

PART TWO

THE ASPHALT WORLD

30

The dogs howled and snarled as their handlers attached sturdy chain leads and dragged them back to the side of the clearing. Two teenage boys set about the temporary fencing, yanking out the supports and lifting away the metal barriers.

A thickset middle-aged man took a shovel and began to transfer a pile of dirt back into the edges of the recessed pit area, lit by two tripod halogen lamps.

He peeled off his polo shirt and turned to a group of men lurking beneath the trees in a cloud of marijuana smoke. 'Anthony! Clean up the fucking mess and get your arse in the van. You can smoke that shit later.'

Anthony's mates shoved him forward, cackling. He snatched up a metal bucket, sloshed soapy water over the earth at the centre of the pit and scrubbed at a patch of gore with a large hand brush. He was skinny, all elbows and knees, with a grimy, loose-fitting T-shirt. 'Fuck's sake. There's *teeth* down here. What the fuck are we cleaning up for, anyway, Uncle Mark? No cunt will find this once you've filled it in.'

A pick-up truck crawled down from the dirt track at

the edge of the wood. Mark Bishop stopped shovelling and waved it through. The headlights picked out his lank hair and white, flabby torso, in contrast to his sunburned cheeks. 'Anthony, I swear you're fucking special needs.' He got back to the shovelling. 'Do you want to go away for six months? If they investigate, they'll dig all this up. This way there's no evidence, see? Thinking ahead. If we could breed fighting dogs that don't bleed, it would be a lot easier.'

'It'll happen one day,' said one of the teenagers, as he gathered up the barriers and slid them onto the truck's cargo bed.

'Yeah, in your fucking head,' said Anthony.

Bishop smiled. 'Definitely nothing happening in there. Don't think there ever has been.'

He laughed, dry and breathless. Anthony snorted his approval, but the other teenagers shrugged and wandered away, dragging a couple of stocky dogs with them.

'What's this, Uncle Mark?' said Anthony, holding up a long wooden pole with a loop of rope attached to one end.

'Break stick. Chuck it in the back with the other stuff.'

A small crowd of fight fans lingered, laughing and smoking. Bishop called to one. 'Drinks on you, Dex?'

An elderly man in a crumpled trilby waved a hand. 'You're having a laugh. I'm down two hundred quid. Where'd that canario come from? Fucking ringer.'

'The one with the cropped ears? It's been doing the rounds. Owner says it's one win off Grand Champ.'

'Shouldn't allow them,' said Dex. 'Not fair on the other dogs.'

Bishop laughed. 'That's the whole point, mate. Fair fights would be dull as fuck. I've seen some last nearly two hours. Dogs breathing out their arse, pissing blood. Nobody's a winner. I've had to finish a few off with this before.' He held up the shovel. 'Kennels in Ukraine and

Bulgaria, in-breeding off winners' bloodlines. Usually pit bulls.'

Dex sneered and walked away.

Bishop wiped sweat from his head with a hairy forearm. 'You'll be back. Next time, don't just bet on the big fuckers.'

The barking faded as the handlers moved off in separate directions, into the trees. The watchers drifted away, and Anthony finished scrubbing and joined the teenagers as they shuffled towards the sparse woodland at the edge of Hayfield village.

Bishop latched the flip-up door on the truck and pumped his fist twice on the side. The vehicle rattled up onto the track and drove away.

Despite the hour—just gone 2am—the air was parched and soupy, and Bishop felt the age in his calves as he trudged down the walking track towards the security lighting at the wool factory perimeter. He could have jumped in the pick-up, but it was his habit to slip away alone after a fight, hoping it might strengthen a claim of casual involvement if the worst happened.

———

A sizeable broad-shouldered man had peeled away from the onlookers near the close of the final fight and waited in a clump of trees at the base of the slope, where the walking track joined the factory road. He watched Bishop slope away from the track and turn the corner towards the housing estate.

The man followed at a distance, hurrying through the pools of street lighting, slowing as he passed through patches of darkness where a few vehicles were parked. He ducked along a side road, unlocked a bottle-green compact van and took out a backpack. Ahead, Bishop stopped to light a cigarette, then carried on past a row of converted semis.

The man caught up and slipped into an alley, out of sight, as Bishop scaled the steps to his house and jangled his keys. He unlocked and opened the front door.

The man dashed up the steps behind him and jabbed something into his back, illuminating the porch in a crackle of blue light.

Bishop yelped in pain and shock, and stumbled forward into the hall, dropping to his hands and knees. He rolled to one side, trying to turn and face upwards, but the man loomed in and hit him with a heavy punch to the side of his head, knocking him unconscious.

————

Bishop jolted awake, gasping for air. A second torrent of icy water splashed into his face, and he twisted his head to the side, spitting and spluttering.

He lay propped against a cold stone wall, still topless, wrists clamped together by a metal cuff, and his legs locked into a chain by clasps around his ankles. He kicked at the floor, pulling the chain taut against its base link, which was locked onto a metal plate at the foot of the wall.

The place was dark, with a faint dawn light peeking in through a grubby window. A male figure moved in his peripheral vision, and bent forward over a storage unit in the corner.

Drawers opening and closing. Clattering metal.

'Hey!' Bishop shouted. 'What am I... Who are you?'

The man went over to a sink and turned on a tap. After a few seconds, he carried a large pan of water over to a workbench and set it down.

Bishop blinked and shook his head, trying to clear his vision. The man struck a match and lit a portable gas stove on the workbench. He lifted the pan onto the stove.

'Oi! I'm talking to you. Where the fuck am I? Who are you?' Bishop winced. 'My fucking face! It hurts to talk. You must have broken my cheekbone. Was it you?'

The man stood over the stove with his back to Bishop. 'Why don't you fight yourself? With other people?' The voice was deep, resounding.

'What?'

'You force the dogs to fight. Why not yourself?'

Bishop shook his head. 'I... What am I doing here? Where are we?'

'You target the powerless because you feel no power yourself.' The man raised himself back to his full height; he was still mostly in silhouette, and the shape of his head seemed to have changed, grown. 'Because it makes you feel powerful.'

Bishop lapsed into a coughing fit. 'Hey. If you say so, right? Now, listen. Get this fucking chain off me or...' He shifted position, tugged at the chain.

The man turned off the stove and lifted the pan. 'Now you close your eyes. You don't look at me. You don't see anything.'

'I'm not closing my eyes. Unlock this fucking chain!'

The man walked over and set the steaming pan of water down on the floor. Bishop looked up, trying to see his face. He caught a flash of shadow. Something beast-like, with horned tips either side of the top of the head.

The man reached down and flattened a strip of opaque masking tape over Bishop's eyes.

'No, no, no. No!'

Clanking metal. Bishop screamed; an unconvincing howl of outrage, the anger now blending into terror.

'You can make noise,' said the man. 'But I won't stop. And this place is remote. Nobody will hear you. I promise you that there is no possibility of rescue or salvation.'

The man leaned over to the wall and flicked a switch, casting the room in feeble electric light.

Bishop writhed and tugged at the chain. 'Fuck you! Let me go! You fucking...'

The man lifted the pan.

Iron scraping on stone.

Bishop paused for breath. The man waited in silence, holding the steaming pan of water, watching him.

Bishop looked around sightlessly, listening for the man.

He leaned in, close to Bishop's ear. 'You can scream now.'

He stripped the tape from Bishop's eyes.

31

Sawyer shouldered through the heavy double doors into the relatives' room. Lewis Vaughan stood alone, staring up at the wall-mounted television that displayed a static image with multicoloured icons and a bright logo in an uneven font: *CAVENDISH HOSPITAL INTERACTIVE.*

'How is she?'

Vaughan turned and ran a hand across the back of his neck. His blond hair was still immaculately quiffed, but his eyes were wild and reddened. 'She's unconscious. I wanted to call you because...' He dropped his head.

Sawyer stepped into the room. Beech coffee table with tissues. Stack of old magazines. Blank walls in pastel and teal. 'What happened?'

Vaughan fumbled for the back of one of the three chairs and took a seat. 'I haven't seen her yet. Haven't spoken to her. She's been sedated. The doctor said she was agitated and rambling. He said he wants to rule out, uh—'

'Head injury.' Sawyer sat down opposite. 'Is she otherwise okay? Physically?'

Vaughan rubbed his knuckles around the corners of his eyes. 'They don't know. They're doing tests or whatever. I only saw her in the bed. She looks thin.' He sucked in a deep breath. 'Fuck!'

'Maybe she's malnourished. She'll be on IV fluids. They'll take care of her. How did she get here?'

'Someone dropped her off in a car. Ginny had her purse, and my number on an emergency contact card.'

Sawyer frowned. 'Who dropped her off?'

Vaughan looked at Sawyer, confused. 'Some old couple. They left. I only spoke to them for a minute or two. The woman said that Ginny flagged them down by woods up near Slackhall.'

Sawyer's phone buzzed in his pocket. 'Did she say anything to them? Or to the doctor?''

No. Just kept asking them for help and crying. They brought her straight here.'

Sawyer looked at the message, from Jordan Burns.

Time running out need an ANSWER

He pocketed the phone. 'Can I see her?'

A voice from behind. 'Why would you want to do that, Detective Sawyer?'

Sawyer sighed, and turned. A scrawny man in a light grey suit entered. He stopped, too close to Sawyer, smiled, and adjusted his wire-framed spectacles. He took out a warrant card and turned to Vaughan. 'I'm Detective Constable Ross Moran. You're Lewis Vaughan?'

'Yes.'

'Mr Vaughan, we're keen to understand how Ginny found herself at the hospital today. I'm sure you're aware that she's the subject of a missing persons investigation.'

Vaughan nodded. 'Yes, but—'

'Detective Sawyer is currently inactive, under suspension pending an investigation.'

Vaughan closed his eyes for a few seconds, opened them again. 'I... want him to help. We've met before.'

Moran smiled again. 'I'm afraid that's not relevant. Have you been nominated as Virginia's next of kin?'

Vaughan looked at Sawyer. 'No.'

'Well, then I'm sorry to say that neither you nor Detective Sawyer have any leverage here.'

Sawyer scoffed. 'Leverage? It's not a business deal, Moran. His girlfriend has been missing for over two weeks. She's just been found in a terrible state.'

'Of course.' Another smile. 'But that's the emotional perspective. I'm here to focus on the practicalities. The police procedure. We need to find out the extent of any illegalities, and regardless of your connection to Detective Sawyer, Mr Vaughan, I would urge you to restrict your dealings to official police channels.' Vaughan looked to Sawyer. 'And, as I say, at the moment that doesn't include Detective Sawyer, who is currently serving a suspension.'

Sawyer stood and headed for the exit. He turned at the door. 'Lewis, can I have a quick word in private?'

Moran sighed, but Vaughan got up and followed Sawyer out into the corridor.

Sawyer led him to an alcove opposite and spoke in a low voice. 'Lewis, can you get me a contact for the couple who brought Ginny to the hospital? I'm entitled to help you privately, but I need to know a bit more about where she was picked up.'

Vaughan nodded. 'I'll text you.' He hesitated. 'Doesn't seem like you're exactly best of friends with the other guy.'

Sawyer smiled. 'You should give him all the information he needs. DC Moran is a good detective. We just got off on a bad foot.'

32

JUNE 2012

Sawyer side-stepped through the crowd, holding his plate aloft. He squeezed through to a raised block of paving at the far end of the outdoor pool, where Frazer Drummond presided over a charcoal barbeque, the forks and spatulas toy-like in his hulking hands.

'Can I interest you in some protein?' Drummond flipped a line of burgers in succession and tugged at the neck of his short-sleeved Hawaiian shirt. 'Hotter than Satan's arsehole today, Sawyer.'

Sawyer held out his plate and prised open his sesame bun. 'You don't get that quality of customer chat at McDonald's.'

Drummond sniffed. 'You don't get PGI Scotch beef at McDonald's.' He slid a burger onto Sawyer's bun.

'What's PGI?'

'Protected Geographical Indication. It's a benchmark. Assurance that the beef was reared and processed in

Scotland. If we're going to justify our place at the top of the food chain, we should at least give the animals a decent life. A bit of dignity.'

'Before we kill them?'

Drummond lifted his sunglasses onto his shiny forehead and narrowed his eyes. 'I don't recommend trying to eat live cow.'

Sawyer looked across to the house's cantilevered porch, where the hired DJ nodded to the music: seventies funk, disco standards. 'So are you exclusive to Keating now?'

Drummond dug a fork into a bowl of salad, mushed it around. 'For police work, yes. Home Office-registered, finally.'

'Prestigious.'

Drummond shrugged. 'Few more letters after my name.'

'More numbers on your bank statement.'

'Cheeky fucker. But, yes. It's why we can afford this place. Just. I hear you're off down to the Smoke soon?'

Sawyer took a bite of burger. 'London calling.'

'You'll learn a lot more there. Ditching the yokels for the mean streets, eh?'

Sawyer pointed down to the distance, beyond the rolling open fields at the side of the house. 'What's that?'

'Broomhead Reservoir. Sophia always said she wanted to live near water. I think she meant of the salty variety, but it's a start. As for me...' He leaned forward. 'Do you know one of the things that attracted me to this place, Sawyer? The address. We are technically in the area of Wigtwizzle.'

'Isn't that a kids' TV show?'

Drummond laughed and took a slurp from a can of beer. 'I was born in a place called Queenzieburn. North of Glasgow. But I think this is actually an upgrade, in the comical place name stakes.'

'*Detective Sergeant*!'

Sawyer turned. A young woman in a paisley beach dress glided out from a porch at the back of the house. She stopped just short of Sawyer, tipped her tortoiseshell shades down her nose, and stuck out a hand.

'Sophia'. He smiled and shook her hand, jingling the array of gold bangles looped around her slender wrist.

'Well done, you. I was so thrilled when I heard the news.' She swished away her long black hair. 'You'll soon be Chief Constable.'

Drummond mock-choked on his drink. 'His hair's too long for that. And he hates uniforms.'

Sophia smiled. 'True to your own spirit, eh, Jake?' She winked and angled her head back towards the house. 'Let me give you the tour.' She took Sawyer's hand and guided him back across the porch into a large dining room with a view of the reservoir below. 'I'm in love with this house. Ben and Emma can't quite believe we actually live here. The other day, Emma asked me if we're still on holiday. I'm dreading them growing up. I wish kids could just stay kids forever.'

A gaunt man in slack shorts and a loose white T-shirt turned from the wooden bannister at the edge of the porch. He took off his silver-framed glasses and used the edge of the T-shirt to clean the lenses, all the while watching Sawyer and Sophia Drummond as they entered the house.

Inside, Sawyer followed Sophia through the dining room into the cavernous kitchen. The central bar had been crammed with bottles of liquor, and the work surfaces held several bowls of mixed salads and finger foods.

Sophia flipped shut the blind that looked out onto the pool area, where the guests had formed a number of cliques in the suntrap at the top of the garden. She turned to Sawyer, tilted her head back. 'Do you like my new earrings?'

He leaned in and lifted them both, resting them flat on his fingertips. Jewelled angel wings. 'Divine.'

She smiled. 'You smell good.'

'Higher pay grade. Ditched the Lynx Africa for Eau de Lacoste.'

Sophia lifted Sawyer's hands away from the earrings and rested them on her shoulders. 'It's been a hectic few weeks, with the move. The kids have been difficult. Too much work, not enough play.'

He nodded. 'Probably not a good time. Sex among the crudités. Could get messy.'

Sophia sighed and pulled back, letting his hands fall away. 'Do you still see me as "play"?'

'Plato said that life must be lived as play.'

She moved to the bar, poured two glasses of red wine, handed one to Sawyer. 'Montoya Cabernet. Frazer's favourite.'

Sawyer sloshed the wine around in the glass. He took a sip, winced.

She laughed. 'No?'

'You want to cool things off a bit.'

'What?'

He set down the glass. 'You're looking for affirmation, in a setting where there's little chance of anything getting too heated.' Sawyer stepped closer to her. 'New house. New beginnings. Husband drawing greater respect. You take the *Observer*, vote Lib Dem, but I think you're more status-centric than you care to admit, Sophia. Must be confusing, now I've been elevated, too.'

Sophia sipped her wine, stalling. 'It all feels too reckless now. Risk is only exciting when the worst-case scenario is endurable.'

'I'm moving.'

'Where?'

'To London. The Met.'

'When?'

'Few weeks.'

She took a slug of wine. 'Well. These things happen for a reason.'

He moved in close. 'No. They don't. Things happen because we make them happen. There's nobody behind the scenes, shuffling the pieces around on some celestial gameboard.'

Sawyer slipped his hands around her hips. Sophia set down her glass. She leaned forward, rested her chin against his shoulder and whispered in his ear. 'I can't let you leave without—' She startled and pulled back. 'Ross.'

Sawyer turned. The thin man from the porch stood at the door, smiling. 'Sorry. Just using the bathroom.' DC Moran nodded at Sawyer and hurried away, back out to the porch.

Sophia closed her eyes and snatched up her wine, draining the glass in a single gulp. 'Fuck!'

Sawyer gripped the edge of the sink. 'Does Frazer—'

'Of course he fucking doesn't.'

'It's just a drunken clinch.'

She barked a bitter laugh. 'Good story.'

'Your housewarming party. Bit too much to drink. Plausible deniability.'

'Yeah. For you, maybe. I'll still get the grief.'

Sawyer headed back out of the door, onto the porch. He squinted at the glare from the low afternoon sun, and shook away a twinge of nausea. The DJ had upped the tempo. 'Tossing and Turning' by Windjammer. Melancholic pop soul.

He walked towards the pool, towards the silhouetted guests. A small group danced beneath the trees at the end of the driveway, arms whirling.

'Jake!'

Sophia from behind. Sawyer kept moving, looking for Moran.

He tried to push through the crowd, but a large, bear-like hand squeezed his shoulder, spinning him round.

Drummond shoved him out into the open and drew back his arm.

Sawyer stepped across Drummond, out of the punch's range, causing Drummond to stumble forward, off balance.

They faced each other: Drummond with flushed red cheeks, breathing hard. He stared Sawyer down, venom tainting his pale blue eyes.

'Frazer!'

Keating's voice from somewhere, off near the front of the house.

A shout of distress from Sophia. Gasps and murmurs, as the crowd tuned in to the confrontation.

Drummond launched himself at Sawyer, who stepped to the side, onto a puddle of pool water. He tried to steady himself, but slid forward onto the tiles at the rim of the pool.

Sawyer heard a loud crack, and yelped at a shot of pain through his chest. He tried to push himself upright, but the pain scythed up into his shoulder and he flopped back down.

A hand on the back of his neck, trying to drag him upright.

He managed to flip onto his side, as Drummond was jostled away by Keating and two other men. He broke free, and held both hands up in the air, indicating submission.

Drummond crouched beside Sawyer. 'You're one lucky fucker, you know that? I'm hoping it's your collarbone, but you've probably only chipped a rib or two.' Sophia stood beside them, hands over her mouth. Drummond glared up at her. 'You think I didn't suspect something?' His head swayed, and he blinked in drunken slow motion, stabbing a chunky finger in Sawyer's direction. 'You made a good choice there, my love. This one. He's fucking *poison*. Takes pleasure where he feels like it. Doesn't care if it causes other people pain. Easier than dealing with your own pain, eh, Sawyer?' Drummond stood up. 'Hurry up and fuck off down to London, where nobody gives a shit about anyone but themselves. You'll fit right in.'

He wheeled away, pursued by Sophia.

Sawyer rolled over, wincing at the pain in the side of his chest. The guests watched at a safe distance as he hauled himself upright.

DC Moran pushed through the crowd and caught Sawyer's eye for a second. He offered a sour little smile, then headed off into the back of the house, after Drummond.

'Okay, lover boy.' A male voice from behind. Sawyer turned. DI Martin Pittman ground a cigarette into a poolside ashtray and slipped an arm around Sawyer's shoulders. 'Let's get you out of the blast zone.'

———

Pittman led Sawyer down the drive, where his blue Subaru Outback was parked at the front of the house. 'How did you get here?'

Sawyer clutched at his side. 'Taxi.'

'I'll give you a lift home. But you should probably drop in to A&E first.' Pittman opened the passenger door and Sawyer eased himself in. Pittman looked back towards the house as he ducked into the driver's side. 'That's one way to leave your mark.'

He closed his door and they sat in silence for a moment. Sawyer closed his eyes and breathed in deep through his nose. Leather upholstery, the flat citrus of Pittman's cologne. The car interior had been baked in the summer heat. Sawyer brushed pool water off his arms and looked for a manual window roller.

Pittman half-turned the ignition key and pressed a button which rolled down both windows. 'When's your last day?'

'Not sure yet. It's all done in principle, but the brass are still working out where to put me.'

Pittman whistled. 'Keating saw some of that. Might be awkward.'

'I don't think it brought the service into disrepute, trying to not get punched by a drunken man who thinks—'

'I'd rather not know, Sawyer. Can't hurt me then, eh?' He lit a cigarette and held it out of the window. 'Haven't had a chance to congratulate you yet. DS is a strange one. Kind of like middle management.'

Sawyer laughed, winced. 'It's taken me a long time to rise to the middle.'

Pittman blew a neat jet of smoke out of the window. 'It's tough at the middle, y'know.'

Sawyer nodded. 'Crowded, too.'

Pittman laughed. Music throbbed from the house. 'Forget Me Nots' by Patrice Rushen. 'You'll do well in London. But they're not as sophisticated as they like to think.'

'Dunning-Kruger effect.'

'You what?'

'Never mind. I'm just in a big-city mood at the moment. I like the idea of a bit of anonymity.'

'Easier to keep your secrets. The cases will be more complex, though.' He drew on his cigarette, puffed away more smoke. 'Hey. Remember that thing last year? Missing professor.'

Sawyer frowned. 'The neuroscience guy?'

'Yeah. Pope. The place we checked out, where the professor's phone had pinged? The old abattoir. It was closed in 2009. The guy who ran it when it was operational, a fella called Sherratt. Vanished. Been missing for almost a week now. Out of character, usual.'

'Did Sherratt have any connection to Pope?'

Pittman shook his head. 'No. The trail on Pope is ice cold. Apparently, his wife has shacked up with another academic type. Didn't waste much time.'

Sawyer shuffled round to face Pittman. 'And does Keating see this bloke's disappearance as a lead?'

'More of a possible link.'

'I could look into it. Go out on a high.'

'No chance. You're as good as on garden leave now, depending on Keating's mood over what he saw in there. And I don't want any jurisdiction grief if you dig up something and then piss off down south.'

'We might also be joining imaginary dots. A lot of mispers do turn out to be runaways.'

Pittman finished his cigarette and threw the stub out of the window. 'C'mon, Sawyer. We're big, tough detectives. The FLOs like to play it soft for the families, but we both know that most people don't just disappear. They get disappeared.'

33

PRESENT DAY

Bruce leapt up onto the bed and marched back and forth across Sawyer's chest. Sawyer checked the time on his phone —10:15am—and rolled out onto the floor. Bruce jumped down and wound around his ankles, purring.

'Breakfast, big man. Not far off lunch.'

Lately, Sawyer's sleep was longer but fragmented: an hour of vivid and baffling dreams, followed by a period of tossing and turning before the next hour. He padded through to the kitchen, rolling his head around his neck, cracking his muscles. He was tense, tenderised. Rested but not recharged.

He scooped out Bruce's food and made coffee, staring into the cup as the machine huffed and hissed. His phone buzzed against the bedside table and he hurried through to take the call.

'Yo!' the caller greeted him as he set the phone onto speaker and dug out some clothes.

'My own personal Jesse Pinkman.'

'Gayest name ever,' said Ash. 'What you saying?'

Sawyer smiled and sat down on the bed. 'So you know *Starsky & Hutch* but not *Breaking Bad*? Kids today.'

Ash sighed. 'Don't know, don't care. Look. Your man, Price. Yeah?'

'I'm aware of his work.'

'This shit about selling your boy "something stronger". He was talking about the Big H, yeah?'

'Haribo?'

Ash sniggered. He had the laugh of an older man, phlegmy and abrasive. 'Nah, man. Smack. Heroin. Well, sort of heroin. I heard it might be fentanyl disguised as heroin. Nasty shit.'

Sawyer sipped his coffee. 'When did it start and stop?' A sizzling sound from Ash's end. 'Are you smoking dope? Bit early, isn't it?'

'Vaping. Bubblegum. Look, Price said that Darren bought the smack off him, but he didn't think he was a junky. He wasn't doing it himself. None of the tell-tale signs, like.'

Sawyer sat forward. 'So, was he selling it on?'

Another laugh from Ash. 'Nah. He was an errand boy. Picking it up for someone else. Sort of an inbetweener.'

Sawyer looked through the window. A boxy, mustard-yellow Range Rover pulled in to the side of the lane.

'You still there?' Ash continued. 'Do you want to know who the someone else was?'

'Thanks, but I already know.'

He ended the call, not waiting for a confirmation. DS Ed Shepherd got out of the Range Rover and ran the palm of his hand along his scruffy goatee.

Sawyer tapped in another number; the call connected instantly.

'Sir.'

'Matt. The address you gave me, for Stuart Sutton. He wasn't there. I think he was using Darren Coleman to pick up his drugs, after the exclusion. Look into further drug convictions. Did he cross paths with any local rehab facilities?'

A knock at the door.

'Do you think Sutton had something to do with Darren's disappearance?'

'I don't know, but I'd like to put it to him in person. See the whites of his eyes. Cross-ref all the possible drug convictions, rehab programmes. We need to find him.'

'We?'

Sawyer walked to the front door. 'Does Shepherd know we've been talking?'

Walker hesitated. 'No.'

'Let's keep it that way.'

Sawyer opened the door. Shepherd nodded, and stepped into the sitting room, closing the door behind him. He hovered at the back of the sofa and grinned at Sawyer.

'What?'

Shepherd nodded. 'Bed hair.'

Sawyer swiped a hand across the top of his head. 'How are things back on the bridge?'

'Now I'm thinking of Keating as Captain Kirk.' He shrugged. 'Not great. You'll love this.' He hurled himself into an armchair, causing Bruce to startle and bolt into the bedroom. 'In a meeting about the Hardwick case, Myers actually suggested we consult with you. Farrell flipped.'

'Farrell is involved in the case?'

'Yeah. While he's working on your thing, Keating wanted to double him up on the Hardwick murder. He's pretty chummy with Moran.'

Sawyer perched on the sofa arm. 'Gruesome twosome.

How did your DC get on? Serious crime related to the meat industry? Animals?'

Shepherd took out his pad. 'Pulled out a few unsolveds. 2006. Guy who ran a puppy mill from his farm near Hartington. Murdered. Beaten pretty badly. Plenty of items stolen, though. 2008—'

'The broiler chicken farm guy.'

'Yes. Beaten badly, but also tortured.'

Sawyer nodded. 'Partially flayed.'

Shepherd continued. '2010. A spate of attacks on legal badger-culling staff. Man traps. No deaths but a couple of the injuries were life changing.'

'I interviewed one of them.'

'Really?'

'Yeah. Up at Cavendish. Pittman sent me.'

Shepherd checked his notes. 'Fenwick?'

'Rings a bell.'

'There's a couple more. 2010. Neuroscience professor. Milton Pope. Missing.'

'What's the animal angle?'

'His university lab was involved in animal experiments. I think he got the usual grief from the ALF before his disappearance. And then in 2012, Mervyn Sherratt. Owner and General Manager of the old Sherratt & Sons abattoir, outside Hayfield. Decommissioned a few years earlier.' Shepherd looked up from his pad. 'Missing.'

Sawyer closed his eyes, casting through memories. 'I looked into the Pope case with Pittman, too. We had a wander round the abattoir grounds. Couldn't get into the main building.'

Shepherd angled his head. 'Couldn't get in?'

'Well. We could have, but it just wouldn't have been appropriate. So, that was Sherratt's place. It's where Pope's phone signal gave its final ping.'

Shepherd pocketed the notepad. 'Could be a connection, but the trail is stone cold for both. Talking of pings, any luck with yours?'

'Not yet. What was the badger guy's name again?'

'Fenwick.'

Sawyer pondered, shook his head. 'Did Drummond come back with an answer on Hardwick being gagged?'

Shepherd paused, turned to the window.

'Ed. This is for the greater good. It's just solid police work, consulting with your Hero Cop.'

'No gag, according to Drummond.' Shepherd swallowed. 'So he must have done the flaying somewhere private. Because of the screaming.'

Sawyer frowned. 'Maybe he wanted to hear the screaming.' He looked up. 'So, how about Farrell? And Bowman?'

'Farrell still hasn't called me in about it.'

'Keating has probably warned him off because of the Hardwick case. He talked to me again.'

Shepherd puffed out his cheeks. 'Did you lie to him?'

'I was economical with the truth. I think he's assuming you'll co-operate.'

Shepherd's phone rang; he stepped out onto the porch and took the call, speaking in a low voice. Sawyer edged over to the kitchen, watching him.

Shepherd called in through the door. 'Got to go, sir. Urgent.'

'Anything I can do to help?'

Shepherd shot him a doubtful look.

'Can I come along?'

'Of course not.'

———

Sawyer threw on his trainers, watching through the bedroom window as Shepherd climbed into the Range Rover. He waited for the car to move back onto the road, and hurried outside to the Mini.

Shepherd U-turned and drove off towards the Hayfield crossroads. Sawyer crossed the driveway bridge and idled until he saw Shepherd turn left, away from the town. The flat, wide fields around the road to Sparrowpit made it easy to keep the Range Rover in sight at a distance, and when Shepherd turned into a lane guarded by two uniforms, Sawyer pulled over and made a call.

Dean Logan slurped at something before speaking. 'Jake Sawyer.'

'Dean Logan. Vodka tonic to warm up the engine?'

Logan laughed. 'Fuck off, Sawyer. Way too early, even for me. Coffee, black.'

'Like your soul.' Sawyer watched the uniforms wave Shepherd through. 'Enough with the baby talk. Information.'

'As in, you want it?'

'As in, I've got it. Cordon set up off Winnat's Pass. Woodland, looks like it. The outer perimeter is set way back. Nobody getting anywhere near the side road.'

Logan slurped again. 'Sounds big.'

'Get me the details and you can have your ripper story.'

34

Sawyer parked in Hartington village square and turned off the car engine. He sat for a few moments with his eyes closed, listening to the final section of *Banstyle* by Underworld: downtempo electronica, with a drowsy, stream-of-consciousness vocal. But the cinema behind his eyes unspooled its resident horror: bloodied faces, looming forward through flared sunlight; his beloved dead, forever alive and forever re-dying in an abysmal loop of flailing and screaming.

'You went missing once.'

He opened his eyes. Jessica sat in her usual place, in the back seat, head leaning on the window, framed by a torrent of coal-black hair. This time, she wore a faded T-shirt. Green with a patchy black print and the legend *IRON BUTTERFLY* in a psychedelic font.

She smiled, but didn't look at him. Because she didn't see him. Because she wasn't really there.

'You were with some older lads.' She gave a warm smile of recall. 'Some quarry or waste ground, not too far from the house. Michael was with you. He said there was some kind of pit, with shallow sides. Not that deep. And you'd all been launching yourself off the edge, daring each other to land at the deepest spot.'

Sawyer watched his mother's lips. Not real but moving. Not there, but somehow conjuring the words.

'You jumped a long way and they thought you were hurt, so they legged it.' She laughed. 'Michael came running home and Dad came to find you. But you'd gone. They looked all over and Dad was close to calling the police when Michael found you in a mini digger that had been left there by the workmen, luckily without power. You said you wanted to use it to make the hole deeper, because it was "too easy". You were only five, my darling. You've been making things hard for yourself ever since.' She lifted her eyes to him, and he felt the urge to smile, to show her he still had the dimple. 'That poor woman. Find her boy, Jake. All she can do is look back. Find her boy so she can start to move forward again.'

Sawyer turned away, gazing out of the passenger window at the stone cottages lining the main street. 'What am I missing? I can't see it. Help me remember, Mum.'

Tap, tap, tap.

He startled. A squashed, elderly man wearing driving gloves leaned in at the driver side window, making a prodding, downward motion with his finger. Sawyer pressed a button and the glass slipped down.

'You just got here, son? We've got an hour left on this.' The man passed a small parking ticket through to Sawyer. 'It'll save you 80p. All adds up, eh?'

'Yes. Thanks. That's kind of you.'

The man gave a dismissive wave and walked away. 'No problem at all. You take care of yourself.'

Sawyer studied the parking ticket, braced, and checked the back seat in the rear-view mirror.

Empty.

———

'Are you sure you don't want a cup of tea?'

Sawyer hovered by the window of the cottage sitting room. Across the road, the sandwich board outside The Nut Tree café asked, *IS EVERYTHING OKAY?* with arrows emerging from both *YES* and *NO* into an image of a steaming mug and the solution: *COME IN AND HAVE A COFFEE.*

'I'm fine, thanks.'

'At least sit yourself down, then.' Lillian Fowler gestured to a puffy armchair with embroidered antimacassars.

Sawyer smiled and sat.

Lillian took her place on a matching sofa facing a vast stone fireplace with dormant wood burner. She was mid-sixties, with a hairsprayed whip of dyed auburn hair. 'Have you been to The Nut Tree?'

Sawyer nodded. 'Yes. I sometimes meet my friend there.' A pang of something. Guilt?

'It's been there for a fair few years.'

'Mrs Fowler. As I said, I'm working with Lewis Vaughan, the partner of Virginia Mendez, the young woman you picked up last night.'

Lillian toyed with her wedding ring, sliding it up and down against her knuckle. 'Oh, it was awful. The poor woman. I don't know what she'd been up to. My husband thought she was on drugs or something.'

'Is your—'

'Ron is resting. He sleeps quite late, anyway, and I think it was a bit of a shock for him.' She leaned forward. 'You're a detective, yes?'

Sawyer nodded. 'Detective Inspector. But I'm helping Lewis, the woman's partner, on a private basis. Exactly where did you first see Ms Mendez?'

'Oh, we were driving back from a friend's house in Chapel. Ron mentioned the woman up ahead. He said he thought she was walking too near the roadside. She turned and saw the car and just stepped out, waving her arms and shouting for us to stop. He slammed on the brakes and she ran around and got into the back seat. She kept looking behind her, into the woods.'

'Did she say anything specific?'

Lillian dropped her eyes to the worn Havana rug in front of the fireplace. 'She was sobbing and pleading. She kept saying, "Go!" and "Please!" And she tried to lock the doors from inside, but they're automatic. Only the driver can do that, you see.'

'And was she walking in the direction of Hartington?'

'Yes. I'm sure I saw her coming out of the woods. Just before she saw us. I thought she was, you know, doing her business.'

Sawyer managed a polite smile. 'Was there anything near the location where you picked her up? Any landmarks?'

Lillian thought for a moment. 'There was a traffic cone, across the road. Just opposite the spot where I first saw her.'

Sawyer looked at Lillian's hands. She was twisting the ring now, loose around her finger. 'Did Virginia look hurt?'

'She had a nasty bang on the head. I gave her my bottle of water and she drank it in one go, then just sat there with her mouth pinched shut, staring out of the window. Ron turned the car round, heading back towards Buxton, and said he was going to get her to a hospital. She nodded but didn't look at us.'

'Did she say anything else?'

Lillian shook her head. 'She was whispering, muttering. I thought she was saying a name or something. Deborah, maybe. Or Dabbler.'

35

'Have a seat, DC Moran.'

DCI Farrell glanced up from his computer as Moran closed the door behind him and perched on the edge of the padded chair facing Farrell's desk.

Farrell stabbed at his Return key with a flourish and pivoted to face Moran, grinning. 'You wanted to see me.'

Moran adjusted his glasses. 'Sir. I've been reading the ballistics on the Sawyer investigation.'

'Ah, yes.' Farrell wriggled out of his suit jacket and hung it on the back of his chair. 'I spoke to our good friend Detective Sawyer about the findings.'

'Did he say anything interesting?'

Farrell took out his breath mints and flicked one into his mouth. 'Oh, he's always interesting. Just nothing useful. He was closed tight, as ever.'

Moran took a notepad from his inside pocket. 'Have you heard of a man named Tony Cross, sir?'

Farrell bit his top lip with his teeth. 'The name is vaguely familiar.'

Moran took out his phone and pushed it across the desk. 'Here's a story from a few years ago. The short version is that Cross was an elite marksman and AFO who took out a career scumbag in Hackney in 2016.'

Farrell browsed the news report on Moran's phone. 'Oh, yes. There was a public enquiry.'

Moran nodded. 'The ruling went against him because the dead man had a MAC-10 under the seat, but he wasn't actually holding it at the time of the shooting, and it turned out to be unloaded, anyway.'

'Cross said he thought he was carrying.'

'Yes. But he got an unlawful verdict, stood trial for murder. Acquitted. He's now freelance. Does a lot of work for private security in the States.'

Farrell sat back, tipped his head forward. 'So how does this relate to the Sawyer situation?'

'Cross was part of the Met's SCO19 elite firearms squad. He worked with Sawyer on a couple of cases.'

'And you think he might have helped Sawyer on the Bowman raid?'

Moran shrugged. 'Seems possible. Ballistics report says that the axe was struck by a round from a high-powered rifle. Cross was one of SCO19's snipers. As it says in that piece, the Met Commander called him "the longest arm of the law".'

Farrell winced. 'It's good, DC Moran. But conjecture. Intelligent conjecture, but still—'

'I can put him near Sawyer on the day of the Bowman raid.'

Farrell frowned, put out by the interruption.

Moran continued. 'I have an ANPR hit on the car registered to Cross near Dovestone Reservoir on the day of the raid. This is around an hour before the official AFOs went in. There's another hit around half an hour later, outbound.'

Farrell grinned. 'Okay. Now that is interesting.'

'Should we talk to Cross, sir?'

'It would have to be voluntary. I see no grounds for arrest. I may have something myself. I received a message from Jordan Burns, the husband of the woman held by Bowman and recovered by Sawyer. He's asked for a private meeting. Unofficial, I assume. Perhaps, along with your information and whatever Jordan Burns wants to talk about, we can get the full picture and open Detective Sawyer up a little.'

36

Sawyer sped along the Snake Pass, away from Slackhall village. As he rounded a long corner, he spotted a single traffic cone planted beside a break in the roadside barrier, with a warning triangle: *ROADWORKS 400 yds.*

He parked on a verge and climbed up over the opposite barrier, into the sparse trees lining the road. The terrain opened out into a vast open field, with distant woodland dividing the White and Dark Peak. He pushed through the long grass, scanning the ground, heading for an isolated copse a few hundred yards into the centre of the field. The slate-grey clouds loomed low, and he squinted into a scattering of fine rain.

Despite the encroaching autumn, the group of trees was still in full leaf, and Sawyer conducted a slow spiral search, walking in a circle from the outermost point of the copse perimeter towards the centre, eyes fixed on the ground, head swaying from left to right with each step.

There. Something neither green nor brown. He crouched, snapped on a pair of latex gloves and carefully extracted a dirty white rag from a tangle of bracken. It looked like a tea towel, torn in half, and smelt strangely fresh and earthy. He held it up to the light; one edge had been tainted by soaked-in blood.

Sawyer flapped open a plastic Ziploc bag with one hand, and dropped the rag inside. He finished his search, and walked out of the trees across the field towards the dense woodland in the distance. The treeline was at least half an hour's walk away. He let his mind rise away, imagined himself hovering above the scene like a drone. Had Virginia Mendez escaped from someone, and made it here from there? The rain stepped up, spattering onto the shoulders of his jacket. He turned, and walked back to the car.

———

Later that afternoon, Sawyer set up his laptop on the coffee table and navigated to the HOLMES login screen. He entered Shepherd's ID and password as usual, but instead of loading the main dashboard area, a pop-up window informed him that either the password or login were incorrect.

They were all advised to change passwords every thirty days as routine. Few bothered, apart from the fussy, process-driven sorts. Like Shepherd.

He tried a couple more possibilities, then abandoned the effort in case the system locked Shepherd's account and warned him about the unauthorised access attempts.

Sawyer pulled on his workout bottoms, stripped to his waist and stood before the full-length bedroom mirror. He slowed his breathing and, with great care, eased into the first Wing Chun form, *Sil Lum Tao* ('Little Idea'). One hundred and eight separate movements, flowing into each other. Optimum efficiency, nothing classical or theatrical, always seeking the shortest path.

He executed the form with his usual precision, but while the discipline usually induced a meditative sense of serenity, powering down the background noise to allow him to focus, today the session seemed to irritate him, inflaming a sense of something rattling around in the back of his mind, refusing to settle.

He warmed down, showered and dressed. It was certain to be a treacherous evening ahead, and his mental chatter was tetchy and fragmented when he needed absolute focus, unclouded by emotion.

His phone rang. He connected the call; Dean Logan spoke first.

'It's your friendly neighbourhood future Pulitzer Prize winner.'

Sawyer scoffed. 'Isn't that a young man's game? The dogged pursuit of moral outrage. Naive idealism.'

'If you're going to be rude, Sawyer, then I'm not going to tell you what I know about the new case you're not allowed to be involved in.'

'And you won't get that exclusive ripper takedown story from me. The first step on the road to Pulitzer glory.'

Sawyer switched the phone to speaker and set it down on the coffee table. He dropped into the sofa and unwrapped the block of Ash's dope, began to roll a joint.

Logan cleared his throat. 'Mark Bishop. Fifty-two. Dumped in a ditch in a different patch of woodland. Near Mermaid's Pool again, though. He managed a couple of hardware shops. One in Hayfield, one in Ashbourne. "Mark Bishop Home & DIY". Snappy.'

Sawyer burned off the marijuana and crumbled it into the joint. 'COD?'

'What am I, the fucking pathologist? I know the body was partially buried again, and I imagine it seriously ruined the day of the elderly walker who found it.'

'How do you mean?'

Logan paused. 'According to my source, it was similar to Hardwick. The killer took off most of his skin. And not just his limbs this time. He gave the poor bastard a really close shave of his chest and back.'

'Refining the fantasy.'

'You what?'

'Nothing.' Sawyer muted the call, struck a match and lit the joint, then unmuted.

'One more thing on the unfortunate Mr Bishop,' said Logan. 'I had a little nose around his particulars, so to speak.'

Sawyer took a silent toke. 'Thanks for that image.'

'He had a previous for animal cruelty. Cautioned last year for keeping dogs in unsanitary conditions. RSPCA visit after a neighbour complaint. He's also got two fines on record. One for contravening the Dangerous Dogs Act, and another against Section 8 of the Animal Welfare Act.'

'Dog fighting.'

'Gold star. Curiouser and curiouser, eh, Sawyer? What's your assessment?'

Another drag. 'I couldn't possibly comment, without a full victimology analysis. The dog stuff might be nothing to do with why he was killed.'

'Okay, then. Now, how about a foaming pint of ale later. And you can tell me all about the day you took out the nasty ripper man.'

Sawyer coughed on a sharp patch of smoke. 'Washing my hair tonight. But we'll set something up soon.'

'Promise?'

'I promise to try.'

He hung up and lay back on the sofa, finishing the joint, inhaling deeply, savouring the fuzzing edges, letting his mind swirl and dip into its darker recesses.

He paused on a thought, dropped the joint end into a can of yesterday's Diet Coke, snatched up the phone and tapped in a new number. As usual, Walker answered immediately.

'Matt.'

'Sir.'

'You really don't need to call me that, you know.'

'Force of habit.'

'Nothing to do with respect, then?' Walker hesitated. 'Joking.'

'I haven't found any other address for Stuart Sutton yet. But his name has popped up in a link to a local rehab initiative that started up a few years ago up in Hathersage. An SIS.'

'Supervised Injection Site. Safe and hygienic places to shoot up. They're usually run by charities to prevent overdose. As you can imagine, they're controversial.'

'Yeah. I spoke to someone at the Hathersage place who recognises the name. But there's obviously a lot of anonymity involved, so I need to dig carefully.'

Sawyer reached for the can of Coke and just about stopped himself from taking a sip. His head spun, and he closed his eyes, trying to clear his thoughts. 'I wanted to ask you about the Hardwick and Bishop murders.'

Chatter in the background. The sound of Walker closing a door. 'Sir. I'm not sure—'

'I know you're on the case. You don't need to compromise yourself. Just a thought.' A flash of nausea. He took a deep breath. 'I think there might be a connection between a few other cases going back quite a few years. Shepherd has the details. And, yes. He's been talking to me. You've probably been following lines of enquiry that I suggested. Maybe he's even taken the credit.'

'Well, he—'

'Doesn't matter.' Sawyer forced himself to slow down, measure out his thoughts. Sweat prickled on his forehead. 'In 2006, a guy who ran a puppy mill was murdered in Hartington. In 2008, the owner of a broiler chicken farm was tortured and murdered, using similar methods to that shown on Hardwick and Bishop.'

'Yes. I know these. In 2010, there were several attacks on a badger-culling group, and in 2010 and 2012, two mispers. One connected to animal experiments, and the owner of the old abattoir outside Hayfield.'

Sawyer deepened his breathing. 'Look into prison or psychiatric hospital releases from the early 2000s, up to 2006.'

'The puppy mill murder.'

'Yes. Cross-ref the releases with connections to animal charities, activist groups, ALF. This is someone who started his work in 2006, and so his fantasy should be refined by now. What started him off? There would have been violence in his past, and a lack of love or some kind of domestic complexity that led to the withdrawal of love, or a betrayal as he saw it.'

'You've said before, focus on outlying detail.'

Sawyer sat back. 'Go on.'

'The gap. Between the 2012 misper and the Hardwick murder. If it's the same man, then—'

'Yes. Good work. Why the gap? Whoever is doing this, it looks like he stopped for a few years, but has now started up again. And I don't see any sign that he might be about to stop again anytime soon.'

———

Sawyer drove through the dimming daylight, listening to his mood-settling playlist: ambient Aphex Twin, Stars of the Lid, The Beloved. He skirted Buxton town centre and parked in an anonymous industrial estate with a cluster of numbered structures that looked more like container crates than buildings.

He walked to the far side of the grounds, and entered a three-storey, glass-fronted building with a sign over the main doors: *SCIENTIFIC SERVICES.*

Sally O'Callaghan stood at the front desk, talking to a male receptionist who, given his build, had clearly been hired to double up as a security guard. She spotted Sawyer and headed over. 'If we were in a relationship, I would insist on more notice before being summoned to bend to your will.'

He smiled. Dimple. 'You don't strike me as the submissive type, Sally.'

'Astutely deduced. My first husband made that mistake.'

He held up the Ziploc bag with the torn tea towel from the copse. 'Pretty please?'

'You want me to make you a bloody bandana?'

'DNA. Prints. The works.'

She took the bag. 'And when would sir be requiring my findings? Last Tuesday, I assume.'

Sawyer swayed in place, and had to put his foot to the side, steadying himself.

Sally's eyes narrowed. 'You okay? I know you're technically off duty, but I thought you didn't drink.'

The room fogged over for a second, then cleared. Sawyer reached out to a nearby table; the beefy security guard raised his eyes to them.

'I'm not drunk. Just... bad sleep. Busy head.'

'You do realise this is the second independent favour I've done for you in the last few weeks. When do I get some kind of reimbursement?'

'If they send me away for the Bowman thing, you can have my cat.'

Sally leaned in, studying his eyes. 'So, what *are* you doing with all your free time? Idle hands. You know the saying.'

'I'm helping with a cold case. I wanted to ask, do you remember Detective Inspector Martin Pittman?'

'Why?'

'There might be a connection with a couple of things we worked on together a few years ago. He was sort of an early mentor for me. I'd like to talk to him.'

She angled her head. 'Fresh out of Ouija boards, I'm afraid. Pittman died a couple of years ago. Lung cancer.'

37

Dale Strickland sized up his shot. Blue into the corner looked like an in-off.

'Brown?' Jerome stood over the table, resting his gigantic hands over the point of his cue.

Dale shook his head. 'No easy red.' He checked his watch. Almost 10pm. 'Our guest is due. You ready?' Jerome gave a slight nod. 'Let's head up.'

They locked the private snooker room, walked through the busy public area, and climbed the stairs to the carpeted corner office on the top floor. It was dark outside, but Dale drew the blind on Deansgate and settled into the revolving chair behind his glass-topped desk. Jerome stood at his side, facing the door, his muscled bulk barely contained by a tailored white shirt.

Dale took off his glasses and cleaned the lenses with his cuff.

Jerome raised his head, keeping his eyes on the door. 'Do we know his position?'

Dale slotted the glasses back over his eyes, taking time to adjust them to his liking. 'Position?'

'About the woman.'

'I'm assuming he's made the link to Fletcher, yes.'

'So why the meeting?'

Dale shrugged. 'I'd say he wants to see if we know anything about Fletcher's movements and plans. If he's accepted that Maggie was attacked by Fletcher, then he'll assume that Fletcher is past caring and will be targeting him next.'

Jerome snorted. 'Maybe he'll ask for protection.'

A buzzer rang. Jerome pressed a button on a wall panel and studied the video image. He held his thumb onto a second button for a few seconds. The image went blank and Jerome resumed his position at Dale's side.

'Switch on,' said Dale. 'He doesn't look like much. But remember, he's on suspension because of his involvement in the death of a suspect.'

Jerome shook his head. 'I'll snap him in half if he tries anything.'

Footsteps in the corridor outside. Sawyer walked into the office and took a spot on the mock Persian rug before Dale's desk.

Dale sat back and knitted his fingers together, holding his hands up to his chin. 'Always a pleasure, Detective Sawyer.'

Sawyer smiled. 'Let's start this how we mean to go on, Dale. With a little honesty. Time to square things, don't you think?'

'We've done this. There's nothing to square.'

'I'm sure you have the gun. The one used on the unfortunate Shaun Brooks. Probably taken from the cave by The Mountain here.'

Jerome frowned, glanced at Dale.

'It's from *Game of Thrones*,' said Dale. 'The TV show.'

'I say, "mountain",' said Sawyer, studying Jerome. 'More of a hillock.' He turned to Dale. 'The gun keeps you clean, and it takes away my insurance. I assume you're hoping that I'll take out Fletcher, or vice versa. Either works for you to sweep up the mess and commune with your new colleagues in high office, without fear of hindrance.' He stepped closer to the desk. 'I think you know that Fletcher won't come for you. But you don't want to take him out directly if you can help it. Which is why you had my friend beaten up and tried to make it look like Fletcher's work. So I'd take him down for you.'

'Why are you here?' said Jerome.

Sawyer smiled. 'You trained him in basic grammar. I thought he was just a coffee bearer.'

Jerome folded his stocky arms, and tilted his head to the side.

'None of us needs this. We have to find a way out before something irreversible happens.'

Dale bowed his head forward, revealing the bald patch on his scalp. 'You have a unique way with threats, Sawyer. It's a shame you're so virtuous. You'd make a decent enforcer for... a strip-club owner.'

'Thing is,' said Jerome. 'There's one of you and two of us. So you're not really carrying a lot of weight, in negotiation terms.'

Sawyer looked over his shoulder. Austin Fletcher entered and took a spot just inside the room, his broad frame blocking the door.

Dale slapped his palms onto the desk. 'Loving the theatre, Sawyer! Are you two best friends now? Or is there something more?'

Jerome sniggered. Fletcher fixed his icy blue eyes on him.

'Disengagement,' said Sawyer. 'Amicable separation. You get on with your new political career. This is all a bit of a mess started by good old-fashioned sexual jealousy. I'm sure you've got the pick of the interns at the mayor's office, Dale. We all need to access our inner grown-ups and get on with our lives.'

Dale's expression darkened. 'There's a lot of beef flying around this little office, Sawyer. Hard to see how we can limit the damage. There's just so much still unresolved.'

Sawyer glanced at Fletcher: he still had Jerome in the full beam of his glare, and Jerome returned the look with interest. Fletcher's forehead had reddened, the colour seething beneath his scraped-back blond hair.

'For one,' continued Dale, 'Austin. I was hoping to speak to you about the fates of Marco and Hector.'

Fletcher ignored Dale, kept his eyes on Jerome.

A faint smile flickered at the edge of Jerome's lips. 'How's your daughter, Fletcher? How's little Emma?' He took a step forward. 'All grown-up now. Although she's been that way for quite a while, hasn't she? Thanks to Marla's friend, Mr Wagner. Although who's to say she wasn't broken in by someone else before then?'

Fletcher's breathing accelerated. His shoulders rose higher, fell further. Sawyer tried to catch his eye, but he couldn't be diverted.

Jerome stepped closer to Fletcher. He was the taller man, but Fletcher's boot heels raised him close to eye level. 'Thing is, Fletcher. Maybe *you* don't care about the consequences of your executive decisions. But not-so-little Emma might soon bear the cost on your behalf.'

Fletcher let fly a bludgeoning right hook. Jerome tried to swing his head away, but Fletcher's fist crunched into his cheek, sending him crashing into the back wall by the window. Dale pushed his chair away and opened the desk drawer.

Jerome slipped out a dark-bladed dagger. Fletcher reached into his jacket and produced his serrated hunting knife. Jerome passed the dagger into his left hand, lunged forward and slashed at Fletcher, forcing him to jerk his head away. As Fletcher corrected himself, Jerome caught him with a punch to the jaw that dropped him onto the rug. Fletcher reached out a hand to push himself back upright, but the fabric slipped against the floor and he sprawled onto his side, momentarily helpless. Jerome stepped in and wrapped one hand around Fletcher's jaw, pushing his head back, exposing the soft flesh of his neck for the dagger.

Sawyer shifted around close to the desk and, with rigid fingers, flashed out a *biu gee* strike to Jerome's throat. The big man staggered back into the desk, choking, but keeping a grip on the dagger. Sawyer covered the distance in an instant, grappling and immobilising Jerome's knife arm beneath his own forearm, and snapping back his face with a palm strike to the chin. As Jerome forced his head back around to face his attacker, Sawyer raised himself and crashed the top of his head into the bridge of Jerome's nose, forcing him to drop the dagger to the floor. Jerome bellowed in fury, and shook his head, spattering the glass-topped desk with blood.

Fletcher was on his feet now, moving in on Jerome.

'Gentlemen!' Dale had taken a boxy black Glock handgun from his desk drawer. He aimed the weapon at Fletcher, pushing himself into the far wall. Jerome doubled over, groaning, holding his hands over his crumpled nose. Dale grinned, pointed the gun at Sawyer. 'Let's save this for pay-per-view sometime.' Fletcher staggered backwards and made off down the corridor. Dale cocked the gun. 'I don't advise a sideline in conflict resolution, Sawyer. I appreciate your time, though. We'll be in touch.'

———

Fletcher had disappeared by the time Sawyer made it down to the club entrance. Head whirling, he charged out across the back streets, past the glass-fronted Podium building and under the rusted iron bridge, to the small car park.

Dale had taken the gun, not Fletcher; it had probably been acquired by his new sidekick. Sawyer had lost all security over his knowledge of Dale's involvement in Shaun's death. And what of Fletcher's motive? The scene in Dale's office had looked planned, but Sawyer had been just as surprised by Fletcher's arrival as Dale.

He took out his phone. Text message from Walker, sent a few minutes earlier.

Got some info.

Sawyer climbed into the Mini and called Walker; he answered instantly.

'Are you ever not available?' Sawyer opened the glovebox and dug a lemon bon-bon from a paper packet.

'Late shift, sir,' said Walker. 'But I do have a life, too.'

Sawyer slid the sweet into his mouth. 'What have you got?'

Again, the sound of Walker closing a door. He lowered his voice. 'A few names clicked with your criteria, but one really sticks out. Scott Walton. Past violence, meat industry connection. It's colourful stuff. Released from HMP Doncaster in 2002, after three years. Aged twenty-one.'

'Crime?'

'Involuntary manslaughter. Killed his father in a

domestic incident. I haven't had a chance to go further back. I wanted to see if you thought it fit.'

Sawyer gazed out at the lamplit car park, keeping his eyes away from the rear-view mirror. 'What's the animal angle?'

'Walton stayed at a place called Norfolk Park Probation Hospital in Sheffield. It's an AP. Approved Premise.'

Sawyer nodded. 'They used to call them probation hostels.'

'Yeah. Run by social workers. But then Walton was assigned a job at ProPak Foods in North Yorkshire. Ready meal factory, basically. He was supervised for a while until they believed he wasn't a risk. I've lost the work paper trail there, but the ProPak place was warned by Food Hygiene about meat-handling practices. I cross-reffed Walton with animal charities, like you said. At the time of his stay at Norfolk Park, he was a member of PETA, and a donor to something called Blue Cross.'

'Abandoned pets.'

'As far as I can tell, he hasn't renewed his memberships since 2004. He had a public order D&D caution in 2006. Gave the address of his mother's house in Crookesmoor. Doesn't look like he's there any more.'

Sawyer chewed on the sweet. 'Who signed off his psychiatric report from the probation hospital?'

'Dr Edgar Bullmore. He left there when he retired five years ago, at sixty-seven. Stayed on quite late. I'll send you his address if you think he's worth talking to.'

'Please, yes. I'd like to know more about Walton's past. But... I suppose you'll need to feed this work back through official channels.'

Walker hesitated. 'Yeah. Sooner or later.'

'Let me talk to Bullmore first. If it doesn't go anywhere,

it doesn't matter. If it's interesting, you can take it to Keating. How about Stuart Sutton?'

'No addresses. But he has been to the Hathersage SIS as recently as three weeks ago. I could push a bit further, see if he has another appointment coming up.'

Sawyer started the engine. 'Great work, Matt.'

'How's Maggie, sir?'

A second flush of guilt. 'I'm sure she's fine.'

38

MARCH 2014

Sawyer set down Maggie's glass of red wine and slid into the booth. 'And now, the end is near.'

Maggie forced a smile, sipped the wine. 'Don't.'

'Don't what?'

'Are they really so short of Detective Inspectors down in London?'

Sawyer took a slurp of Diet Coke. 'They probably have plenty of bad ones.'

She gave him a look. 'Will the Drummond thing stay on your record?'

'Thing? I didn't lift a finger.'

'It still held up your transfer.'

He pulled open a packet of smoky bacon crisps and spread them across the flattened wrapper. 'It's gone. I've already met my new colleagues. Moving into the future, remember? Informed by the past but not defined by it.'

'It's all about the day by day when you have young kids.

The hour to hour, sometimes. Mia is six going on twelve. Freddy has skipped crawling and cruising and is concentrating on breaking things. I'm hoping Mia will be able to dress them both for me soon. I'm all set up for the private therapy side now. Bit more work from home. Easier to give them attention.' She sloshed the wine around her glass. 'Just looking for my first client.'

Sawyer crunched on a few crisps, smiled. 'No way. You're too close to me. You couldn't be objective.'

'Don't worry. I have a few potentials lined up.'

'You might be needed by Keating even more. He's setting up the Buxton MIT soon.'

Maggie tucked her hair behind her ear. 'Well, this is the thing. You're leaving at such an exciting time.'

He held her eye contact. 'I need to get away, find a bit of distance. But don't worry. I'm like The Terminator.'

She smiled. 'You'll be back.'

They shared a silence. Sawyer licked his finger and dabbed at a few crisp fragments. 'Klein's up for release in less than five years.'

Maggie rested her fingertips on the back of his hand. 'That shouldn't be your concern.'

He looked up at the chalkboard food menu. *Welcome to the Prince of Wales, Baslow. Pie of the Week, Soup of the Day.* 'How can it not be my concern? He didn't kill my mother. Somebody else did. And maybe they're still busy, killing other people's mothers.'

'Is this you moving into the future?'

He shrugged. 'Maybe I'll investigate it myself one day.'

She shook her head. 'Excellent idea. Focus on cases that don't resonate too deeply.'

Sawyer took his time over another mouthful of crisps, kept his eyes on her. 'I thought I was pretty good at sarcasm. But you taught me all I know.'

'Are you being sarcastic?'

He laughed, took another sip of Coke. Maggie squeezed his hand, then withdrew her fingers and picked up her wine.

Sawyer looked away. 'So, have you completed all your work for Keating?'

'Almost. I was helping with the case of a local lad from Matlock who's been missing for a while now. Darren Coleman.'

'I think Pittman mentioned that.'

She nodded. 'He was SIO. I worked with the family. His *mother*. Jesus Christ, Jake. It must be like a living death.'

'Any other kids?'

'No. Father a bit hands-off, too.'

Sawyer finished his drink. 'Most people's lives don't work out the way they hope. Because you build your fantasy when you're young. And nobody adds shade to the light. They all focus on the things that they want to go well, but don't factor in the unexpected. And that's what makes up most of life.'

'The unexpected?'

'Yeah. Partly because we can't see inside each other's heads, and we're good at only showing the version of ourselves we want people to see. But you don't know what people are going through. You can never know the full picture. In fact, you sometimes have to avoid listening to people who claim to know someone well. Their viewpoint is too clouded with emotion. How long has he been gone for?'

'Just over a year.'

He dropped his gaze to the table. 'Yeah. Living death. She's in limbo. Neither one thing nor another. And after all this time, you and I both know he's probably gone for good, and his mother will probably go to her grave with the mystery unsolved. But there's no shelf life when it comes to love. The best thing his mother could get would be to have her son alive and well, back in her loving arms. The second best thing would be for her to know what happened to him, good or bad.'

39

PRESENT DAY

Sawyer hung the heavy bag chain over a rafter in the corner of the sitting room. He secured the straps and pulled on his padded sparring gloves. Topless, he worked around the bag, sidestepping, pummelling it from multiple angles—jabs, hooks, combinations—all to his angry playlist (Nine Inch Nails, Suicide, KMFDM). As the blows landed, his mind flicked through the worst of his embedded horror show: his brother, crawling, hands leaving smears of blood across the grass; his mother's shouts of shock, of panic, of pain; the terrible peace in his father's eyes as he raised the shotgun on himself. Perhaps it was faulty logic, to try and soothe it or smother it; instead, he would take it on directly, punch it all out, force it into the fabric of the bag.

He groaned and roared with each impact, squinting into the early morning sunshine as it broke through the blinds. He collapsed to his knees, muscles screaming, hair matted with sweat. Shower, then smoke. Only then, out into the world. Purged, fortified.

His phone vibrated on the coffee table. Sawyer draped a towel over his shoulders and took the call.

'Okay,' said Sally. 'It's morning. Heavy breathing. I hope I'm not interrupting anything.'

'Just been working out.'

'Disappointing. I thought it might at least be aimed at the thought of me. I'm calling about your rag.'

'Anything on it?'

She lowered her voice. 'Well. Unlike your mysterious cigarette end, yes. There is something on it. Only one set of prints. I cross-reffed them with our Virginia Mendez file. They're hers. The blood is also hers. DNA match. And there's the teeniest, tiniest hint of someone else. I got a hit from NDNAD. Male. He was swabbed for a minor offence well over ten years ago. Fella called—'

'Scott Walton,' said Sawyer.

Sally sighed. 'If you already know all this, Sawyer, why disrupt my beauty sleep? And don't say I don't need it.'

Sawyer towelled his face. 'He let her go.'

'Sorry?'

'Virginia.'

'She's still unconscious, Sawyer. We don't know what happened to her, why she went missing for two weeks. But the hard part of that one is over.' She hesitated. 'There's another thing heating up.'

Bruce poured himself through the cat-flap; Sawyer watched him prowl over to his food bowl. 'Why not kill her?'

'Kill who? Virginia?'

'Yes.'

Sally clicked her teeth. 'I guess we'll find out when she's well enough to talk.'

Sawyer stood up. 'I think I can find out sooner than that.'

———

'You're most welcome, Detective Sawyer.' Dr Edgar Bullmore groped his way across the two basic chairs facing his desk, and eased himself into a large padded armchair on the other side. 'I warn you, though. I fear my obsolescence is now so established, face-to-face visitors find it difficult to shut me up once I get going.'

Sawyer stepped into the office. Bullmore had designed his workspace in sitting-room comfort at the back of his roomy bungalow in suburban Dronfield. A large window looked out on a tidy garden with a closely shorn lawn and miniature potting shed.

Bullmore rubbed at the bridge of his nose. He was seventy-odd: slight and wizened, with a scruffy crop of thick white hair. But he dressed like a wedding guest: grey tweed suit, spotted blue-and-white tie. He took an overstuffed folder out of a drawer and thunked it down on the desk. 'You've caught me at a good time, in that I'm still alive. I was recently diagnosed with some ghastly tumour or other. Something beyond the remit of modern science, anyway.' He opened the folder.

'Sorry to hear that,' said Sawyer. 'We all have our compromises.'

Bullmore jerked his head up. 'Oh, no cause for sorrow. My wife... died earlier this year. I almost said "passed", but she is still very present for me. We thoroughly enjoyed our life together, but all good things come to an end. If they didn't, they would soon cease to be good things.'

'The pleasure principle,' said Sawyer.

Bullmore brightened. 'Absolutely. I'm just grateful that

I might expire in the space we shared together. I can't bear the idea of fading away in some desolate care home.' He smiled. 'But you're not here for my life story.'

'As I mentioned on the phone, I'm interested in a man named Scott Walton. I believe you treated him when he was at Norfolk Park Probation Hospital.'

'I did indeed. Many years ago. Psychiatrists are always advised to retain an emotional distance from patients, particularly those who have committed aberrative acts. But it was difficult not to empathise with Scott, given the horrendous circumstances that brought him under my care.'

'Empathise?'

'Well, yes. His experiences were so vivid. With some patients, my response can go beyond sympathy.' Bullmore shuffled through some papers. 'He'd come from HMP Doncaster. I signed him off his licence when he was twenty-one, I believe. There was a scheme connecting new releases to the ProPak Foods factory. Not pleasant work, so they struggled with recruitment.'

Sawyer leaned forward. 'And Norfolk was an Approved Premise.'

Bullmore scoffed. 'Approved Premise, Probation Hospital. Forgive my unreconstructed side, but there's a lack of robustness. They tend to be run by very young people, and the labels change with the current sensitivities.'

'Did you carry on seeing him after his release?'

Bullmore hesitated. 'I did. But as I remember, he stopped coming to our sessions and we fell out of touch. He was desperately ill, Mr Sawyer. Mental illness is not necessarily a precursor to criminal behaviour, of course, but the inadequate management of a mental illness can lead to poor choices, often criminal in nature.'

'What was his background?'

Bullmore drew in a deep breath, held it, released. He browsed the folder. 'I believe that he was suffering from an integration disorder. As I say, changing labels. Back then, we called it schizophrenia. But there's more sensitivity now, given the stigma attached to that term.'

'Rightly so?'

Bullmore nodded. 'Oh, indeed. There are many other examples. "Health anxiety" over "hypochondria". The focus today is on the behavioural dysfunction over the diagnostic vernacular. Since his time in HMP Doncaster, Scott had been self-medicating with alcohol and marijuana. Sadly, those habits form in prison, as I'm sure you know. When he started at ProPak Foods, he seemed relatively stable, and his supervision was high quality. But I assume you're more interested in what sent him to prison in the first place?'

'He killed his father,' said Sawyer, glancing out at the garden. 'Domestic abuse?'

'Yes. He was fourteen at the time. He had suffered dreadful physical and emotional violence from his father. And a CT scan showed frontal lobe impairment, possibly as a result of the violence. Scott found solace in nature and animals. It's common among children whose domestic world is rendered toxic. The simplicity and predictability of the natural world, in contrast to the ever-shifting realities at home. In our conversations at Norfolk, Scott told me he dreamed of becoming a vet, treating and caring for animals. He said he'd wanted a pet of his own, but his father wouldn't allow it. He retreated into the rural areas around his home, studying animals and wildlife, identifying with them.'

'Projection.'

Bullmore smiled. 'Not quite. It's a defence mechanism, but perhaps closer to displacement, or sublimation. It's certainly delusional. As we mentioned before, there's a strong element of empathy. Some people believe that they have more in common with other species, and that they are in the process of transforming into one. They call it clinical lycanthropy. It's a rare disorder, but I felt that Scott's complexities fell close to the diagnosis. In crass terms, you might suggest that for someone with literally nowhere to run or hide from domestic abuse, they retreat into an alternative reality. One which feels safer.'

'An animal self.'

'Yes. With a deep enough delusion, there might even be a sense that the animal self acts as a screen, or filter, justifying behaviour. Or at least as a way of muting the worst excesses. Many people wear clothing that identifies them with animals, and some achieve sexual satisfaction through costumes and masks.'

Sawyer held Bullmore's gaze. 'Tell me about his father.'

Bullmore wrinkled his nose. 'One of those people who gets described as an "authoritarian", "fierce", "strong character", "a man's man". All codified language for an abuser, of course. According to his mother's testimony, Scott's father did allow him to own a stray dog that followed him home one day, but then killed it when it fouled the carpet.'

'How?'

'He beat it to death with a heavy pan, in front of Scott. To his father, that would have been a decisive action, a show of strength to demonstrate to his son what happens when he dares to dilute his affection. His mother was frequently beaten in sight of Scott and his older brother, Philip. And one day, after he watched his mother take a particularly vicious beating, Scott took the same pan and bludgeoned his father to death with it. Apparently, he struck him once to the back of the head, and the force was sufficient to kill him instantly.'

Sawyer shuddered at a flash of his childhood dog, Henry, snuffling into his own belly. Exposed intestines.

'As a minor, where did he go before Doncaster?'

Bullmore checked his notes. 'Aldine House Secure Children's Centre, Sheffield. Basically a prison for children. Not the best suited for treating trauma. Scott began to experience auditory hallucinations at this point.'

'Hearing voices?'

Bullmore shrugged. 'Again, Mr Sawyer. Labels. Then Doncaster Young Offenders, then to grown-up prison when he turned eighteen. I felt there was a degree of progress in our work together, but over my many years in the profession, I've come to the conclusion that there may be some trauma which is too deep-seated to overcome, particularly the type that develops in formative years.'

The skin on the back of Sawyer's neck prickled. Bullmore: reclining in his chair and talking, talking. He seemed simultaneously near and distant.

Not enough air.

'Did Scott tell you what the voices were saying?'

Take deeper breaths. It'll pass.

'For many people with integration disorder, their internal chatter begins as benign. As if they are invoking an imaginary friend as a coping strategy.'

The space in front of Bullmore's desk shimmered, as if a heat haze was forming.

'But often, a trauma renders the voices malevolent.'

Sawyer screwed his eyes shut, opened them again. The room had compressed into a circular tunnel view, surrounded by a blurred aura.

'And some say it's like they have a devil in their head, speaking to them and directing their actions.'

Bullmore's speech pattern remained normal, but he appeared ballooned and bloated at the centre of Sawyer's vision of the room.

Inhale slowly, five seconds.

Exhale slowly, five seconds.

'This is why there's a high suicide rate among schizophrenics. Anything to silence the voices or visions.'

Sawyer sprang to his feet. 'Do you mind if we open a window, Dr Bullmore?'

'Of course not.'

Sawyer stumbled towards the window and turned the handle up, then down. No luck. He looked for a latch.

Bullmore's words now floated in from behind, faint and wavering, fighting for clarity at the centre of a familiar audio collage: his mother's screams, his dog barking.

Metal on skull.

Metal on teeth.

'People talk about escaping their demons, Mr Sawyer. Purging themselves of darkness. But with mental illness, like any dark force, I believe that if you turn away, if you simply try and run, then you'll never be free of it.'

He found the latch, threw open the window.

The fresh air hit him like a jet of icy water.

'I used to think that the idea of "evil" was just a tabloid buzzword. But it does exist. And it relishes darkness, secrecy. You have to pursue it, hunt it down, bring it out into the light. And sometimes you do have to fight evil with evil.'

Inhale.

Exhale.

Sawyer turned. The room had normalised, the sounds receded. Bullmore tidied the papers into the folder.

He looked up, smiled. 'Now. Mr Sawyer. Are you going to tell me why you're interested in Scott?'

Sawyer took a slow, steady breath. 'I think you're right about evil, Dr Bullmore. And I need to bring Scott out into the light.'

40

Shepherd took a steadying breath and stepped into the interview room. Farrell sat behind the central desk, typing on a laptop, with Keating beside him in full uniform.

Shepherd waited by the chair, keeping his eyes away from Keating's gaze.

Farrell finished his typing, striking the final key with a flourish. He looked up. 'Have a seat, Detective Sergeant.'

'Thank you, sir.' He settled into the chair.

Farrell waved a hand towards the two men at the temporary desk in the corner. 'As before, IOPC Lead Investigator Callum Whitehead. Federation rep DC Simon Gail. And of course you know DSI Keating well.' He leaned back in his chair and placed his hands on the desktop, knitting his fingers together. 'Questions. Let's get the big one cleared up first. Were you, or were you not, in attendance on the day that DI Sawyer conducted his... independent investigation into David Bowman's kidnap of Stephanie Burns?'

Shepherd glanced at Keating. No help. 'In attendance?'

Farrell offered a waspish smile. 'Did you go with him to Dovestone Reservoir?'

DC Gail held up a hand. 'DS Shepherd, you're not under caution, but if you choose not to answer—'

'I choose not to answer.'

Keating raised his eyes.

Farrell typed as he spoke. 'I had Digital Media Adviser Karl Rhodes take a look at your IT.' He looked up. 'Due diligence. Completely within remit. Nothing to definitely place you at the scene with DI Sawyer, but something caught my eye. I had Rhodes run some software on your HOLMES system, tracking recent activity. DS Shepherd, have you shared your login details with anyone else?'

'Of course not, sir.'

'Well, can you explain why your account has been accessed three times over the past week, from a location in the Edale area? As far as I'm aware, your family home is in Thornhill. Some distance from Edale. Is that correct?'

'Yes, sir.'

'And so would you have any idea why your HOLMES account might have been accessed by someone in the Edale area?'

Shepherd locked eyes with Keating. 'No, sir.'

'Really think, Detective,' said Farrell. 'Are you sure you didn't share your login details with someone? With, perhaps, DI Sawyer? Doesn't he live in the Edale area?'

'He does, sir.'

'I'm guessing that if we impounded DI Sawyer's laptop, then my suspicion would be confirmed. And, given your association, it would be difficult to prove that you hadn't shared your login details with him.' Farrell tapped out a short drumbeat on the desk with his hands. 'Please think very carefully, Detective Shepherd. I do understand your loyalty. But it would seem that Detective Sawyer doesn't reciprocate the respect you clearly have for him. Granted, he has apprehended some dangerous criminals, and proven himself an excellent detective. But his actions on the Bowman raid are unacceptable, and as an upstanding—'

'Julius Newton confirmed his connection to Bowman,' said Shepherd, avoiding eye contact with Farrell. 'He insisted that he knew where he would be holding Stephanie Burns. DI Sawyer felt that we needed to take swift action to preserve life. He assured me that we would call in assistance if there was any concrete sign of Bowman.'

Farrell bristled. 'Assistance? You mean inform your commanding officers. Or, in this case, me. As the senior officer in charge of the Greater Manchester area.'

'Sir.'

'And so what exactly happened?'

'While DI Sawyer was otherwise detained, Julius Newton attacked me and got away, confronting Bowman at the house. By the time DI Sawyer had caught up with him, Bowman had been alerted.'

'What do you mean by DI Sawyer being "otherwise detained"?'

Shepherd shuffled in his seat. 'He stepped out of the car, to... take a phone call.'

Farrell took out his canister of breath mints and popped one into his mouth. 'Was DI Sawyer, I wonder, talking to Tony Cross?'

'Sir?'

Farrell studied Shepherd, rolling the mint around his mouth. 'We have a ballistics report showing that the axe wielded by David Bowman was struck by a high-calibre bullet. Given DI Sawyer's connection with Cross, it seems plausible that he might have called him in for back-up.'

'Tony Cross... appeared when Sawyer pursued Newton after he attacked me.'

'"Appeared"? In a puff of smoke? DS Shepherd, I suggest that you and DI Sawyer travelled to the Dovestone location with Julius Newton. DI Sawyer then had Tony Cross attend to provide armed back-up. A wise decision, given Cross's eventual contribution.' Farrell dug his fingers through his oily hair. 'I also suggest that DI Sawyer had an agenda that he was reluctant to share with you. An ill-advised confrontational approach to the apprehension of Bowman based on the similarities of Bowman's crimes to the method of Jessica Sawyer's murder—'

'DCI Farrell...' Keating turned to face him.

Farrell continued. 'And, given the widespread testimony on DI Sawyer's recent behaviour, I would also question his mental state at the time.'

Keating held up a hand. 'Okay. Let's wind this up.'

Farrell composed himself. 'I apologise for the voracity. But you've been extremely helpful, DS Shepherd. It's my view that you've been mismanaged by a highly skilled manipulator, and your testimony will ensure that he receives a firm but fair sanction.'

Shepherd glanced at Keating: again, no help. 'What do you mean by that, sir?'

'I'm hoping to secure further evidence to support my view that DI Sawyer executed this operation with the full intention of eliminating David Bowman with prejudice, and that his claims of self-defence are spurious at best.'

'If that holds, sir, DI Sawyer might lose his job.'

'He might even go to prison,' said Whitehead.

Farrell took a breath. 'I take no pleasure in this, DS Shepherd. But if that does transpire, then you should see it as the wider force benefiting by disciplining an officer who either feels that the rules don't apply to him or is mentally unfit to follow them. We are civil servants. We are salaried to serve the public. Given his actions, if Detective Sawyer is taken out of service, then it will be his loss but the public's gain.'

41

Sawyer eased the Mini into a tight space at the corner of the Evelyn Medical Centre car park. The facility, on the edge of Hathersage village, was a standard rural clinic: one-storey, stone-built to blend with the surrounding cottages. Several windowless Portacabins had been set up in a recessed area off the far side of the car park, and Sawyer's position by the perimeter path gave him a good view of anyone entering or leaving.

He squinted to read a sign beside the single door leading into the cabins: a large pink letter A with an underscored legend.

ACTION AGAINST ADDICTION

After a few minutes, a short, skinny twentysomething man emerged from the door and walked out onto the path, a little unsteady. He wore an ageing black Adidas hoodie, ill-fitting tracksuit trousers, scruffy red-and-white trainers. Sawyer studied him as he shambled past, stopping to light a cigarette near the front of the car. But it was difficult to see any facial features with his hood up.

Sawyer got out of the Mini and called to the man. 'It's The Great Explorer!'

The man stopped and turned. 'Eh?'

Sawyer walked over, through a small iron gate. He offered a broad smile. 'YouTube. Urbex. I'm a big fan.'

The man flipped his hood back. He was pallid, prematurely aged, with sunken, heavy-lidded eyes and a patch of blond fluff on his chin. Up close, his sportswear was stained, with sagging pockets.

Sawyer stepped forward and held out a hand. 'Lloyd Robbins. Don't worry, Stuart. I'm not a serial killer or anything. Just looking for a bit of information.'

Sutton eyed Sawyer's hand, looked him over, then submitted his skeletal fingers for the shake, allowing Sawyer to move in a little closer.

Gold stud in right earlobe.

'Are you a copper or something?' said Sutton, checking the car park behind.

'I'm a journalist, Stuart. I'm writing a book about a lad who went missing a few years ago. Darren Coleman. I believe you were good friends, weren't you?'

'I don't do the exploring any more. I'll have to take that shit down.'

Sawyer nodded. 'More of an inner voyager, eh?'

'What?'

Sawyer nodded to the Portacabins. 'Supervised Injection Site.'

'They call them Drug Consumption Rooms now, and I'm not doing it for a laugh. I'm an addict and I don't need your judgement.'

Sawyer held his hands up. 'I'm not judging. Just trying to make a connection with something.'

Sutton frowned. 'How do you mean?'

'You did a bit of urbex with Darren, didn't you?'

Sutton hesitated, wiped his forearm across his nose.

'It's a rhetorical question, Stuart. It's on YouTube, remember?'

'Yeah. Fucking long time ago, though.'

'How fucking long? When was the last time you saw Darren?'

Sutton's eyes drifted to the side, back towards the car park. 'About the time we did the last video.'

Sawyer smiled. 'You're lying.'

'I'm not!'

'You're still lying.'

Sutton flipped his hood back up. 'Look. I was good mates with Darren for a bit. It was ages ago. I remember doing the urbex, and the video shit.'

'And you got him to buy drugs for you. Didn't want to risk it yourself.'

'He helped me out, yeah. But addicts do shit like that, okay? It don't mean that I done him in or something.'

'You were close. Was he in any other trouble? Did he mention anything?'

Sutton shifted his weight from foot to foot. 'No. You know what? These are seriously sounding like copper questions. I've got to go.'

'On one of the videos, Stuart, you say that the place is haunted. Do you remember that?'

Sutton scowled. He looked ready to run. 'Just saying shit to freak him out. I don't believe in ghosts.'

'How about demons? Devils?'

Sutton barked a laugh. 'Right. You're freaking *me* out now. I'm going to say goodbye, yeah?' He offered a sarcastic salute. 'A pleasure to meet you.'

Sutton hurried away down the path. Sawyer watched him all the way to the front gate of the medical centre. As he turned and walked through onto the pavement, he glanced back over his shoulder, then disappeared behind the main wall.

Sawyer jumped into the car and drove out of the gate, keeping his distance as Sutton crossed the road and entered a side street behind the tall, Neo-Jacobean building on the corner, which now contained the Bank House pub. He waited for Sutton to gain some ground, then crawled the Mini along the same route, until he saw him enter a flat block off a hill that climbed towards the sunset hotspot of Surprise View.

Sawyer drove past the building and noted the sign out front: *KOTECHA HOUSE.* He pushed on, up and around the spiralling road to the viewpoint car park and the widescreen sweep of the Hope Valley and Padley Gorge beyond.

He killed the engine and made a call. It rang for a long time before connecting.

'If you're too busy to talk,' said Sawyer.

Walker kept his voice low. 'Lots going on here. I was going to call you, actually.'

'First thing, though. Can you get me a clear address for Stuart Sutton? I saw him go into a block near Hathersage. Kotecha House. Might be a mate or a girlfriend's place, but if he's on the census you should be able to dig him out.'

'Okay. Did you meet him?'

'Yeah. He's holding something back, but I don't want to push too hard now.'

A door closing at Walker's end. 'Sir. DS Shepherd called me in, with Keating. They told me I should avoid all contact with you.'

'So, that's going well. Did they say why?'

'Compromising the suspension case.'

Sawyer screwed his eyes shut. 'What were you going to call me about?'

235

'Scott Walton. I tracked his movements after leaving ProPak Foods. Tax records show that he transferred to an abattoir, outside Hayfield.'

Sawyer's eyes sprang open. 'Sherratt & Sons?'

'Yes. There was a meat industry awards event there in the mid-2000s. One of Walton's line managers was commended for blowing the whistle on unsafe and unethical practices there in 2007. The place closed in 2009. Probably related to the investigation. I've got a contact for the whistle-blower. He works for a farming standards agency in Crosspool.'

Sawyer glanced at his rear-view mirror. 'Send me the details. I'll go and see him. I can be there within the hour.'

'Trail goes a bit cold for Walton, so maybe he can help to pick it up. I can keep digging, but... Sir. If this transpires as a solid lead for the Hardwick and Bishop killings... I'm—'

'Caught in the middle, yes. I'll talk to the abattoir guy and feed back. I'll also brief you on Bullmore. Don't worry. I'll use a burner. You can take it from there.'

'Thank you, sir.'

He started the engine, dug into his pocket. 'For now, though. Do what Shepherd says. Cut me off. Don't contact me again. Cover yourself until the suspension thing blows over.'

Sawyer took out a small transparent bag filled with a grainy brown powder, lifted from Sutton. He turned it around in his fingers.

'You think it'll blow over?'

'I'll be okay.'

42

Sawyer fixed his eyes on the road ahead, and let the music drown his thoughts. An overlong playlist of nineties UK dance music: toytown rave, landfill trance, club bangers. Here on a dank autumnal afternoon, the soundtrack was florid and off-mood, but he needed something stifling, surrounding.

Eyes forward, away from the rear-view mirror.

In his periphery, the wide, open farm fields and dry-stone walls gave way to garden centres and golf clubs, as he descended through the Crosspool suburbs.

He found a parking space at a village square shopping parade and ducked out of the Mini, locking the door by pointing the transponder key over his shoulder, heading for a separate section of the mall that had been converted into cheap office space.

A chunky man in a short-sleeved shirt emerged from the office at the end of the row. He slipped on a pair of sunglasses and hitched a canvas satchel over his shoulder.

'Hi,' said Sawyer. 'Trying to find the DFSA. Derbyshire Farming Standards Agency.'

The man nodded. 'You've found it. Who are you after?'

'Gary Holloway.'

'You're doing well. You've found him, too. I was just about to head home.' Holloway tilted the sunglasses forward off his eyes, and looked Sawyer up and down. 'Unsolicited visit. That's never good.'

'I'm a journalist. Lloyd Robbins. I was hoping you could spare a few minutes to talk about Sherratt & Sons.'

Holloway's head gave a subtle jerk to the side; a nervous twitch. 'I don't mean to be rude, Mr Robbins, but I'm all talked out about that. Who do you work for?'

'Myself. I'm writing a book about the people who work in food production, the meat industry. I wanted to get your thoughts on the culture of slaughterhouses, what needs to change.'

Holloway checked his watch.

'I'm interested in issues surrounding the mental health of workers. I believe you were responsible for exposing unethical practice at Sherratt & Sons. As a central figure in the progression of the last ten or so years, it would be irresponsible of me to write a book that doesn't take account of your experience.'

Holloway drew in a deep breath, held the moment. 'Twenty minutes.'

———

Holloway pulled the blind over the window at the back of his office, muting the late afternoon sun. 'Drink? Tea? Coffee? If you're after stories, you might need something stronger.'

'I'm fine, thanks.' Sawyer took a seat in the rickety foldaway chair facing Holloway's corner desk. The office was small and smelt of wet socks and cheap detergent. An open gym bag had been thrown into the corner. Holloway clearly favoured an uncluttered workspace: recent-looking desktop PC, a neat stack of wire mesh trays, no posters or pictures. 'Nice place.'

Holloway laughed. He sat down and pivoted his chair towards Sawyer. 'It's okay, Mr Robbins. You've done the buttering up. It's a dump, but it's all about the work.'

'How long were you at Sherratt & Sons?'

'About ten years in total. I was in Quality Control, but I worked with the slaughtermen. Supervised a few.'

'The slaughtermen?'

'They do what it says on the tin, yeah. They're killers. It's horrible, dangerous work, and we are still not taking proper care of them. We like our meat, but we don't want to know how it got onto the plate. These guys are the start of the process. We kill one hundred million animals for meat in this country every month.'

'Every *month*?'

'Yeah. Month, not year. Imagine that. One hundred million killer blows. Thousands of slaughtermen. Human beings, like you and me. This place isn't going to win any awards for Workplace of the Year, but these guys, and they are all guys, have to work in filthy, dirty conditions. There's animal shit on the floor. You see the guts, there's blood all over the walls. And there's nothing to describe the stink. It's like a punch on the nose, the first time you smell it. And then it just clings to you, hanging in the air like a fucking soup. The stench of dead and dying animals. And there's always a tang of iron in the air, from the blood. Even when you're not in the preparation areas.'

'And you came forward to expose the poor practices?'

'I did. And it's the best thing I've ever done, despite all the shit I got for it. I took secret film. Terrified sheep wriggling free from their restrainers before being chased and recaptured and slaughtered. I got footage of a sheep being killed on the blood-soaked floor, because the slaughterman couldn't be bothered to get it back in the restraints. Unsafe equipment, unsanitary conditions. And no attention paid to the psychological effects. I used to have nightmares about the things I saw all day. Then I started to get mental health problems because of the way I'd trained myself to *not* feel anything.'

Sawyer glanced at the closed blind, again craving an open window.

Holloway caught his gaze. 'Sorry it's a bit stuffy in here. The window is fixed. Won't open.'

'What happened after all the investigation into your exposé?'

'I put some distance between myself and the place. Went to Australia for a few weeks while it all calmed down. Luckily, it was in the days before social media. I couldn't escape so easily these days, of course.'

'Did you work with a man named Scott Walton?'

Holloway frowned, studying Sawyer. 'I did, yes. I was his manager in Quality Control. Haven't heard that name in years. He came from ProPak, didn't he? A lot of the slaughtermen came from processing factories. It's like an apprenticeship.'

'Desensitising.'

'In a way, yes. Scott had a difficult start, as I remember. In life, I mean.'

Sawyer nodded. 'Abusive father, spent time in prison at a young age.'

'He seemed like a decent bloke, but he never quite settled. It's a very male culture. Everyone is terrified of showing weakness. There's a lot of drinking, and weird things like addictions to energy drinks because many of the slaughtermen hold down multiple jobs. There's a frequent turnover, but Scott stayed longer than most. Probably too long. There was a guy... Pat something. He worked with Scott. Topped himself. I kept an eye on Scott after that. Went for a few drinks with him. He told me that when he first started, some of the older blokes sent him into a storage room to fetch something, because they knew what was in there. A big skip full of cow's heads, flayed for all the available meat, but with the eyeballs left, staring. They all found it hilarious, but he said he had nightmares for weeks after.'

'What kind of work would Scott have to do on a daily basis?'

The sun squeezed through the blind, casting a strip of light across Sawyer's eyes. He shifted his chair back into shade.

'Restraining, stunning, killing. The bleeding can take hours. Then you have to get all the innards out, throw it together as contaminated waste. Barrels of guts hanging around. Then there's de-skinning, de-furring. Dicing and bagging. It's like a production line. They stun everything now, before killing. They used to use bolts through the brain, but they realised that the animals could sense what was coming and they'd get agitated. The worst thing is a stressed animal that knows it's about to be slaughtered. Low lactic acid, ruins the meat.' Holloway took a breath. 'I remember one time, Scott went home early, sick. One of the other lads said he'd cut into a freshly killed cow and a fucking calf foetus had fallen out. Then there was BSE. That was apocalyptic.'

'Mass killing?'

'Yes. We had to go round to farms and kill many, many animals in one day, then burn the bodies. Scott missed that. But we often had to deal with cases where an animal had tested positive for TB, and they would bring whole families in to be culled. Bulls, heifers, calves. Probably the worst thing I've ever overseen was when we had to slaughter this group of five calves. Scott and a couple of others were trying to keep them within the rails of the pens, but they were so tiny and bony they skipped out and trotted around, all wobbly on their newborn legs. They were sniffing around us like puppies, because they were young and curious. I remember Scott stroking one, and it suckling his finger. And so, when the time came to kill them, it was unbelievably tough. Slaughterhouses are designed for killing large animals, and the stun boxes are the right size to hold a cow that weighs around a ton. But the calves only came around a quarter of the way up the box. We got them all in at once, then we killed them. Everyone stood around, staring at their bodies. Scott was sobbing his heart out.

'There's a thing they call perpetrator-induced traumatic syndrome. Basically, PTSD suffered by slaughterhouse workers. I became really worried about Scott after the calf killings. He just seemed to be drifting around the place. He started to talk about how he wasn't going to be around for much longer.'

'He wanted to leave?'

'I took it as a lot darker than that. But then he changed, and said he was going to take action, to help animals.'

Sawyer realised his breathing had quickened again. He fought to slow it down. 'He worked for animal charities.'

'I believe he did, yes. Is he okay, Mr Robbins? You seem quite focused on Scott.'

'He's a strong candidate for a case study. For the book.'

Holloway paused, and regarded Sawyer with something close to suspicion. 'I'm afraid I don't have any contact details for him. As I say, I haven't seen him in years. They closed Sherratt & Sons in 2009 after the investigation. I attended an FSA hearing in 2010 and I heard that Scott had been given keyholder status by the place's owners. Basically a glorified caretaker for a building where demolition isn't feasible.' He stood up and re-opened the blind. Sawyer squinted at the flare of light. 'Anyway. I hope that's been helpful. Please let me know if you need anything more from me. I'd be happy to help. I can give you contacts for some of the ex-Quality Control staff if you like. It might be worth trying to track Scott down and speak to him directly.'

Sawyer rose to his feet, in a daze. 'I'll certainly do that.'

43

Sawyer bowed his head as the lift lurched and began its descent to the basement level at Sheffield's Northern General Teaching Hospital. He took out his phone and opened a new text message from Jordan Burns.

Call me this evening - URGENT

The lift car clunked against the walls of the shaft, and Sawyer sifted through his memories, nagged by a connection he couldn't quite make: something standing plain and clear, but always just outside his vision.

He tugged open the inner security door and stepped out into the labyrinth of empty and unloved corridors. Not that the lack of adornment was an oversight; down here, the patients were past caring about peeling paint or obsolete signage.

As he passed the immense chemical storage room, the colours shifted from pastel to primary, and he followed the sound of a female voice into the refurbished lobby area: anonymous reception desk, unmarked side rooms, the sting of something acrid in the air. Holloway had spoken about the raw stench of animal death; here, the prevailing odour came from the materials that masked human decay, holding the bodies in a state of purgatory until every molecule of forensic worth had been extracted.

A young woman in crisp business dress spotted Sawyer and ended her phone call. She tapped something into her computer. 'Detective Sawyer. How lovely to see you again.'

'Gina. Is he around?'

She looked surprised. 'Is that it? No small talk?'

Sawyer sighed. 'Been anywhere nice on your holidays this year?'

Gina opened her mouth wide. 'Oh! We did. Mykonos. Expensive, but such a beautiful place. Crystal blue sea. Lovely people. The sort of food you only eat in your dreams.'

'Must be hard to come back here.'

She managed a thin smile. 'The view's not so good, but I enjoy the work. How about you? Have you managed some downtime since... all that business?'

'Sawyer isn't a downtime sort of guy.' A voice from the corridor behind the reception desk: deep, sonorous, faint Glaswegian burr. Frazer Drummond stabbed at the control panel of a coffee machine. 'To what do we owe the dubious pleasure?'

'It's not a social visit.'

Drummond gave an exaggerated toothsome grin. 'That's a shame. The people round here. Honestly. No personality. You have to do all the work, you know? And you get nothing back.'

He angled his head and walked into a side room, letting the pale green door close behind him with a slam. Sawyer followed. As he entered the tiny break room, Drummond set his coffee down on a central coffee table and fell backward into a sunken chair pushed against the far wall.

Sawyer nodded at the book on the table. '*The Antidote*. Don't tell me you're embracing the ways of Stoicism, Frazer?'

'I'm not keen on any single "way". I like the ideas, though. It basically boils down to three words: fuck positive thinking.'

'You get more value from assuming the worst, working back from there, counting your blessings.'

Drummond slurped his coffee, winced. 'You make it sound like a motivational plaque, Sawyer. The problem with Stoicism is that everyone goes for the easy message of focusing on what you can control, but nobody picks up on the idea of *logos*, which was central to Epictetus's thinking.'

Sawyer sat down in the other chair. 'It just means that we're all part of the natural order of things. Spring follows winter, then summer, then autumn, then things die off again in winter. Repeat.'

'Until the heat death of the universe.'

'Christians have just placed all of this in the hands of some imaginary divine being. We came from stardust, we're living our Earthly lives now, and soon, like the seasons, we'll die off, our blood relations will die off, and then we'll be nothing but memories in the minds of the people who knew and loved us. We're all part of that natural order, and so we shouldn't get too wrapped up in our own importance.'

Drummond braved another sip of coffee. 'We should do this life-affirming communion more often, Sawyer.'

'I'm just saying that it shows how the only thing that really matters is our connections on Earth, and how they will eventually translate into memories in the minds of our loved ones, how they'll carry us around once—'

'We end up in one of those drawers.' Drummond

nodded to the wall, and the mortuary and autopsy room next door.

'Like Duncan Hardwick and Mark Bishop.'

Drummond raised his eyebrows. 'Nice segue. You know we can't talk about that, though. Not while you're off Keating's Christmas card list.'

'You know that we can. Your secretary isn't the type to have a glass pressed against the door, and the clients are hardly listening. Hardwick and Bishop were both obviously the victims of the same killer. On the day I first started at Buxton, I met you in a meeting room where you were helping with a case. Martin Pittman was the SIO.'

Drummond nodded. 'I remember Pittman, but not the case.'

Sawyer edged his chair forward. 'It was a guy who ran a broiler chicken farm. The killer flayed him.'

'You think it's the same psycho?'

Sawyer smiled. 'I was hoping you could take a look at the old file, see if there's any connecting detail. It's like there's all of these links and similarities with other cases floating around, but I can't quite find the element that snaps it into place.'

'Hardwick and Bishop were in horrendous states, but Sally and crew have found no trace evidence.' Drummond tugged at his short-sleeved shirt, loosening the fit. 'Flaying has been around for a long time, you know. The Aztecs did it, the ancient Greeks, medieval Europe. You've got around a thousand nerve endings in one square inch of skin. We don't have any living testimony, of course, but it has to be one of the most painful ways to die.' He leaned forward. 'You have to soften the skin first, to loosen it from the muscles and make it easier to peel off. The Aztecs just left the poor bastards out in the sun until the skin reddened and burned. Of course, that also tenderises the skin and makes the pain worse. Our medieval cousins were a bit more efficient. They dipped the victims alive in boiling water, but pulled them out before they were boiled alive. Because that would have spoiled the fun. Although they would probably have been blinded, suffered nerve damage, scorched lungs. That's before anyone has even made a cut. This is not someone drowning in compassion here, Sawyer. If he doesn't enjoy it, then he's chosen a pretty stressful method of murder.'

Sawyer's eyes drifted to the streaks of damp in a top corner of the break room. 'Maybe the suffering is the point. He's been refining it over a long period. He's tried different approaches, taken breaks. But now something has changed. Something has tripped a switch.'

'You think he's killed more but we haven't found them?'

Sawyer nodded. 'So why are we finding them now? The half-burials. It's almost as if he's inviting discovery, upping the risk. It's sloppy, in contrast to the rigorous control of the sadism and torture. I also think he captured someone and let them go, because he couldn't go through with it, for some reason.' He looked up, held Drummond's eye. 'He's either tired of it, or something is pushing him to stop.'

44

A mid-morning mist hovered over the farm fields surrounding the Manifold Valley. Sawyer trudged through the soggy earth and joined the well-trodden walking track from Wetton village, keeping a respectful distance from the clusters of grazing sheep. The sun was stirring later now, with a dampened intensity, taking its time to burn off the cloud. But, despite the early showings of fallen leaves, the air was still balmy and rich with pollen, and the grass remained untarnished.

The ground steepened, and he left the track, stumbling down the final section in an unflattering crouch. He jumped down onto the roadside, screwed in his earphones, and followed the old railway track to the stairs embedded in the crag, up to his childhood safe space.

Thor's Cave was a natural karst cavern at the top of a peaked limestone crag. Its ten-metre-high circular front entrance had stared down on the valley below for ten thousand years. Sawyer took out his earphones and scaled the smooth rock, deep into the central cavern, where he perched on his favoured flattened section of rock and looked out through the cave mouth at the swaying treetops.

He sank into the isolation, listening to the rushing river, the plangent hoot of a curlew. He inhaled the cave's primordial essence: empty peat, blank stone. Undisturbed, unchanging. It was an emotional epicentre; a place where he could quiet his mind, dismantle a case, study the moving parts.

A wind whistled through the slitted natural window at the side of the cave, and Sawyer hitched up his hoodie, covering his head, tunnelling his vision to the centre of the valley view.

'The first time we brought you here, you didn't want to come in.'

He turned towards the sloped chamber at the back. Sunlight reflected off the patches of rainwater, revealing his mother's silhouette, curved into the rock wall.

Sawyer turned away, looked back out of the cave mouth. 'I'd fallen in the river. Got soaked.'

Jessica chuckled. 'It was a hot day. You dried off quickly. You got over it. You asked me if bears lived here. Dad said there were monsters. He was joking, but that only made it worse. So you climbed the path that goes up around the top. The really steep bit, with sheer drops. I was terrified, but you were too far ahead for me to follow and stop you.'

He smiled. 'Making things hard for myself again.'

'And now you're seeing things, my darling. Hearing things. Talking to yourself.'

'First sign of madness.'

'You're close. To remembering.'

'I'm scratching the surface. Nothing's showing.'

'You're fixating. You're not paying attention to the surface. You're too focused on what might be underneath, lurking in the darkness. Like you were with this place.'

'What if I pulled back? Viewed it from a distance?'

He turned. The chamber was empty.

———

Sawyer took the steep road back up to Wetton, turning near the top to look back across the valley to the cave entrance. He stood at the roadside for a few minutes, staring, straining for focus. Thor's Cave loomed across the valley, implacable. The impassive façade: a portal to history.

A car swished by behind, and he turned, quickening his pace, forcing himself up the final, flattening section of road as it met the edge of the village. He found the Mini where he'd parked it by the road and leaned on it as he took out his phone.

Text message from Walker.

Sutton is Flat 14. Looks like his girlfriend's place.

Sawyer closed his message inbox and made a call. The phone rang for a long time before it connected.

'Paul Barton.'

'Paul. It's Jake Sawyer. We met at the coffee shop a few days ago to talk about urbex. I was wondering if the word "Devil" made any connection for you. Any association.'

Barton hesitated. 'Yeah, I remember.'

Sawyer took a breath. 'You do remember, Paul. You have a thing you do with your hands. Lathering them together as if you're washing them. When I mentioned the word "Devil" it was the only time in our chat that your hands stopped moving for a few seconds.'

'I... Look, I really don't—'

'There's a desperate mother, Paul. She needs to know what happened to her son. This might really help. Strictly between you and me.' Sawyer got into the car and closed the door.

Barton puffed out a breath. 'It's a stupid thing. You just reminded me of... You hear stories. Silly legends. Things get passed on, and take on their own logic. The facts get twisted and exaggerated. There's a place down by Ashbourne. Lots of urbexers have tried to get in, take some pictures. Some claim that they have, but I've never seen a decent visual report with definitive pics. One or two dirty shots, couple of Goon Tuber vids.'

'So most definitely a hot place?'

'Most definitely. It used to be a slaughterhouse. Abattoir.'

'Sherratt & Sons.'

'Yeah. It's one hell of a prize, because the rumours are they never really took it apart, so there's bound to be some amazing stuff in there. But it's really well secured and there's this stupid legend that keeps people away.'

A sharp glare of sunlight pierced the clouds overhead, and Sawyer flipped down the driver's eye shield. 'What's the legend, Paul?'

'It's going to sound stupid. People say they see a beast. A creature. With horns. Something that walks upright. Urbexers say they've seen it inside the abattoir building, and also around the grounds. I've heard various reports, but most people say it's tall and looks pretty powerful.'

'Horns? Like the Devil?'

Barton sighed. 'Yeah, like a demon. Or a minotaur or human bull or something. Seriously, I've heard a lot worse. It's just bullshit. It was probably put about by the building owners to keep people away.'

Sawyer started the engine. 'Paul, that's a huge help.'

'I don't see how—'

'So, you don't believe the stories?'

'No, I don't.'

'Do you believe in the Devil, Paul?'

'No.'

'Me neither.'

45

Sawyer drove into Hathersage and parked back at the Evelyn Medical Centre. He walked through the fading daylight, down into the village, and bought a cheap PAYG phone from an electronics shop, and a notepad and pen from the newsagent next door. On the way out, he slipped a miniature can of Diet Coke into the pocket of his hoodie.

He headed back to the Medical Centre and sat on a low wall near the car park, slurping from the can and sketching in the notepad. A group of medical workers eyed him as they separated and climbed into their cars.

Sawyer pulled out his own phone and took a photo of his sketch. He sent the image to a number, which he called as soon as the transfer was complete. The call connected immediately, but the reception was vague and crackly.

'Lewis?'

'Mr Sawyer. Let me just get outside.' Noises as Lewis Vaughan opened a heavy-sounding door. The reception fluttered, then cleared. 'Sorry. At the hospital. Service is—'

'Are you with Virginia?'

'Yes. They're not keen on phones in the ward. Reception is bad, anyway.'

'How is she?'

'Not good, Mr Sawyer. She sleeps a lot. Still under sedation. I've been here pretty much since she was brought in. The bruising has eased a bit on her head, but I don't think it's her physical injuries that they're worried about.'

'Has she spoken?'

Vaughan sighed. 'Nothing that makes much sense. She knows who I am, and we talk a bit. One-word answers, mostly. She... won't let me touch her. She just pulls back her hand whenever I... The other guy, Moran, was here, trying to get something out of her. He asked if she was driven to the place where she was found, and she nodded. I think they're getting a trauma specialist or something. But the doctors want her left in peace to recover.'

'Is she awake now?'

'Yes. She's just had some food.'

'Can you go back in to see her, Lewis?'

'Okay, but she won't—'

'I want you to show her something.'

'I'm here.' Vaughan kept his voice low. The phone reception stuttered again.

'Did you get the picture I sent?'

A pause. 'Yes. Okay. What's this?'

'Could you show it to Virginia? Ask her if she recognises it.'

A crackle as Vaughan moved the phone.

'Baby? Could you open your eyes for a second? One of the policemen, he wants you to take a look at something.'

A long pause. The reception faded, but hung on.

A loud crack, distorted. Ruffling and crunching. Vaughan's voice, imploring. And another sound: Virginia, screaming and shouting in Spanish.

'Baby, baby. It's okay. It's okay.'

A loud thud and a dramatic drop in volume. More

screaming, from the background, fuzzed over. Another female voice, urgent.

The sounds receded. The heavy door squealed open again.

'Mr Sawyer,' said Vaughan. 'She went crazy, wide-eyed. What was it? Why did you—'

'I saw Lillian Fowler. One of the couple who picked up Virginia and took her to the hospital. She said she was whispering and muttering in the back of the car. She caught the word "Deborah" or maybe "Dabbler".'

Sawyer looked down at his sketch: an oval head shape with two large curved horns sticking up at the top.

'*Diablo*. Devil.'

46

Sawyer slipped into the main doors of Kotecha House, past a departing male resident with his head in his phone. He climbed a poky stairwell to the first floor and tapped on the door of Flat 14.

Murmurs from within. A young woman threw the door open wide. Angry eyes, unwashed bleach-blonde hair hustled into a ponytail.

She angled her head at Sawyer. 'Yeah?'

'Looking for Stuart.'

'And who are you?'

'His hairdresser.'

Stuart Sutton peered over the woman's shoulder. He rolled his eyes at the sight of Sawyer. 'Mate. We've had our chat, yeah? Piss off and write your book.'

Sawyer took out his phone and accessed a copy of the video shown to him by Darren Coleman's father. He turned the screen to Sutton, and let the first few seconds play out.

'*Right. Yeah. We're here again. There's me, The Great Explorer. And my colleague, who has promised not to shit out this time when he hears a little noise.*'

'*Fuck off, Stu.*'

Sawyer stopped the video, stared down Sutton. 'I can tell your time is precious, Stuart. If you can spare me a few more minutes, I promise you'll never see me again.'

———

They sat in a small, stale bedroom with eye-straining black-and-green criss-crossed wallpaper; Sutton on the bed, Sawyer in a chair in the corner. Sutton's girlfriend thumped around next door in the sitting room, then left the flat, slamming the door.

Sutton lit a cigarette. 'Off to work.'

'What does she do?'

'Tesco. All sorts.'

'Do you rent this place?'

Sutton shrugged. 'She does.'

'You trying to get clean?'

He dragged a forearm across his nose. In the overhead light, the cracked skin was visible. Track marks, dark veins. 'Nobody gets clean. You're always between fixes. You just try and make the gap longer. Fucking lost a whole score the other day. Lucky it was just after I'd been to the injection site.'

Sawyer leaned forward, elbows on knees. 'Help me find Darren, Stuart. Give your soul a spruce-up for autumn.'

Sutton tapped his cigarette into a tin ashtray on the bedside table. 'Look. If you're looking for a bit of honesty, let's have some from you, too. You are a copper, aren't you? Way too confident for a fucking journalist.'

'I'm a detective, yes. My real name is Jake. I'm not on duty at the moment. I'm helping Darren's mother.'

'Sam.'

'Yes. It's been over seven years. So the case is officially

258

cold, and Darren is registered as dead. Whatever happened to him, you can't undo it. But you can close the circle for her, give her some answers. On the video—'

'Where did you get it? I didn't put it up online.'

'Darren's father took it from his camcorder.'

Sutton nodded, bowed his head, revealing the razor nicks across his scalp. His shoulders tremored, and when he lifted his head again, his eyes had reddened. He screwed up his face, forcing back tears. 'Ah, fuck.' He sniffed and swiped his arm across his nose again.

'How long have you been an addict, Stuart?'

Sutton gave a bitter laugh. 'All my life. Anything to numb the fucking pain. I had a sister, couple of years younger. Josie. She was run over when I was little.' Tears trickled down both cheeks; he rubbed at his eyes. 'I saw it happen.'

'How old were you?'

'Seven or eight. Fuck knows. One day she was there and the next she wasn't. I never heard her voice again. Never heard her laugh. She was lovely. I was too far away.'

'To help her?'

Sutton caught Sawyer's eye. 'Yeah. Other side of the road. Car sent her flying. Oh, fuck. *Fuck*.'

'Take your time. And don't be embarrassed by the tears.'

Sutton composed himself, sat upright; a pose of dignity. 'I got into the drink. Fighting, all that. Started smoking my nan's fags. Then some lads at the youth club gave me a bit of smack. I snorted it. Fucking horrible. Then got into smoking it, then injecting. Classic, really.'

'And you were friends with Darren?'

'Yeah, we were really tight. Watched a lot of mad horror together. Zombie stuff. We got into urbex and I started the

259

channel. When I got kicked out of school, I was cautioned to stay away from known dealers.'

'So Darren started to get the drugs for you.'

He winced. 'Yeah. He was younger than me. Hard to believe it now, but he used to look up to me. Not the best choice of role model.'

'The video was filmed at the old abattoir, wasn't it? Down near Ashbourne.'

'Yeah. We got in with cutters, through the mesh fence. The urbexers wouldn't be happy with that. You're not supposed to do any damage. I suppose I thought I could get a of a reputation as an outlaw. Stand out from the crowd a bit.'

Sawyer kept a close watch on Sutton's eyes. 'It looks like you tripped an alarm in the YouTube video.'

'Yeah.' He laughed. 'Shit us both right up. We got out of Dodge straight away. Good for the vid, though.'

'And you tease Darren about the place being haunted, saying there's a "weird guy" who haunts the place. A demon.'

Sutton raised his gaze to the ceiling. 'Just taking the piss.'

Sawyer stood up and walked to the window, peered around the edge of the thin curtains. Almost dusk. 'A strange figure has been seen around there, though. I've heard the stories. Is it printing the legend, or no smoke without fire?'

Sutton held his head in his hands, scraped his knuckles over his scalp. 'I don't know—'

'When did you last see Darren, Stuart? Really?'

Sutton took a deep, shuddering breath. 'We... We went up there one night. I took the cutters. I wanted to try and get into a different part of the main building, see if we could find anything really harsh. Fucking animal skulls or whatever. I cut through the fence, and Darren slipped in first. While I was tidying up the fence, I lost sight of him. I followed, around the edge of the main building, thinking he was hiding, messing around. I heard him cry out.' Sutton turned his bony face to Sawyer, his cheeks shining with tears. He grimaced, bit into his bottom lip. The angle of light rendered his features haggard and cadaverous. 'I saw that fucking thing, dragging him away.'

'Thing?'

'The man with horns. Big and strong-looking. He was a long way off, under a bright security light, so it was mostly shadow. But he'd got Darren. And he was pulling him up a ramp, by the fucking legs. Dragging him inside.'

Sawyer walked back to the chair and sat down. 'Then what?'

'I shouted. And the... thing's head jerked up, saw me, and started to run towards me. I jumped back and forced my way out through the hole in the fence, then ran through the woods.'

Sawyer frowned. 'Did you not—'

Sutton jerked his head up and glared at Sawyer. 'No! No, I didn't. I didn't help him. I didn't tell anyone. I was too scared for myself. Getting into trouble.'

'You could have helped him. You could have saved him.'

He shook his head. 'No way. You didn't see this thing, Mr Robbins... Jake. I don't know how I managed to get away. It was like I was paralysed, by fear. But something got my legs moving, thank God.'

'And you never reported it? Went back to check? Told Darren's family?'

'No, mate. I didn't. I... Look. I was high, see? When it happened. I was so fucking gone I couldn't tell if what I saw was real or not. Fucked me up for months afterwards. Years. The dreams, memories. And, I guess, the guilt. For not saving him.' He shuddered. 'Only smack takes that shit away.'

They were quiet for a moment, each in his own private hell.

Sutton broke the silence. 'Look. I'm... sorry. For Darren's mum. But is this really the kind of answer she's looking for? Isn't it just going to make it worse for her?'

Sawyer snapped out of his reverie and stood up again. 'It's not really an answer, is it, Stuart? We know what happened to Darren. But we still don't know where he is.'

47

Sawyer slid his forearms through the struts of the wooden man dummy; thrusting, parrying. He pushed down on the obstacles with his cupped palms, shifting his bodyweight, simulating blocking and grappling, mirroring the praying mantis fighting motions witnessed by the originator of the Wing Chun style.

He put on his sparring gloves and sat on the edge of the bed, shoulders rising and falling. The *Loveless* album finished, and flipped back to the beginning. At the four opening drumbeats of the first track, 'Only Shallow', Sawyer sprang to his feet and laid into the heavy bag, pummelling hard with wide hook punches, jabs, combinations. As the track faded, he fell back onto the bed, slick with sweat, and listened, as his thoughts reformed around his plans for the evening.

He switched off the music, showered and dressed, slipping on a Kevlar vest over a black T-shirt. Old jeans, hoodie, walking boots.

In the sitting room, he opened the wrap he had lifted from Sutton and laid it out on the coffee table. The heroin was grainy, impure, far removed from its source. If he was lucky, it would have been cut with baking soda, starch, powdered milk. If he was unlucky, the original supplier might have slipped in a potentially dangerous impurity, like fentanyl. Maybe even a dash of rat poison.

He took a wrap of tinfoil from a kitchen drawer and cut off two handkerchief-sized sheets, then burned each of them over a lit gas hob, killing any chemicals on the foil. He sat on the sofa and rolled one sheet around a pen to form a long, tight tube.

After folding the second sheet in half twice, Sawyer then opened it out, creating a criss-cross of grooves. He lit a candle, pinched the corner of the sheet and tipped out some of the powder, running the foil backwards and forwards over the candle flame, taking care to melt the heroin and not burn it. He kept the flame beneath the melted bead as it trickled along the groove, tilting the foil to keep the heroin on track around the criss-cross pattern.

Sawyer leaned in and sucked the white smoke up through the tube, inhaling it deep into his lungs, holding it, then releasing slowly. He stared up at the ceiling, and sank back into the sofa.

The rush seeped over him; a fever of euphoria. His skin prickled and flushed, and his legs and arms grew leaden and distant. He heard a loud laugh, and looked around for the source, then realised it had been his own voice, his own private joy.

He had only used a small amount of powder, but the after-effects of the high clung to him for a couple of hours. He lay in a stupor, wallowing in a state of temporary insulation, incapable of summoning concern or care for external matters.

The clank of the cat-flap stirred him, and he rose to his feet, unsteady. He fed Bruce, disposed of the foil and hid the remaining heroin behind a loose brick around the side of the house.

It was late—11:30pm—but he called Shepherd. The phone rang and rang, without going to voicemail.

Sawyer's mouth was dry, his lips cracked. He drank a full pint of Diet Coke and stood over the sink, breathing slow and steady. He took a pair of hair clippers from the bedside drawer and adjusted the length attachment to Number 2 then stood before the bathroom mirror and ran the clippers in long, continuous sweeps from the front to the back of his hairline.

He swept up the dark patches of hair and stood at the front door, rolling and cracking his shoulder muscles.

Inhale.

Exhale.

Time to go.

48

Sawyer drove at speed through the narrow, unlit roads, with the Mini's lights on full beam, ignoring the angry flashes of oncoming cars. More Suicide: 'Dream Baby Dream', 'Frankie Teardrop'. Mesmeric beats, squalls of guitar: always shifting and changing, hijacking his attention, diverting and distracting.

The neurosurgeon's words rose up. *'We give our very best... Sometimes it isn't enough... We can't save everyone.'*

Sawyer parked near Parwich village, at the south-eastern tip of the National Park, in the same lay-by occupied by Pittman's Subaru almost ten years earlier. He headed up the steep dirt track, navigating by the light of his phone, keeping the brightness low and always trained on the ground directly in front of his feet.

The road curved, and he glanced up at the pale half-moon before ducking into the trees. The walking track he'd taken with Pittman was now overgrown, but he kept moving until he caught sight of the security light at the abattoir's main fence some distance ahead.

A rustling sound from somewhere behind.

Sawyer froze, listening. Nothing. He pressed on.

The sturdy gate still stood at the entrance to the private road, with the same *KEEP OUT* sign. He paused for a while, listening again, then headed forward into a final patch of dense woodland, before emerging into the clearing.

The main abattoir building sat in the centre of the large patch of open ground. Most of the upper windows had been smashed, and those at the lower level were boarded over.

Sawyer turned off his phone light and approached the main building. The covered passageway was cracked and blighted, but the connecting structure seemed robust.

He crossed a patch of fallen leaves, taking care to make each step silent. The barbed-wire fence surrounding the main building showed no sign of breaches, and Sawyer pressed on, heading for the barn-sized outbuilding at the far edge of the grounds.

The stone surface of the brickwork was tainted by patches of grey mould, and a rim of spindly vegetation had colonised the lower section of the outer walls.

Sawyer checked the door; the old padlock had long been replaced by a sturdy external bolt, and he cursed himself for not bringing cutters.

He headed over to the passageway and pushed his face up against the small window, now almost completely opaque with grime. As before, he could only make out the vague shapes of shelves and fittings in the connecting passage.

He took out his phone and activated the light, hoping to get a clearer look inside.

A hint of movement in the window, caught by his phone light. Something over his shoulder. He turned, and lowered himself into a side-on fighting stance, ready to spring back and increase the distance between himself and any potential attacker.

A tall, bulky figure loomed up and barrelled into Sawyer, pushing him back into the door with tremendous force, causing him to drop his phone.

A small blunt object dug into his side.

A bright flare of blue light, like a lightning spark, transformed the clearing into an over-exposed flash photograph for a millisecond.

Crackling, static.

Sawyer roared in pain, as a paralysing cramp gripped his muscles, holding him rigid, then releasing him. He fell to his knees and toppled forward, face-first into the leaves.

49

'Who are you?'

The question carried a weary tone. At first, Sawyer thought that it wasn't addressed to him. Had he even heard it at all?

He opened his eyes to the dim interior of the barn; a faint glow from the main building security lighting filtered in through the tiny skylight.

'Who are you?'

The question again. A deep, impassive voice, drifting over from the dark corner of the barn, by the closed door. A figure lurked there, crouched over a table, working on something.

Sawyer recognised the place, but not the voice.

He pulled himself upright, against the wall. A solid metal clasp surrounded each ankle, and his wrists were secured by a metal cuff. The ankle clasps were connected to a thick chain, fixed to a metal plate embedded in the stone wall. His head throbbed from the electric shock.

A scraping sound from the table near to the figure. Metal, stone. Sharpening.

Sawyer squinted, trying to adjust to the dark. 'Health

and safety. Ombudsman. I need to speak to your line manager.'

The figure paused, then resumed work. 'I've seen you before. A long time ago.'

Sawyer rubbed at his forehead with both hands. The wrist cuff was so tight he could barely separate his palms. 'I was here with a colleague.'

'Police?'

'He died too quickly, didn't he?'

The figure paused again. 'What?'

'Your dad. You've always felt he got off lightly. You hated him. But he never suffered, like he made you all suffer. You, your mum, your brother.'

The figure paused for longer this time, then resumed work. Long scrapes of metal grinding across stone. Sparks flashed around the table, and Sawyer caught a momentary glimpse of the figure's outline, sitting in a chair, hunched over a workbench.

Sawyer shuffled further upright, squinting harder, trying to discern more detail. 'That's why you torture. You never got to do that to him. You hit him with the pan, and turned out his lights instantly. It was his final indignity. Denying you the satisfaction of watching him suffer.'

The figure stood and walked over to Sawyer, looking down on him. The moonlight shone through the roof window, picking out the oversized head, the horns. His arm hung at his side, and he held a knife with a long, tapering blade.

'You want to take off the mask, don't you, Scott?'

Scott Walton reached out to a shelf on the wall behind Sawyer and lit a candle. He crouched down, just out of Sawyer's reach. He wore a shabby brown jacket, with the upper two-thirds of his face covered by a black enamel mask, moulded to resemble the top half of a bull's head.

Two large eyeholes, a broad snout, with flared nostrils modified for breathing. Two long, hooked white horns sprouted from the top of the mask. Walton's mouth and neck was exposed beneath the snout: dark stubble, bulging neck muscles.

Walton glared out through the eyeholes, studying Sawyer. He moved the pointed tip of the knife blade close to Sawyer's chest and applied slight pressure, pushing inward. He withdrew the blade and stood upright. 'You're wearing a stab vest. But if you're police, why would you come alone?'

'I don't abuse animals. So I hoped you'd give me a pass.'

Walton turned and walked back to the bench. 'I can't let you go. I'm sorry.'

Sawyer nodded. 'I understand.'

'Why would you think I'd want to take off the mask? What do you mean?'

'I think you want to stop. You want it to be over. Something made you stop before, didn't it?'

Walton walked back to Sawyer. He leaned over and dug the blunt object into his side.

Another flash of blue light. Sawyer's muscles spasmed, and a wave of agony rolled through him. He cried out, as loud as he could, hoping to stay conscious this time.

The sound of his shout pulled him back to his dream. The beach. His mother wading out.

'Who are you?' said Walton.

Sawyer said nothing. He took slow, deep breaths, riding the pain, willing it to subside.

Walton shocked him again, holding the object against him longer this time. Sawyer writhed and roared. His vision fuzzed over, and he came close to blacking out. He dug his nails into his palm, jolting himself alert, trying to distract from the pain in his limbs.

Walton stepped back, watching Sawyer as he fought for breath, for consciousness. 'Who are you?'

Sawyer spat to the side. 'I met Gary. Gary Holloway. Remember him, Scott? You worked with him here.'

Walton dipped his head, held up the device. Grey plastic, tubular, with two metal prongs at the far end. 'This is an electric cattle prod. We used them to stun animals. The voltage isn't too high, but a prolonged shock can knock you out, and repeated shocks run the risk of damaging your heart. I got the knife from Duncan Hardwick. He used it for filleting fish. I used it to make the initial incisions, and I switched to a serrated slicing knife to open the wounds deep enough for me to peel off his skin.'

Sawyer steadied his breathing. 'A proxy. For your father. Like the others.'

Walton squatted down. 'Abusers. Bullies. Killers. The world is brighter without them. You will not be able to break free. I remember you picked the lock here. Those clasps are beyond that.' He leaned in closer, almost within reach. 'Tell me who you are, and I'll make your death quick and painless. I have an old captive bolt pistol in my bench. Non-penetrating. I'll apply it to your forehead. You will be instantly concussed. Then I'll slit your throat, deep and clean. By the time you're aware of what's happening, you'll be gone.'

'It's a tempting offer. And what if I don't tell you who I am?'

'I'll soften your skin with boiling water, and you can watch as I peel it away. It will be an unbelievably painful and stressful death.'

Walton dropped his head again. Sawyer looked around the floor, trying to focus in the candlelight. The chain fitting was strong and immovable, and his shackles were practically medieval, with no practical option to break them open.

'What about the boy, Scott? His name was Darren. Was *he* an abuser? A bully? A killer?'

Walton raised his head slightly, the tips of the horns pointing directly at Sawyer. His eyes shifted behind the mask. 'Boy?'

Sawyer nodded, wincing away the pain in his side. 'He was here, exploring. Seven years ago. With a mate, who ran away. Whatever happened to him, whatever you did to him, it made you stop for a while, didn't it? Until Hardwick.'

Walton sprang to his feet and fell on Sawyer, striking him with a heavy punch to the jaw. Sawyer saw it coming and managed to jerk his head away, dampening the worst of its power, but it was a sickening confirmation of Walton's strength, and he followed it by jabbing the prod into Sawyer's side again, this time holding it for several seconds while Sawyer bared his teeth and bellowed with pain.

Walton pulled away and steadied himself on the shelf behind.

Sawyer gasped for air, leaning into the pain, grinding his teeth. His heart fluttered and raced. 'What happened to Darren, Scott?' He spat to the side again: hot bile.

Walton kept his back to Sawyer, head lowered.

'If you're going to kill me, then I have a last request. Please let Darren's mother know happened to him. Give her some way of restarting her life. You've become an expert in inflicting pain on the guilty, as you see them. Give an innocent woman some peace.'

Walton walked towards the locked doors which linked to the connecting passage. He turned to Sawyer, his features buried in the gloom, his outline surreal and bestial.

'I had someone here.' Walton dropped his head, fell silent, his shoulders rising and falling.

Sawyer's head throbbed. 'Darren?'

Walton looked up. 'My old boss. Sherratt. He ran this place. A fucking animal Auschwitz.'

'That's not a view that will find many sympathisers in court.'

Walton nodded. 'We justify it by viewing the animals as separate and distant, in service to our needs. Food, farming, clothing, sport.'

'Scott. What did Darren see?'

Walton paused, turned away. 'I'd had Sherratt here for some time. I took him up to the old bleeding rooms for a while, to work on him in a place he used to control. One night, I heard voices and went up to one of the high floors to look down on the woods. Two lads came through. One ran ahead of the other. By the time I'd got down there, he'd seen Sherratt. He was still alive, but I'd peeled his face, his arms. The boy cried out and I clubbed him. The other one saw me but got away.'

Sawyer twisted to face Walton. 'What happened to Darren, Scott? Where is he?'

Walton walked back over to the shelf behind Sawyer. 'He's out in the woods somewhere, with the others. I killed him that night. Quickly. He never came round. There was no suffering.'

Sawyer closed his eyes.

His mother, with a sad smile, in the back seat of the car.

'You're too focused on what might be under the layers, lurking in the darkness.'

He opened his eyes. 'And there I was, thinking the gap might have been something to do with you being emotionally affected.'

'What?'

'But it was because you thought the other boy would start an investigation, wasn't it? So you laid low for a while, soothed yourself by working for animal charities. But when nobody came—'

'I read about that cunt, Hardwick, and his chicken farm. Millions of chickens die every year in those places. They separate day-old male chicks because they can't lay eggs and so have no use to the intensive farming industry. They gather them up into massive bags and they tip them into a maceration machine. An industrial grinder. In some places, they gas them.'

'Darren Coleman's mother will struggle to find consolation in your concern for animals.'

Walton spun round to face Sawyer, raised his voice. 'We're the animals. Humans. We're the ones who can switch off our caring for other living creatures and just feed our own needs.'

Sawyer rubbed at his chest. A burning pain pulsed around his heart. 'Is this why you couldn't kill Virginia Mendez?'

'The woman?'

'Yes. The woman. You held her for a while, but you couldn't do it.'

'She was innocent.'

Sawyer smiled and shook his head. 'That's not why you let her go, is it? That's how you justify it to yourself. You let her go for the same reason you only half-buried Duncan Hardwick and Mark Bishop, the dogfight guy.' He tugged at the chain, pulled himself around, square on to Walton. 'Because you want to take off the mask. You want it to be over.'

Walton lunged forward and punched Sawyer on the jaw.

Sawyer absorbed it, took a breath. He raised his eyes to Walton; bloodied, defiant. '"He who makes a beast of himself gets rid of the pain of being a man." You've done this for so long now, and you've built up all this justification. But what's really happened is that you've started to enjoy it for what it is. Pleasure from suffering. You fantasised about that with your father, and you never got to deliver it to him. And now you've rationalised everything by selecting targets who you feel deserve the suffering. But now the compulsion has overtaken the logic, and you're scared of it. You want it to stop. The mask used to be your shield, part of a different personality. But it's become your prison. And you want to take it off.'

Walton lunged for Sawyer. He zapped him again, driving the prod into his stomach this time. Sawyer screamed, helpless. He kicked and squirmed as Walton pushed his face close, staring through the eyeholes of the mask, scrutinising his torment.

He pulled away, and walked to the workbench.

Grinding. Sharpening.

'Who are you?'

Sawyer chewed on his tongue, riding the pain again. His chest tremored, and he had to flex and strain his muscles to stabilise the streaks of shooting pain. He spat again. 'You're very ill, Scott. And you know it. And you want it to end. If you carry on, then your father has won. It will be like he's reaching out from beyond the grave, ruining your life, just as he ruined your mother's, your brother's, your own.'

The grinding stopped, and Walton's head rose from his work.

He froze.

A noise from outside. Breaking glass?

Walton picked up the cattle prod and strode to the door. He unlocked the bolt and pulled it aside, then stood in the open doorway, listening. 'You are police. You didn't come alone.'

Sawyer looked around in the pool of light cast by the

candle. Walton had left nothing useful within reach. He always carried a paperclip in his back pocket, but his hands were secured at his front. He rolled onto his side, hoping to stand and check the wall shelf above, but his movement was restrained by the chain.

Footsteps outside. Running.

The door slammed shut, then shuddered with a heavy impact.

A shout from Walton.

The door flew open. A blue flash lit up the night.

A howl of pain from another voice, male.

Walton stumbled into the barn. He lunged for the workbench and snatched up the filleting knife. As he turned back to face the door, a figure ran in from outside, head down, and drove into him, tackling him to the floor.

Walton managed to hold on to the knife and twist around to face his attacker, who gripped his arm, holding it firm.

The attacker climbed higher up Walton's chest, pinning him beneath his knees. The two figures grappled in the gloom, and Sawyer shuffled across the floor, closer to the centre of the candlelight, straining to see more detail.

The man on top held Walton's knife arm in place and reached out with his other hand. Walton tried to bat him away, but he gripped one of the horns and tore off the mask, throwing it across the floor. He drew back his head and brought his forehead down into the centre of Walton's face.

A wet crunch. Walton roared and pushed himself back, keeping his grip on the knife. He slashed it around in a narrow arc, just missing his attacker's face. The second man stumbled back and hauled himself upright, at last giving Sawyer a clear view.

Austin Fletcher raised his head and set himself as

Walton scrambled to his feet, his face dripping blood. He held the knife upright, and edged forward. Fletcher caught Sawyer's eye, and Walton lurched towards him. Fletcher read the movement and stepped aside, but too late to dodge the knife as it skimmed away from the original target—his chest—and plunged into his shoulder.

Fletcher howled in pain and reared away, pushing Walton back and pulling out the knife. He threw it aside and ran forward, face flushed red. He hit Walton with a right hook, sending him crashing into the workbench, glancing his head against the side as he went down. Fletcher fell on him, gripped the front of the T-shirt to hold him in place, and hit him with another blow, then another.

'Fletcher!' Sawyer cried out, but the blows kept coming, full force into the side of Walton's face, sending spatters of blood flying into the side of the bench.

Sawyer pushed forward, straining against the chain. 'Stop!'

More punches, just as strong but less and less frequent.

Sawyer bowed his head and waited, until Fletcher let Walton's body slump to the floor and fell back, exhausted.

Another minute passed, as Sawyer listened to Fletcher's ragged breathing.

Fletcher got to his feet; Sawyer looked up. 'Nice move with the headbutt. I wonder where you got that from.'

Fletcher stood facing Sawyer, the moonlight at his back.

'Did you track me?' said Sawyer.

Fletcher nodded. 'Car.'

'And is this you saving my life or finishing me off?'

Fletcher pulled a small torch from his pocket, and aimed the beam at the workbench. He opened a side cupboard, then a drawer and rummaged around, eventually taking out a set of keys. He trudged over to Sawyer and crouched beside him. After several tries, Fletcher hit on the key that unlocked the wrist cuff. He dropped the rest of the set on the floor beside Sawyer and stood upright. The filleting knife had fallen near to the back wall shelf, in the centre of the candlelight, and Fletcher's eyes moved to it. He looked back at Sawyer, then walked over to Walton and squatted at his side.

Sawyer tried a few keys and released the ankle clasp.

Fletcher placed his hand on Walton's neck, checking for a pulse. He looked back at Sawyer and shook his head.

———

They carried Walton's body, with the mask resting in the centre of his torso, through the trees, back to the road, where Fletcher had parked his Fiesta behind Sawyer's Mini. They bundled the body into the boot.

Fletcher closed the boot, paused, and laid a hand on the driver's door handle, the other clutching his injured shoulder.

'So we're square?' said Sawyer.

Fletcher's pinhole eyes narrowed as he reached up to touch the scars on his neck. He sighed and opened the door.

'Before you go,' said Sawyer. 'I've got a present for you.'

He opened the Mini, pulled a wallet out of the glovebox, and held it up for Fletcher. 'I took this from Jerome in the altercation at Dale's place. He's Czech. Real name is Marian. No wonder he changed it.'

A hint of a smile on Fletcher's lips. He took the wallet.

'We might be square,' said Sawyer, 'but I'd say you still have one piece of unfinished business. Do it your way, but I checked. Marian's immigration status is... open to question. It wouldn't be hard to get him deported. But I'm sure you can think of something more creative.'

50

THREE DAYS LATER

'What happened?' Michael looked up from his handheld game.

'You mean with the bruises?'

Michael nodded, returned to his game.

Sawyer shrugged. 'What *didn't* happen?'

He got up from the bedside chair, wincing at the pain in his chest. The room held a slight chill from outside. Sawyer closed the window, and gazed out at the wooded slopes of the Goyt Valley, blurred behind a morning fog.

'The heather is flowering,' said Michael. 'Turning purple.'

Sawyer turned, gave his brother a quizzical look. 'Autumn's on its way. New colours. Yellows, reds. Orange. Mum's favourite.'

Michael sighed. He had trimmed his hair down to a uniform fuzz, mirroring Sawyer's.

'Had any bird visits?'

Michael's shoulders twitched with something close to a laugh.

Sawyer raised an eyebrow. 'Not that sort. Finches, nuthatches, lapwings.'

Michael shook his head.

'Dad told me that Mum used to go down to Fernilee Reservoir by herself. Reading, watching the wildlife. Is that glue?' Sawyer nodded to a small plastic bottle on the bedside table.

'Yeah. Medical glue. It's therapy. You paint it onto your skin, peel it off when you feel the need to self-harm.'

Sawyer walked around in front of his brother and squatted down to look directly into his eyes. 'Mike. You could live at my place for a while. Get away from Rosemary House and Chris Hill. Transition.'

Michael kept focus on his game. 'Your place?'

'You know. Edale. Near Kinder. I'm thinking we could go out walking, reforge our brotherly bond. Pints and pies in the local.'

Michael looked at him, blank. 'What happened?'

Sawyer frowned. 'You asked me that. Difficult case. A suspect wasn't keen on submitting to enquiry.'

Michael shook his head. 'To me.'

Sawyer frowned. 'You mean at Rosemary House?'

'Jake.' Michael set down the handheld. 'I don't know that. I don't know what that is.'

'It's where you live, Mike. It's a care facility. You've been unwell. Since...'

Michael closed his eyes, rubbed his stubby fingers around the sockets. 'I know you. I don't know Rosemary House. Or Chris Hill. And I don't know why I'm here.'

'What's the last thing you remember?'

Michael kept his eyes closed, pondering. 'I remember

coming here. Doctors' voices. Nurses. You say I've been unwell.'

Sawyer shifted his weight, looking up into his brother's haggard face. 'You tried to hurt yourself. Do you not remember that?'

Michael opened his eyes. 'No. I don't.' He looked at Sawyer. 'There's nothing, Jake. It's all just... white. Nothing.'

'Do you remember Mum? Dad?' Sawyer stood up. 'Do you remember what happened to us?'

Michael gave a strange, elongated grunt, shook his head. 'You'll have to tell me. Take me back. Jog my memory.'

Blinking, Sawyer walked back to the chair. 'It'll take time. Mum said you had a "head like a sieve".'

Michael stared down at the carpet, ran his hands across his scalp. 'How long have I *been* here? How long have I been like this?'

'The doctors say it's normal to have some memory loss at first. How do you feel?'

Michael looked at Sawyer. 'I feel better.'

———

Sawyer bought a double-strength coffee in the hospital Costa and took it to a table outside, in a grubby smoking area. He called Walker on the burner phone he'd bought in Hathersage. It rang and rang, and he was close to giving up when the call connected.

Walker spoke in a low voice, close to a whisper. 'That you, sir?'

'Anything?'

Movement at Walker's end. A squeaky door opening and closing. Low traffic noise. 'They cordoned off the woodland around the abattoir buildings. Cadaver dogs found one body. Then Keating authorised GPR. Two found in total so far. One IDd as Milton Pope. The other is the young lad. Darren Coleman.'

Sawyer sipped his coffee, watched a visiting family gather round a table. A mum, dad, teenage girl, younger boy. Milkshakes, muffins.

Walker cleared his throat. 'You found him, sir.'

'Are they still digging?'

'Yes. No sign of Scott Walton. Did you—'

'Is Shepherd involved?'

Walker hesitated. 'Yes. Farrell told us again not to contact you. There's been a lot of meetings. Farrell and the IOPC guy, the Federation rep. With Keating and Shepherd, Moran.'

'Moran?'

'Yeah. Don't know why he's involved. They're not telling me anything. But, just saying. Getting a vibe. Be careful.'

51

Sawyer parked at the top of road overlooking Hall Leys
Park. He waited, watching the crowd around the
bandstand. Steel drums, covered food stalls. Some kind of
festival. He listened to the album *Dog Man Star* by Suede,
repeatedly glancing up at the rear-view mirror. But the back
seat remained empty.

After half an hour, two young women emerged from
Samantha Coleman's house. A detective he vaguely
recognised, and Patricia, one of the FLOs. Heads down,
they trudged over to a car parked opposite and drove away.

Sawyer took one last look in the rear-view mirror. He
got out, walked to the house, and made his way down the
path to the front door. Samantha opened it before he could
ring the doorbell. She looked dazed, desolate, clutching a
tissue.

'He was...' She fought back another wave of tears. 'They
found Darren, Mr Sawyer. They found my boy. Did you—'

He shook his head. 'Nothing to do with me. I think
they had an anonymous tip-off. I'm so sorry, Samantha.'

She flinched, caught in a spasm of grief. Dark laughter

through the tears. 'It's okay, it's okay. They say it looked like he didn't... He didn't suffer.'

'That's good.'

'I don't want anyone... I don't want you to come in. I'm sorry. I don't mean to be rude.' Sawyer held up a hand. 'I need to make calls. Arrange things.'

'Samantha.' Sawyer resisted the urge to hug her. 'The life you gave to Darren, the love you shared. It will always be real. It will always be a part of you.'

Samantha dropped her head, started to sob. 'Like you said, it's better that I know I'll never spend time with him again, apart from in my memory.'

'You lost Darren too soon, but you gained so much by giving him the gift of that time. And now you have an answer, you can try to restart your own life.'

She wiped at her nose with the tissue. 'There's a woman I used to speak to online. Val. We talked about the limbo of not knowing, the way you shift from hope to hopelessness. Val called it "the beast within". Her son came back after a year away, alive and well, late last year. She said it was weird, like having a stranger in the house. But she also said that her beast within had been tamed, and she could finally start again. I hope I can do the same.' She gave a weak smile. 'I think you're being humble, Mr Sawyer, saying you didn't have anything to do with it. And if I'm right, then thank you. We couldn't bring Darren back, but you've saved my life.'

52

Sawyer cut out two squares of foil and burned off the chemicals over the gas hob, as before. He laid them out on the coffee table and rolled one around the pen to form the smoking tube.

Metal on teeth.

He lit a candle, and folded the other sheet in half twice, forming the base for the melted heroin.

Sun flare. Screaming, screaming.

He turned up the volume on his smart speaker: 'Giant' by The The. Immense, rolling drums, muffling the sounds and visions.

He tipped the powder onto the foil, held the flame beneath the bead as it traced the grooves in the criss-cross pattern. He leaned forward, sucked up the smoke, inhaled, dropped back onto the sofa.

The drums, pummelling and pounding.

Matt Johnson singing of being a stranger to himself.

His mother's face. Pulped, lurid red.

The patch of gore on his father's ceiling. Oozing, ready to drop.

A surge of bliss as the drug entered Sawyer's brain and

surged to his opioid receptors, banishing pain, slowing his breathing. Again, he laughed out loud, waited for his troubles to soften and recede.

Screaming, barking.

'I'm sorry, son. I love you.'

His brave and brilliant father, pushing a shotgun under his chin.

Matt Johnson singing of choking to death, of a sun that never sets.

'Run, my darling!'

'You've been making things hard for yourself ever since.'

Sawyer jolted upright, grinding his teeth through the rush. He took the packet of heroin and tipped it out onto a magazine on the coffee table. He spread the brown powder around the surface of the magazine, then leaned in and pushed one end of the tube deep into a nostril. He ran the other end of the tube across the powder, snorting, inhaling. He tipped back his head and did the same again, taking a deeper snort this time.

The powder fizzed and liquified at the back of his throat, and he took a drink from an old can of Coke, trying to stifle the bitter taste on his tongue.

'Don't look back!'

Barking, screaming.

Shotgun blast.

'I'm sorry, son.'

Pulped face.

Bloodied tears.

Gore splashing from ceiling to floor.

Matt Johnson singing of God and hell and caving in on himself.

Sawyer stumbled off the sofa, struggling to catch his breath.

Drumming, drumming.

He fought for deeper breaths, but his diaphragm wouldn't contract, wouldn't allow his lungs to take the oxygen he craved.

Drumming.

Matt Johnson singing that nobody can know him, he doesn't even know himself.

A rocket of nausea, flaring in Sawyer's gut, rising up through his throat.

He needed more air, but it wouldn't come.

He opened his mouth wide, trying to force air down his throat. But there still wasn't enough reaching his lungs.

Blackness. Prickling around the edge of his vision.

Muscle convulsions, gut cramps. He was crawling now, heading for the front door.

He managed to reach up, force it open.

He fell forward onto the porch and dragged himself down the stairs, across the driveway bridge, down onto the roadside verge.

Drums, pounding from the house behind.

His hands gripped the grass: skin clammy, nails turning blue.

No air.

No strength left to fight back, to stay conscious.

It all fell away.

'You don't write, you don't call.'

Sawyer opened his eyes. Maggie stood at his bedside, arms folded.

He looked around the private hospital room. A middle-aged man with rolled-up shirt sleeves and a lanyard badge around his neck stood at the door, in discussion with a nurse out in the corridor.

He turned to Maggie. 'You're in your civvies.'

'I was about to leave. Then they brought you in.'

'This isn't your old room, is it?'

She smiled. 'No.'

He pushed himself upright, winced at the pain in his side. His limbs felt tender, hyper-sensitive, and it hurt his ribs to take deep breaths.

Maggie glared at him with a mixture of anger and concern.

'Mr Sawyer. I'm Doctor Randall.' The man approached his bed. 'You've been under sedation for a few hours, so you may feel rather groggy. From the sound of things, you were extremely lucky. The screening shows you ingested quite a large amount of heroin mixed with a powerful drug called fentanyl. It's one of the most common causes of overdose death, particularly among heavy users with high tolerance. You were picked up by an ambulance called by a passer-by, near to your home. You've been given oxygen to counteract cyanosis. That's peripheral skin discolouration. You've also been given a drug called naloxone, which is an opioid antagonist.' He checked a folder on the bedside table. 'I'm guessing you didn't inject? I'm not sure you'd have been so fortunate if that had been the case. Tox screen also showed the presence of marijuana.' Randall glanced at Maggie. 'Apologies. Is this your—'

'Fiancée,' said Sawyer.

Maggie sighed. 'What happens next, doctor?'

'If... there's an issue with dependency, I would suggest you reduce your dose—'

'There's no issue with dependency,' said Sawyer. 'It was a one-off.'

Randall's eyes flicked to Maggie again. 'Okay. Well, I would suggest you explore the root cause of your action. Psychotherapy. Self-care. The circumstances that led you to use the drug in the first place. I'm happy for you to stay overnight, but if you're feeling well enough to go home, I won't stop you. Your heartrate is a touch erratic, but not outside acceptable limits. You're young, Mr Sawyer.' He smiled. 'Relatively. And you're otherwise healthy. I can prescribe a naloxone nasal spray as a precaution, but generally, I would advise you to rest, recover, and try to avoid ingesting Class A drugs of dubious origin.'

He gave an abrupt nod and hurried away down the corridor alongside the nurse.

'It's hard not to take it personally, you know,' said Maggie. 'You have to be on the brink of death before you'll come to see me.'

'Had a lot going on. Sorry. And I did see you.'

'Did you get him for me?'

Sawyer took a drink of water from his bedside jug. 'Who?'

'The man who attacked me.'

'Let's not go there.'

Maggie raised her eyebrows, tucked her hair behind her ear. 'What went wrong with Alex, Jake? Why did you stop the work? When it was working?'

'I got the gist. Avoid triggers. Eat better.'

'She didn't specifically tell you not to use heroin, so you thought that was okay? Which parts of your history did you talk about?'

Sawyer rubbed his hands together, trying to stimulate more sensation. 'I did a stupid thing, but I'm not stupid any more. Not in that way.'

Maggie's smile was pained. 'You promise you'll try not to do it again?'

He took another drink.

Maggie sat down. 'Distraction isn't a good strategy, because it just forces you to pursue more extreme forms of distraction. In other words, self-medication. Traumatised people pursue distraction because of their terror of introspection. Remember what Pascal said?'

Sawyer nodded. 'All our problems come from our inability to sit quietly in a room alone.'

'Yes. You have to get good at that, instead of surrounding yourself with more and more distraction. I think your time with Alex got derailed because you hadn't taken the first step to wellness. Being comfortable with your own thoughts. It's why so many troubled people who are scared of introspection tend to spend time with children or animals. They're not given any time or space to turn their thoughts on themselves.'

'I've been hallucinating, Maggie.'

She grimaced. 'More drugs?'

'No. Just... It happens sometimes. Like before. Past events, reoccurring in the present. People. As real as if they were right there before me. They speak to me.'

Maggie sighed. 'Jake. You're strong, but there's only so much you can take. I'm concerned about the regressive behaviour, and... Seeing things? Hearing voices? This is post-traumatic stress disorder, possibly more. The thalamus works as a subtle gatekeeper in your brain, filtering out sensory information, separating threats from everything else. But in people with PTSD, this filter is faulty, and they're hyper-aware, hyper-sensitive. And when they try to shut this down completely, they throw the baby out with the bathwater. They risk screening out the sources of joy and pleasure along with the things that bring them pain.' She shunted her chair closer, reached out, took his hand. 'You've suffered great loss. But you have to try and absorb the loss, and replace it with a gratitude for the time before. And then use the source of that gratitude to allow you to embrace whatever is left after the loss.' She sat back. 'You're carrying a mountain, instead of learning to climb.'

———

Later that afternoon, Sawyer dressed and signed himself out. As he pulled on his hoodie, he felt a solid weight in the inside pocket and took out the coin given to him by his father. One side was dominated by a profile illustration of a skull, which sat between the words MEMENTO and MORI with an hourglass on one side and a tulip on the other. The tulip represented life, the skull depicted death, and the hourglass exemplified time. On the reverse side, six words were stacked in the centre: a quote from Marcus Aurelius, one of the founders of the Stoic philosophy.

He mouthed the rest of the quote to himself. 'Let that determine what you say and think.'

He took the burner phone from the shelf on the bedside table and switched it on. Several Missed Call alerts from the same number.

Walker.

He navigated to his voicemail and opened the first message.

Commotion in the corridor outside. He recognised one of the voices.

Sawyer pocketed the phone as a short, formally dressed young man crashed into the room.

Sawyer stood back from the door. 'Matt.'

'Sir. They're going to charge you. For Bowman.' He caught his breath. 'They... know about Tony Cross. Farrell is calling it premeditated. Moran spoke to Cross.'

'Did he say anything?'

Walker shook his head. 'No, but they have evidence that Cross was with you on the day of the Bowman raid. And there's something else. Jordan Burns. He's spoken to Farrell. Stephanie Burns has revised her story. She's saying you didn't kill Bowman in self-defence. She's saying it was cold blood.' He swallowed, steadied his breathing. 'Sir.'

––––––

DCI Farrell walked through the hospital reception. DC Moran trotted past him and jabbed at the lift button.

'Let's be clear about this,' said Farrell as they waited. 'Once we have DI Sawyer under arrest, he is to be treated like any other potential criminal. This will already be an embarrassing case, and we have to be completely—'

Farrell caught Moran's gaze, looking up and over his shoulder.

He turned.

DS Walker on the central staircase, coming down.

'Stairs,' said Farrell.

They ran from the lift and charged past Walker, bounding up the stairs to the private ward on the third floor.

Farrell sprinted down the corridor. He stopped at the nurse station. '*Sawyer*. Jake. Where is he?' The young nurse hesitated, and Farrell pulled out his warrant card.

She pointed. 'Room 12. At the end.'

Farrell bolted away, Moran close behind.

They pushed into Room 12.

Empty bed. Empty room.

Farrell turned to Moran. '*Fuck!*'

BOOK SIX IN THE **JAKE SAWYER** SERIES

JAKE SAWYER is in hiding. Wanted for questioning after a death in his custody, he is lying low, forming a plan to clear his name.

When the bodies of several elderly men are discovered, horrifically brutalised, police race to apprehend an insatiable killer with a sadistic streak.

As Sawyer is targeted by devious new enemies, tasked with flushing him out and taking him down, he discovers a family secret which reveals the true horror behind the murders. But to catch the culprit, he must delve deep into his personal trauma, and finally make peace with the past.

http://books2read.com/theskeletonlake

JOIN MY MAILING LIST

I occasionally send an email newsletter with details on forthcoming releases and anything else I think my readers might care about.

Sign up and I'll send you **a Jake Sawyer prequel novella**.

THE LONG DARK is set in the summer before the events of CREEPY CRAWLY. It's FREE and totally exclusive to mailing list subscribers.

Go here to get the book:
http://andrewlowewriter.com/longdark

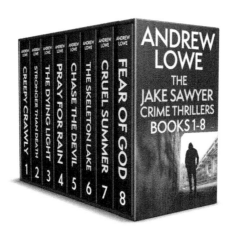

BOOKS 1-8 IN THE **JAKE SAWYER** SERIES

AVAILABLE IN EBOOK and PAPERBACK

READ NOW WITH **KINDLE UNLIMITED**

https://books2read.com/sawyerboxset4

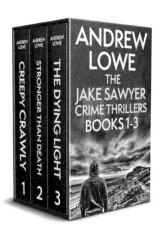

BOOKS 1-3 IN THE **JAKE SAWYER** SERIES

AVAILABLE IN EBOOK and PAPERBACK

READ NOW WITH **KINDLE UNLIMITED**

https://books2read.com/sawyerboxset1

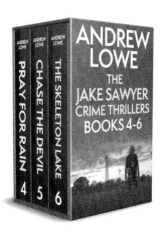

BOOKS 4-6 IN THE **JAKE SAWYER** SERIES

AVAILABLE IN EBOOK and PAPERBACK

READ NOW WITH **KINDLE UNLIMITED**

https://books2read.com/sawyerboxset2

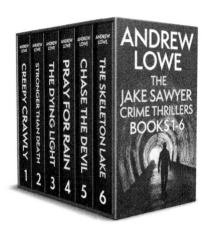

BOOKS 1-6 IN THE **JAKE SAWYER** SERIES

AVAILABLE IN EBOOK and PAPERBACK

READ NOW WITH **KINDLE UNLIMITED**

https://books2read.com/sawyerboxset3

ACKNOWLEDGMENTS

For their insight on issues of animal abuse, my thanks to Ellie Greer and Helen Lewis from **The League Against Cruel Sports**, Debbie Bailey from the **High Peak Badger Group**, and Mark Randell from **Hidden-in-Sight**.

Tom Ford (not that one) was a patient educator on urbex culture. His website **Whatever's Left** is fascinating and definitive, with some beautiful photography.

Bryony Sutherland was my all-seeing editor.

Book Cover Shop made the cover and website.

Special thanks to **Julia**, for listening to me go on about it all.

Andrew Lowe. London, 2020

PLEASE LEAVE A REVIEW

If you enjoyed **CHASE THE DEVIL**, please take a couple of minutes to leave a review or rating on the book's **Amazon** page.

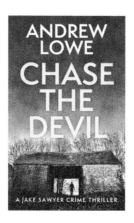

Honest reviews of my books help bring them to the attention of others, and connecting with readers is the number one thing that keeps me writing.

Go here to leave your review:
https://books2read.com/chasethedevil

THE JAKE SAWYER SERIES

THE LONG DARK
CREEPY CRAWLY
STRONGER THAN DEATH
THE DYING LIGHT
PRAY FOR RAIN
CHASE THE DEVIL
THE SKELETON LAKE
CRUEL SUMMER
FEAR OF GOD
TENDER IS THE NORTH
BLOOD NEVER SLEEPS (2025)

BOOKS 1-3 BOX SET
BOOKS 4-6 BOX SET
BOOKS 1-6 BOX SET
BOOKS 1-8 BOX SET

GLOSSARY

ACT – Acceptance and Commitment Therapy. A form of psychotherapy that uses acceptance and mindfulness strategies along with commitment to behaviour change.

AFO – Authorised Firearms Officer. A UK police officer who has received training, and is authorised to carry and use firearms.

ALF – Animal Liberation Front. A political and social resistance movement that promotes non-violent direct action in protest against incidents of animal cruelty.

ANPR – Automatic Number Plate Recognition. A camera technology for automatically reading vehicle number plates.

AWOL – Absent without leave. Acronym.

BSE – Bovine Spongiform Encephalopahy. Colloquially known as 'mad cow disease'. A neurodegenerative condition in cattle.

CCRC – Criminal Cases Review Commission. Independent body which investigates suspected miscarriages of justice in England, Wales and NI.

CI – Confidential Informant. An individual who passes information to the police on guarantee of anonymity.

CBT – Cognitive Behaviour Therapy. A form of psychotherapy based on principles from behavioural and cognitive psychology.

CID – Criminal Investigation Department. The branch of the UK police whose officers operate in plainclothes and specialise in serious crime.

COD – Cause of Death. Police acronym.

CPS – Crown Prosecution Service. The principle public agency for conducting criminal prosecutions in England and Wales.

CROP – Covert Rural Observation Post. A camouflaged surveillance operation, mostly used to detect or monitor criminal activity in rural areas.

CSI – Crime Scene Investigator. A professional responsible for collecting, cataloguing and preserving physical evidence from crime scenes.

CSO – Community Support Officer. Uniformed but non-warranted member of police staff in England & Wales. The role has limited police powers. Also known as PCSO.

D&D – Drunk & Disorderly. Minor public order offence in the UK (revised to 'Drunk and disorderly in a public place' in 2017).

Dibble – Manchester/Northern English slang. Police.

EMDR – Eye Movement Desensitisation and Reprocessing. An interactive psychotherapy technique used to relieve psychological stress, particularly trauma and post-traumatic stress disorder.

ETD – Estimated Time of Death. Police acronym.

FLO – Family Liaison Officer. A specially trained officer or police employee who provides emotional support to the families of crime victims and gathers evidence and information to assist the police enquiry.

FOA – First Officer Attending. The first officer to arrive at a crime scene.

FSI – Forensic Science Investigator. An employee of the Scientific Services Unit, usually deployed at a crime scene to gather forensic evidence.

GIS – General Intelligence Service (Egypt). Government agency responsible for national security intelligence, both domestically and internationally.

GMCA – Greater Manchester Combined Authority. Local government institution serving the ten metropolitan boroughs of the Greater Manchester area of the UK.

GMP – Greater Manchester Police. Territorial police force responsible for law enforcement within the county of Greater Manchester in North West England.

GPR – Ground Penetrating Radar. A non-intrusive geophysical method of surveying the sub-surface. Often used by police to investigate suspected buried remains.

HOLMES – Home Office Large Major Enquiry System. An IT database system used by UK police forces for the investigation of major incidents.

H&C – Hostage & Crisis Negotiator. Specially trained law enforcement officer or professional skilled in negotiation techniques to resolve high-stress situations such as hostage crises.

IED – Improvised Explosive Device. A bomb constructed and deployed in ways outside of conventional military standards.

IDENT1 – The UK's central national database for holding, searching and comparing biometric information on those who come into contact with the police as detainees after arrest.

IMSI – International Mobile Subscriber Identity. A number sent by a mobile device that uniquely identifies the user of a cellular network.

IOPC – Independent Office for Police Conduct.

Oversees the police complaints system in England and Wales.

ISC – Intelligence and Security Committee of Parliament. The committee of the UK Parliament responsible for oversight of the UK Intelligence Community.

MCT – Metacognitive Therapy. A form of psychotherapy focused on modifying beliefs that perpetuate states of worry, rumination and attention fixation.

MIT – Murder/Major Investigation Team. A specialised squad of detectives who investigate cases of murder, manslaughter, and attempted murder.

Misper – missing person. Police slang.

NCA – National Crime Agency. A UK law enforcement organisation. Sometimes dubbed the 'British FBI', the NCA fights organised crime that spans regional and international borders.

NCB – National Central Bureau. An agency within an INTERPOL member country that links its national law enforcement with similar agencies in other countries.

NDNAD – National DNA Database. Administered by the Home Office in the UK.

NHS – National Health Service. Umbrella term for the three publicly funded healthcare systems of the UK (NHS England, NHS Scotland, NHS Wales).

NHSBT – NHS Blood and Transplant. A division of the UK National Health Service, dedicated to blood, organ and tissue donation.

OCG – Organised Crime Group. A structured group of individuals who work together to engage in illegal activities.

OP – Observation Point. The officer/observer locations in a surveillance operation.

Osman Warning – An alert of a death threat or high risk of murder issued by UK police, usually when there is intelligence of the threat but an arrest can't yet be carried out or justified.

PACE – Police and Criminal Evidence Act. An act of the UK Parliament which instituted a legislative framework for the powers of police officers in England and Wales.

PAVA – Pelargonic Acid Vanillylamide. Key component in an incapacitant spray dispensed from a handheld canister. Causes eye closure and severe pain.

PAYG – Pay As You Go. A mobile phone handset with no contract or commitment. Often referred to as a 'burner' due to its disposable nature.

PM – Post Mortem. Police acronym.

PNC – Police National Computer. A database which allows law enforcement organisations across the UK to share intelligence on criminals.

PPE – Personal Protective Equipment designed to protect users against health or safety risks at work.

Presser – Press conference or media event.

RIPA – Regulation of Investigatory Powers Act. UK Act of Parliament which regulates the powers of public bodies to carry out surveillance and investigation. Introduced to take account of technological change such as the grown of the internet and data encryption.

SAP scale. A five-point scale, devised by the Sentencing Advisory Panel in the UK, to rate the severity of indecent images of children.

SIO – Senior Investigating Officer. The detective who heads an enquiry and is ultimately responsible for personnel management and tactical decisions.

SOCO – Scene of Crime Officer. Specialist forensic investigator who works with law enforcement agencies to collect and analyse evidence from crime scenes.

SSU – Scientific Services Unit. A police support team which collects and examines forensic evidence at the scene of a crime.

Tac-Med – Tactical Medic. Specially trained medical professional who provides advanced medical care and support during high-risk law enforcement operations.

TOD – Time of Death. Police acronym.

TRiM – Trauma Risk Management. Trauma-focused peer support system designed to assess and support employees who have experienced a traumatic, or potentially traumatic, event.

Urbex – urban exploration. Enthusiasts share images of man-made structures, usually abandoned buildings or hidden components of the man-made environment.

VPU – Vulnerable Prisoner Unit. The section of a UK prison which houses inmates who would be at risk of attack if kept in the mainstream prison population.

A WOMAN TO DIE FOR

AN EX WHO WOULD KILL TO GET HER BACK

Sam Bartley is living well. He's running his own personal trainer business, making progress in therapy, and he's planning to propose to his girlfriend, Amy.

When he sees a strange message on Amy's phone, Sam copies the number and sends an anonymous threat. But the sender replies, and Sam is sucked into a dangerous confrontation that will expose his steady, reliable life as a horrifying lie.

https://books2read.com/dontyouwantme

WHAT IF THE HOLIDAY OF YOUR DREAMS TURNED INTO YOUR WORST NIGHTMARE?

Joel Pearce is an average suburban family man looking to shake up his routine. With four close friends, he travels to a remote tropical paradise for a 'desert island survival experience': three weeks of indulgence and self-discovery.

But after their supplies disappear and they lose contact with the mainland, the rookie castaways start to suspect that the island is far from deserted.

https://books2read.com/savages

ABOUT THE AUTHOR

Andrew Lowe was born in the north of England. He has written for *The Guardian* and *Sunday Times*, and contributed to numerous books and magazines on films, music, TV, videogames, sex and shin splints.

He lives in the south of England, where he writes, edits other people's writing, and shepherds his two young sons down the path of righteousness.

His online home is andrewlowewriter.com

Follow him via the social media links below.

Email him at andrew@andrewlowewriter.com

For Andrew's editing and writing coach services, email him at andylowe99@gmail.com

f facebook.com/andrewlowewriter

X x.com/andylowe99

⊙ instagram.com/andylowe99

♪ tiktok.com/@andrewlowewriter

BB bookbub.com/profile/andrew-lowe

a amazon.com/stores/Andrew-Lowe/author/B00UAJGZZU